E... Was... But He Knew How To Fight Like A Man.

Bill picked up his dollar and pocketed it. Then he shot out a hand to clutch Ernest's shirt.

"Come along hyar. I'll show you who's a skunk," he growled, and then turned to give his companion a meaningful glance.

"Let go," ordered Selby sharply, and with a powerful wrench freed himself. With the same movement he swung a heavy fist. It took Bill square on the jaw and down he went in a heap, a look of blank surprise on his bearded face. He lay there on the ground for a moment, his eyes filled with mingled shock and hatred.

"Did you hit me, you young jacksnip?" he roared.

"What'd it feel like?" queried Ernest with a laugh. "Want me to help you up and give you more of the same?"

Coming soon from
HARPER PAPERBACKS

ZANE GREY

THE DUDE RANGER

Harper Paperbacks

Harper & Row, Publishers, New York
Grand Rapids, Philadelphia, St. Louis, San Francisco
London, Singapore, Sydney, Tokyo, Toronto

Harper Paperbacks a division of Harper & Row, Publishers, Inc.
10 East 53rd Street, New York, N.Y. 10022

Cover photo courtesy of the Bettmann Archive

First Harper Paperbacks printing: July, 1990

Printed in the United States of America

HARPER PAPERBACKS and colophon are trademarks of
Harper & Row, Publishers, Inc.

10 9 8 7 6 5 4 3 2 1

THE DUDE RANGER

CHAPTER

1

"I'LL palm myself off as a cowboy!" In his excitement Ernest Selby spoke his thought aloud. Then he looked around quickly to see if anyone had overheard him. His fellow travelers paid him no marked attention and he breathed freely again.

A growing elation had been mounting in Ernest ever since the train had climbed the Raton Pass into New Mexico. Now he was fairly in Arizona. This was the West, the real West that had always spelled romance to him; and almost miraculously had come his opportunity to become a part of it.

Time and again, since he had left his home in Iowa, Ernest had pulled out the papers and letter from the lawyer in Chicago. These set forth that his uncle, Silas Selby, had died suddenly of a heart attack and had bequeathed to his nephew a certain property in Arizona called Red Rock Ranch. The lawyer went on to say that just before his death Mr. Silas Selby had decided to make a trip to the ranch to ascertain just why the revenues had so greatly fallen off. The reports of the manager, Hepford, were apparently in good order. They explained why, in the last three years, twenty thousand head of cattle had dwindled to six thousand. But Mr. Selby had felt the discrepancy warranted investigation. Now his death had put the matter squarely up to Ernest Selby, the new owner.

While the lawyer did not commit himself to a definite implication of dishonesty on the part of this Hepford, the facts were sufficiently arresting to give that impression.

Ernest had talked the matter over with his father and mother, and then had permitted no grass to grow under his feet before boarding a westward-bound train. He was extremely grateful to Uncle Silas for having left him the ranch, but still more for the opportunity it gave him to forsake his circumscribed life in a small Iowa farm community for the romance and adventure that the West promised.

But he must be sensible, he told himself; he must curb the exultant leap of his blood and make an effort to figure out the best way to proceed. He knew little or nothing about ranching, and was entirely unfitted to step in and manage a large ranch. He would have to learn the business from the ground up, to gain by actual experience the various activities connected with stock raising, to find out what was going on. He would not even know how to go about uncovering any dishonesty or maladministration.

Then had come the idea: why not, under an assumed name, ask for employment as a cowboy on his own ranch? That would certainly be one way of getting experience from the ground up. Of course, being a cowboy would be new, too; but Ernest had had plenty of experience with horses and farm work; he was strong and husky, and thought he ought to be able to overcome tenderfoot reactions in short order. In that way he could also get the inside track on the ranch management. There might be difficulty in persuading Hepford to employ him, but Ernest was inclined to meet that issue when he came to it. He felt equal to any situation, now that he was really in the West with all its mysterious and glamorous possibilities.

Selby left the train at Holbrook. Sight of several cowboys lounging on a corner opposite the station caught his attention. The cowboys were young, red-faced, sharp-eyed, lazy in movement, and garbed in the usual picturesque, big sombreros, flannel shirts, Levis tucked in high-heeled leather boots to which were attached enormously long spurs.

He stepped up to the lounging group, glad that he was dressed plainly.

"Any place round here to eat?" he asked.

They eyed him without apparently seeing him. "Shore," replied one, pointing across the street. "There's a hotel. An' there's a lunch counter at the depot. If you cain't get enough at them, there's a Chink restaurant down the street, an' a Navaho joint."

"What time does the stage leave for Springer-town?" asked Ernest, risking one more query.

"Wal, it goes at eleven an' then again it don't," was the cryptic reply.

"Thanks for your courtesy," returned Selby, without change of inflection or expression. His speech drew a suspicious glance. But nothing further was said, and he walked off toward the hotel. There he left his bag, and after asking a few more questions sallied forth to see the sights. The first object his eye fell upon, of any particular interest to him, was a handsome red-haired girl. As Ernest passed, half turning to get a glimpse of the western girl's face, he heard her say to a companion: "Sorry, Polly, but I'm taking the stage this mawnin' for Red Rock Ranch. Dad had me draw more money than I like to be responsible for."

That remark interested the new owner of Red Rock Ranch. Impulsively he turned back and doffed his hat.

"Excuse me, Miss—" he began, then broke off abruptly, realizing he had been about to introduce himself.

The girl turned on him a pair of amused green eyes.

The young man from Iowa stuttered, but managed to go on: "W-will you, that is, can you direct me to a store where I can buy a riding outfit?"

"Can't you read, Mister?" she replied, rather flippantly, as she pointed to the large white-lettered signs on the windows directly across the street.

Selby thanked her and started to cross the street, catching a remark as he did so about a good-looking tenderfoot. Part of the laughing remark pleased him and part of it did not. He was sensitive about being taken for a tenderfoot, because he knew he was one.

Choosing the restaurant kept by the Chinaman he went in to get breakfast. The place contained a long lunch counter and some tables. Evidently the kitchen was back of the counter. Mexicans and roughly garbed men seemed to be the only patrons of the place. Ernest took a seat at one of the tables placed along a thin board partition which separated the restaurant from the business next door. It must have been a very flimsy structure for his keen ears caught the sound of low voices from the other side. Every word was distinct.

"I seen Hepford's gurl get it."

"At the bank?"

"Shore. An' she's takin' the Springer stage this mornin'."

"S'pose thar's others goin', too?"

"Wal, Bud'll git it if we don't. He's gone on ahead. But we'll lay low fer a good chanct fer ourselves."

Then came the sound of scraping chairs, followed by footsteps. Selby looked out of the window and a moment later saw two men emerge from the place next door. They were certainly hard-looking customers, and Ernest scrutinized them carefully. He would not be likely to forget either. They went quickly down the street, and such was Ernest's degree of excitement that he could scarcely make the Chinaman understand what he wanted to eat. Then when he finally got it he had lost his appetite. What a wonderful opportunity had been fairly thrust upon him! The girl he had spoken to was the daughter of Hepford, the manager of Red Rock Ranch, and she was evidently going to be robbed. Now that he was in possession of such knowledge, he realized with growing excitement that it was going to be his duty to circumvent the robbers. The bandit referred to as Bud probably intended to hold up the stage somewhere while the two hard-bitten men he had overheard would take passage upon it, waiting until a favorable opportunity presented itself for carrying out their plans. Well, he was going to be aboard that stage, too, and he would watch carefully for a chance to nip the bandits' plot in the bud with little or no risk. To be able to introduce himself at Red Rock Ranch with such a coup to his credit would assure his reception there and the possibility of being employed as a ranch hand. Nothing tenderfoot about that!

The idea possessed him to such an extent that he completely smothered an inward voice which advised notifying the town authorities. He could handle this thing. The adventure would have appealed to Ernest even if the girl had not been involved, and even if she had not been pretty.

He would require a gun, along with the cowboy clothes he had planned to purchase. Thrilled at the prospect he sallied forth to find the store to which he had been directed.

When Ernest entered the store he was surprised to see that the establishment would have done credit to a much larger city. He strolled from the dry goods department into the grocery, from that to the hardware, and thence to the saddle and harness section. This ought to be close to where he could supply his needs. It was a pretty busy place. Finally a clerk accosted him, and the Iowan replied: "Plain cowboy outfit."

It did not take long to purchase what he wanted. The clerk evidently suspected that his customer was a tenderfoot, which hurried Ernest into additional purchases of chaps, scarves, blanket, and finally gun, belt and shells.

The last thing Selby desired was to excite curiosity; and in his hurry to escape from the store with his large bundle he turned a corner so fast that he collided with someone on the sidewalk. It was a girl, and the collision staggered her a little, so that in stepping backward she sat down rather breathlessly upon some grain sacks. To his horror he recognized her to be the Hepford girl. Her beautiful green eyes were certainly now regarding him with undisguised annoyance. She sat there with face flushed, angrily adjusting her hat.

"I—I beg your pardon," stammered Ernest. "I wasn't looking where I was going. I'm very awkward. Are you all right?"

She stood up and shot him a glance that sent the color to his face. As she passed Ernest saw a spot of rich red under the clear brown of her own cheek. His first impulse was to follow her and explain that even his genuine admiration for a pretty girl would not lead him to the extreme of purposely colliding with her. But he decided against it.

Ernest went back to the hotel, got a room, and changing his clothes for the cowboy garb, was so pleased with himself that he quite forgot his embarrassing encounter. Rough garments became him. The effect was not too dudish. He decided he had better leave off the spurs until he had taken a few lessons in walking with them. If he kept them on, he certainly would be bound to stumble and give himself away. The gun was big and heavy. He loaded it and stuck it in his hip pocket. Packing up, he sallied forth to where he had been directed to find the stage. There he was to learn that despite his pessimistic cowboy informant, the stage was to depart in a few minutes.

The vehicle looked to Ernest like a very large spring wagon, with four wide seats behind the driver's seat, and a top with rolled curtains, which evidently were to be let down in inclement weather. Two well-matched teams were hitched to it, and they seemed impatient to be off.

"Whar you goin', cowboy?" inquired the driver, a weather-beaten man of fifty, with twinkling blue eyes.

"Springertown," answered Selby, as laconically as he was able. He took considerable satisfaction at being taken for a cowboy.

"Ten—in advance," demanded the driver bluntly, implying no question as to his experience with range gentry.

"Ten what?" inquired Ernest.

"Say, boy, air you advertisin' the Kansas plains?" queried the stage driver in real or assumed amaze. "Ten bucks. Simoleons! Cartwheels! Pesos! Otherwise good old U.S. coin!"

"Oh, I reckoned you meant ten cents fare," replied Ernest guilelessly, and produced his wallet, out of which he guardedly extracted a greenback.

"Ahuh," grunted the driver, taking the money. "You can have the back seat. Stow your bags under."

Ernest leisurely did as he was bidden, after which he settled back to enjoy the situation. The seat in front was empty, and the one next to it contained the two hard-looking fellows whose plans he had overheard.

Presently, on the sidewalk, he caught sight of the girl with the red hair he had so unceremoniously encountered twice before that morning. She had come out of the hotel with a middle-aged woman, and a cowboy much burdened with bags and bundles. As they reached the stage Ernest averted his face, notwithstanding the fact that he would have liked to see hers when she recognized him.

"Good-by, Jeff, and thanks for everything," the girl was saying.

"Shore sorry I didn't know sooner you was in town an' sorrier you're goin'," replied the cowboy, in a likable drawl. "But shore you'll be in fer the Fourth."

"I'm afraid not, Jeff," she replied regretfully.

"Aw, you're missin' *the* dance!"

"Reckon I'll miss more than that. If it hadn't been for some particular business of Dad's, I'd not have got to town this time.... Fact is, Jeff, we're awfully upset out at Red Rock Ranch these days."

"You don't say, Anne! An' what aboot?"

"Well, I suppose I may as well tell all my friends," said the girl resignedly. She lowered her voice, but her words, nevertheless, fell distinctly on Ernest's ears. "You know we don't really own Red Rock, though it always seemed as though we did. Dad only runs the ranch for that old skinflint Selby. And now it appears Selby died. We never heard about it until a letter came from his lawyer. That letter acquainted us with the fact that we must expect someone to arrive in Arizona, sooner or later, to take charge of the ranch."

"Doggone! Thet's shore tough," ejaculated the cowboy. "Who'd old Selby leave Red Rock to?"

"The lawyer didn't say. I suppose to a tenderfoot son or nephew. But Dad thinks not. Selby had a middle-aged brother," replied the girl bitterly.

"Wal, I'd stand to be a lot myself to get thet ranch left to me," rejoined Jeff, with a mellow laugh. "Cheer up, Miss Anne. Reckon things will go on aboot the same. This heah man won't show up, an' if he does you can marry him. Ha! Ha!" The cowboy roared with laughter.

The ladies joined in the laugh. "That's what Mrs. Jones advised," continued the girl presently. "But it's not funny. Catch me marrying some white-necked tenderfoot, or some bald-headed Easterner, even to save Red Rock."

"Shore, thet's lucky for one of us cowboys," said Jeff, fervently. "Wal, *adios*. Hope after all you get in for the Fourth. An' say, give my love to your little cousin, Daisy Brooks."

"Catch me, Jeff Martin!" she retorted. "You cowboys! . . . Well, *adios*."

Silas Selby's nephew very soberly agreed with the red-haired young lady that this Red Rock inheritance matter was not at all funny. The fact that this attractive western girl, who had a temper to match her hair, was a daughter of John Hepford, who for years had managed the Red Rock Ranch for Uncle Silas, stirred Ernest considerably. At first sight of

Anne Hepford he had been decidedly attracted; at second sight, it seemed he had been rather badly smitten. Weighing her rather sharp remarks about Silas Selby, he decided he was not smitten after all. But when she sat down in front of him with her companion and he saw the blazing hair, and the nape of her firm, round neck, white where it met the gold tan, he feared that at least he was interested. He recognized the symptoms. They had attacked him occasionally up to the time he was twenty-one, and once or twice during the three years since. But this was something different. After all, when had he seen such a gorgeous creature as Anne Hepford?

"Anne, you didn't tell me this news aboot the ranch," the older woman was saying to the girl in an excited voice, as she settled herself in the seat. "Why, everybody round Springer look on it as yours—you bein' the only child. An' it's been your home for so long!"

"Well, it's *not* mine or Dad's either—that's shore," rejoined the girl shortly. "When I threw a fit at the news, Dad let me know pronto where we stand. Oh, he was upset!"

They began to whisper then, and though Ernest listened shamelessly he could not catch a word. And when the stage started, the roll of the grating wheels and the clatter of hoofs drowned even ordinary conversation. Presently they left the town limits for the ranch country.

Ernest fell into a reverie which precluded neither his own problem nor strict watch upon the two plotters in the seat behind the driver. Nevertheless he got genuine enjoyment from the scenery. The four horses clicked off the miles at a good pace, and each mile appeared to lead into more fascinating country. The green pastures, the gray fields dotted with cattle, the occasional little ranch house, situated in a valley or on a wooded knoll, the rolling, cedared ridges and the dark patches of timber, all pleased the Iowan, yet scarcely prepared him for the rangeland. He had been used to unrestricted view, but this vast sweep of rolling gray with its lines of white and its outcroppings of red, leading the eye to the wide upheaval of land, belted black to the sky, made him catch his breath. Arizona! Rangeland! Up to now, the name had been a myth. He had no recollection of his Uncle Silas, though at home they told him how once he had danced Ernest on his knee and said he would some- day make a Westerner of him. The prediction bade fair to come true. But at the moment Ernest was not wholeheartedly sure that this tremendous stretch of wild, lonely and colorful land would altogether ac- count for it.

The stage rolled on. Evidently the ladies in front had talked themselves out for the time being. Miss Hepford seemed pensive. He was certain that she had not noticed him. He felt curious about the moment when she would actually recognize him; he did not know just why, but he imagined something might hang on that. Chance had thrown together the real owner of Red Rock Ranch and the girl who had dreamed herself into owning it. Here Ernest, proving he was a dreamer himself, indulged in a pretty little boyish fancy of how he went unknown to Red Rock, and as a poor cowboy, saved the red-haired lass from being robbed, and in the end won her hand to present her with the ranch she loved so well as a wedding gift.

That dream lingered with Ernest for many miles, far across the valley which had enchanted him, and up a long slope to a rugged summit. The spectacle that met his eyes from this point dispelled Ernest's daydreams. He gazed in awe at the far-flung ranges, and continued spellbound until the stage rolled down into another valley. It pulled into a picturesque little hamlet and came to a stop before a low one-story inn.

"Concha," called the driver. "Only an' last call for lunch."

Mrs. Jones awoke and Miss Hepford came out of her own reverie. Ernest pulled the wide brim of his sombrero far down over his eyes. He divined, as the girl turned around, that she meant to speak to him.

CHAPTER

2

ALL Selby could see of the young redheaded lady from under his sombrero was her shapely, gloved hand, in the extended palm of which lay some silver coins. "Please get me some ham sandwiches," she was saying.

Ernest took the money, mumbling his pleasure, and leaping out of the stage he went into the tavern. A buxom, middle-aged woman delivered the sandwiches to him, not without a speculative glance. The Iowan was thinking that he might as well not seek any longer to deceive the young lady in the stage; and he went out with his sombrero tipped back and a smile on his face.

But Miss Hepford was not looking and did not notice him until he handed her the sandwiches. Then her green eyes opened wide with a puzzled, searching expression. The look of surprise changed into a twinkle. "Well!" she ejaculated, and then she laughed outright. Her vanity had been tickled. Ernest surmised at once that she imagined he had followed her and that such circumstances were customary in her range life. Her assumption nettled him. He watched her whispering something to her companion, who exclaimed: "For land's sake!" After which Mrs. Jones gave Ernest the benefit of an amused stare. Not to be outdone, Selby returned the compliment with a smile and a wink.

At this juncture the two tough hombres in the second seat ahead claimed Ernest's attention. It struck him that his return had been untimely for them. Probably with the stage driver and himself absent they had thought the time propitious for the planned move.

The larger of the two, a hulking fellow with hard eyes and a beard that did not hide his cruel lips and craggy chin, shoved a dollar at Ernest.

"Hey, sonny, fetch us some of the same," he said.

Ernest shoved the dirty hand away.

"Hey yourself. Who was your dogrobber this time last year?" he retorted.

Both men seemed to take distinct umbrage at this rebuff, or at the refusal which may have militated against an opportunity to carry out their plan.

"You insultin' hayseed of a Mizzouri tenderfoot!" ejaculated the one who had requested the sandwiches.

"Make him get them sandwiches, Bill, or bust his pretty mug," growled the other hombre.

Whereupon Bill threw a silver dollar at Selby

who was standing by the back wheel. It struck him hard and jingled on the hard ground.

"Pick thet up an' fetch them sandwiches," he ordered.

"Say, you are a couple of lazy skunks," replied Ernest angrily.

Bill started to clamber out of the stage, coming over the wheel instead of passing the women, who had now become aware of the argument and were watching the three men intently. Out of the tail of his eye Selby saw Miss Hepford watching him and that certainly added to his determination not to back down. He quite forgot that he carried a gun or he would have found the moment a judicious one to draw it. He sensed battle and with the girl looking on he was eager to give these thugs all the fight they wanted.

Once upon the ground, Bill picked up his dollar and pocketed it. Then he shot out a hand to clutch Ernest's shirt.

"Come along hyar. I'll show you who's a skunk," he growled, and then turned to give his companion a meaningful glance. The latter, acting upon it, stood up. He was a short, stocky man with yellow eyes and teeth that protruded.

"Let go," ordered Selby sharply, and with a powerful wrench he freed himself. With the same movement he swung a heavy fist. It took Bill square on the jaw and down he went in a heap, a look of blank surprise on his bearded face. He lay there on the ground for a moment, his hand on his face, his eyes filled with mingled shock and hatred.

"Did you hit me, you young jacksnipe?" he roared.

"What'd it feel like?" queried Ernest with a laugh. "Want me to help you up and give you more of the same?"

The ruffian bounded to his feet and charged like a mad bull, shouting something to his comrade. Selby avoided the savage rush by nimbly side-stepping. A hard left-hand jab stopped Bill cold and a harder right swing knocked him between the wheels of the stage.

"Git the money, Bill," called the man in the stage. "I'll take kear of this bobcat."

Then he leaped out of the vehicle, landing heavily on the Iowan's back and bearing him to the ground. Whether he thought merely to hold Ernest or to beat him into submission the two women in the stage would never know. For the powerful and active young man rolled over with him, and then quickly breaking loose he sprang to his feet. Bill had just arisen but before he could get set Selby had knocked him down again. By this time the short fellow was upon Ernest once more. There followed a furious fight in which the Iowan found himself extremely busy avoiding the bandit's long gorilla-like arms.

"Rustle—Bill—and git thet gurl's—bag!" panted Selby's assailant. "Driver's—"

Here Ernest twisted loose and swung from the heels. The robber went spinning down with a crash. The younger man waited for him to get to his feet. But his antagonist appeared momentarily stunned.

"Gimme thet bag!" Ernest heard Bill growl.

Wheeling, he was just in time to see Miss Hepford rise from her seat with a scream, while with both hands she clung to a small bag which the bearded man had got a hand on.

"Let go—you thief!" she cried furiously.

It was at this instant that Selby bethought himself of his newly purchased gun. He jerked it out of his pocket and pointed it at the robber.

"DROP IT!" he yelled.

Before the man had time to turn the gun exploded with a loud bang. If Ernest's tight squeeze of inexperience had caused the discharge, it also kept it from flying out of his hand. He had not intended to shoot.

"Don't shoot!" yelled the robber hoarsely, letting go of the girl's bag and elevating his hands. His blood-shot eyes stared wildly at Ernest.

"Run fer it, Bill," called the shorter man, struggling to his feet. And without a backward glance he took to his heels, his boots thudding over the baked ground.

By this time Bill had jumped clear of the stage and was heading for the brush beyond the rock. Selby, almost as badly scared as the robber, once more was able to grasp the situation and his opportunity. Whereupon he aimed the gun in the general direction of the two fleeing bandits who were about to reach the cover of a clump of sagebrush, and pulled the trigger. Bang! Bang! Bang! The bullets struck up angry puffs of yellow dust. But all they accomplished was to make the robbers run faster. Before Ernest could get in a fourth shot they were out of sight.

At the sound of firing, the stage driver came

running out of the tavern accompanied by a heavy-booted man. A woman appeared in the doorway. Down the street people could be seen hurriedly getting out of sight.

"Whut's all the shooting?" demanded the driver, approaching Selby, whose gun was still smoking.

"Those two men tried to rob me," declared Miss Hepford angrily, and she extended the bag as if in evidence.

"They'd 'a' got her bag, too, but for this quick-thinking cowboy," corroborated the older woman.

"Wal, I'll be dinged!" ejaculated the man who had run out with the driver.

Ernest put the gun back in his pocket and kept his hand there, so that they would not see it trembling. Otherwise he managed to face them with simulated nonchalance.

"Doggone it! I shore wasn't fooled much by them fellers," exclaimed the stage driver. "Never paid me no fare!"

Miss Hepford sat down composedly, though she appeared a trifle pale. The green eyes, magnificent now, were fixed curiously upon the young man in the brand new cowboy outfit.

"Thanks, cowboy," she said constrainedly. "You shore did me a service. But what'd you shoot for?"

"Well, it seemed about the only thing to do," explained Ernest, finding his voice. "I couldn't lick them both. And that fellow had hold of your bag."

"Oh, but you did lick them both," interposed the older woman stoutly.

"Did you shoot to kill?" asked Miss Hepford, most curiously.

"No, indeed. I—I only wanted to scare him.... But if he hadn't let go I reckon I'd filled him full of lead," Ernest finished off with considerable *sang-froid*.

"Oh, I see," replied the girl, but her eyes said she did not see at all. Ernest wondered if they did not look straight through his monstrous pretension. "I'm shore glad you didn't have to fill them 'full of lead' for me."

"You ought to have been glad if he had," added her companion vigorously.

"Mrs. Jones, I've had cowboys jump at chances to shoot up each other or the town aboot me, and I don't like it."

"But, Anne, this is different," expostulated Mrs. Jones, aghast at the girl's attitude.

"She thinks me ungrateful, Mr. Gunman," said Miss Hepford to Ernest, a warm, flashing smile suddenly lighting up her face, "but indeed I'm not. If I seem so it is only because I hate gossip, and now another story about me will go the rounds of the range."

"I'm very sorry if I seem to have compromised you, Miss," replied Ernest a bit stiffly.

"Anne, this one won't hurt you a heap," spoke up the big man, with a laugh.

"Uncle Brooks, I'll bet you Hyslip will swear this cowboy hired two hombres to pretend to rob me," protested the girl.

"Haw! Haw! Haw!"

"These cowboys!" exclaimed Mrs. Jones, throwing up her hands in mock dismay.

Selby, however, caught an admiring glance from

the older woman. But the Hepford girl was looking in the direction toward which the two bandits had escaped. He got into the stage again, into the last seat. The heavy man, unshaven and smelling of plowed fields and horses, amiably shoved Ernest to the far corner of his seat.

"Don't mind me. Help yourself," said Ernest with a smile.

"Young man, age before beauty," was the reply; and shrewd but not unkind eyes took the young man's measure.

The driver cracked his whip and called: "All aboord fer Springer." He gathered up the reins and shouted at his horses. The stage rolled out of Concha; the red-haired girl put her head on Mrs. Jones' shoulder; and the big man beside Ernest showed disposition to be friendly.

"Where you ridin', puncher?"

"Springertown," replied his seatmate, interested to discover how much clothes made the man.

"Not long out in these parts, spite of this gun play?"

"Not very long."

"Where you from?"

"Iowa."

"Are you on the grub line?"

Ernest did not know what that was, but he answered in the negative, and added that he was hunting for a job. He was glad to talk, feeling shaky and queer now that the recent excitement was over, and he realized what had actually transpired. He had skinned his knuckles and sustained a bruise on the side of his head, and soiled his new cowboy clothes.

"Wal, I reckon thet'll be easy. Hawk Siebert, foreman for Red Rock, needs riders. He has a hard time keepin' his outfit up. Hepford cain't keep men. An' if you don't get on there I'll take you on myself. Course I cain't pay much, but it's a job."

"Thanks," returned Ernest, drawn to this plain, kindly rancher. "Reckon I'll try Hepford anyhow— heard so much about Red Rock. Why can't he keep men?"

"Wal, he used to be different, long ago, but late year's he's the kind of cattleman riders won't ride for unless they have to. You'll find that out."

"I see. Not very encouraging—me being new to the far West. Fact is, I've heard things not exactly— er—well—very complimentary about the way he runs a ranch."

"Huh. He's shore run Red Rock into the ground, as everybody round here knows," replied the rancher, with some bitterness. "It was shore a great ranch when I had charge."

Ernest restrained his astonishment. Without appearing too curious he tried to show the natural interest of a cowboy on the loose. He was to learn that his rancher acquaintance was Sam Brooks, who some years back had built up Red Rock for Selby. At one time there were sixty thousand head of cattle, he was told. Brooks' wife was a cousin of the Hepfords. When Selby bought the ranch he gave Brooks a hundred acres of land at the head of the valley, which land Hepford, when he had ousted Brooks from his job, could not get possession of.

"But he's never stopped tryin' to scare me out," continued Brooks. "I've got thet land, though, an' someday it'll be valuable. You see the creek head's on my land, an' in dry seasons Red Rock shore would run mighty dry but for my spring. I never put any obstacle in Hepford's way. Selby gave me the land an' it was right of me to be liberal with my water. But someday—"

Brooks did not complete his sentence, but his massive jaw set hard. Then leaning close to Ernest, he indicated with a large thumb the person of Anne Hepford, and whispered: "Thet's Hepford's gal. She thinks she owns Red Rock."

Ernest discovered through Brooks' proximity that he had been drinking, which no doubt accounted for his loquaciousness. It seemed to Ernest to be a significant and fortunate chance, this meeting with Brooks, and during the next hour he proceeded to make the most of it. He learned more about Red Rock and the range than he might otherwise have found out in months. Brooks just fell short of intimating that there might be some question about John Hepford's cattle dealings. There was tremendous bitterness here, if not more, and Red Rock's new owner became convinced that he was on the track of something. What with Brooks' talk and the changing and ever growing ruggedness of the scenery the miles appeared to fly by, until at last the stage topped a long rise that looked down into a valley. "Wonderful!" exclaimed Ernest.

"You see them red cliffs an' crags standin' up across there, under the timber?" queried Brooks. "Wal, when Selby seen them he named his ranch Red Rock.... You cain't see my place yet."

"How much of this valley does Hepford own—I

mean—belongs to Red Rock Ranch?"

"Every darn acre of it, an' then some, except my hundred up heah."

"Whew!" exclaimed the young man, gazing around him with wonderment.

Sight of the great ranch evidently had strong effect upon Brooks also, but exactly opposite to Ernest's. Perhaps Brooks, too, had once entertained ambitions to get possession of Red Rock Ranch. He lapsed into moody silence. The stage rolled down a fine wide road that wound by easy stretches and curves down the mountain and through succeeding belts of pine, cedar, oak and maple to the level valley floor. Ernest saw a glistening stream that ran through green pastures and fields, and led up to a white cottage under a red bluff, where the valley narrowed.

The stage stopped at a lane which ran straight in the direction of the cottage. There Ernest caught sight of a girl leaning over the bars of the gate.

"Hyar you air, Sam," bawled the stage driver. "Pile out."

Brooks clambered heavily out of the stage and Ernest handed down his packages. "Wal, puncher, heah's where I get off. What'd you say your name was?"

"I forgot to tell you. I—it's Ernest Howard," replied the young man on the back seat, luckily glib with his middle name.

"Mine's Sam Brooks. Ride up to see me if you land a job in the neighborhood."

"Sure will. And maybe I'll want that job—if Mr. Hepford won't take me on," returned Ernest, loud enough for the benefit of Miss Hepford, who had roused from her nap and was now looking about her.

Meanwhile the girl at the gate was coming rather slowly forward toward the halted stage. She appeared to be about seventeen years old, and she had big, shy, dark eyes. She was barefooted.

"Hello, Dais, heah I am loaded down like a pack hoss," Brooks greeted her and began to load her with some of the bundles. "Howdy, Daisy," spoke up Miss Hepford. "Haven't seen you for ages."

"Howdy, cousin," replied the girl. "I don't get down much these days."

Ernest, listening and watching, suspected that there was no love lost between the cousins. And just as the stage started on again, the Brooks girl looked up to meet his curious gaze. She blushed so furiously that he instantly regretted his stare. Miss Hepford saw the girl's confusion and laughed merrily. After the stage had rolled a few rods down the road the young man looked back, again to be caught staring. But this time he smiled, as if to mitigate his offense, and turning carried with him an impression of dark, melancholy eyes.

The valley was longer and wider than it had appeared from the high point above. Naturally after the first possessive thrill Ernest began to make a closer and more detailed observation of the property which belonged to him. But for the deeds and papers in his bag he certainly would have doubted his senses.

The road wound under a wooded slope and through clumps of pine, and along a swift, clear creek, the size of which, remembering Brooks' assertion that it flowed from a single spring on his farm, astounded him greatly. At the same time Ernest could not but reflect that it certainly had been an oversight on the part of his Uncle Silas to give away the source of the main water supply to his ranch. Ernest thought it might be well to buy back this piece of land, or make some fair and square deal with Brooks for water rights.

He discovered but few cattle, considering the large acreage represented there, and concluded that the stock probably was ranging up and down beyond the hills. He saw not a single fence until he got well down toward the mouth of the valley. Then it became evident that the valley debouched into another of those vast, rolling parks for which this part of the country was famous. Probably that was the real cattle range.

All the cliffs and crags on the opposite side of the wide park stood out in striking shades and tints of red above the green of the range. In a rounded curve of the valley, almost an amphitheater, a wide bench jutted out, and here among scattered pine trees and gnarled old oaks stood the low, rambling ranch house, very picturesquely located, with an assortment of barns, sheds, corrals, and the like grouped farther back under the slope.

Ernest drew a deep, almost painful breath. All this could not possibly be his. But it was! And he had a flash of lively expectancy of the fun and adventure he was going to experience before he revealed himself as the real owner. What, he thought, would this outspoken western girl, this green-eyed Anne Hepford say if she knew? Looking at her as she sat before him, her face excitedly turned in the direction of the

Red Rock ranch house, he wondered how this proud creature would react when she learned the truth.

"Whoa!" yelled the driver, and braked the stage to a halt at a corner of the road where a thick clump of pines obstructed the view of the valley in both directions.

A man suddenly appeared along the roadside. Instantly Ernest's mind reverted to the conversation between the robbers which had intimated that a third member of the party named Bud would secure the money Miss Hepford carried, should they fail in their effort to get it. Selby sat up suddenly, and his hand went to his hip pocket. These rangeland ruffians certainly did not lack when it came to boldness. This man was younger than the other two, and he had a clean square-cut chin and dark face. He might be a ranchman or even a cowboy from his looks, Ernest thought, but he had hard, steady, flinty eyes that reminded him of the other cowboys he had seen that morning on the station square.

"What you want, haulin' me up like this?" demanded the driver suspiciously.

"Ride to Springer. My hoss went lame," was the calm reply.

"Whar is your hoss?"

"Tied back off the road," rejoined the stranger, jerking his hand backward. "I'll come back after him."

"Wal, all right, git in," replied the stage driver reluctantly.

The man leaped up onto the step with one graceful bound and at that moment Ernest felt himself subjected to the most penetrating gaze he had ever encountered. Something in it that the Iowan interpreted as an insolent appraisal of his status as a tenderfoot, inflamed him to the point of rage. Moreover it convinced him that the man who just had boarded the stage was the third robber. He coolly accepted the stranger's challenging look. His eyes did not waver. Glad indeed was he that he had still two shells in his gun. Miss Hepford might see something presently that was not calculated to excite her suspicious vanity over the tricks of cowboys to win her favor.

Selby sat forward, nerved for swift action if it proved necessary, as the man stepped up as if to take the seat behind the women. But he did not sit down. Quick as a flash he bent over Miss Hepford and snatched her bag, which she held in her lap.

She screamed: "Let go of my bag! Help me, somebody!" She was frantically wrestling to regain her bag. But she was too late.

The Iowan leaped up with drawn gun and when the robber wheeled Ernest leveled it at him.

"Halt or I fire!" Selby cried hoarsely, and he had a hair-raising sense of his finger on the trigger. The man's dark face changed, more from surprise and chagrin than fear.

"Up they are," he sang out.

Ernest made no false move here. He knew what he was doing when with his left hand he jerked the bag from the thief.

"Turn round....Now sit down....Keep your hands high!"

These orders were obeyed. Then Selby directed the women to step across into the seat ahead of them.

"I might have to shoot this footpad," he added,

"and I don't want to risk hurting anyone else."

They lost no time in complying. Mrs. Jones nearly fainted and dropped her head against Miss Hepford's shoulder. The redheaded girl turned a pale and wrathful face backward.

"Don't kill—him!" she cried, but there was no compassion in her voice.

"If I have to, I'll be careful not to spatter his brains all over you," replied Ernest coolly. Then he pressed the gun barrel hard against the middle of the thief's back.

"Well, so you're Bill's pard," he muttered. "You may be interested to know that this gun went off of its own accord awhile back."

Here the stage driver came out of his trance with a muttered curse. "Woods seem to be full of these cheap holdup hombres! Cowboy, you're all there! Watch him like a hawk!"

"Drive on to the ranch," ordered Ernest sharply.

In another moment the stage was on its way at a fast trot. As it turned off to the right, the horses came to a gentle slope, above which lay the pine-covered bench where the ranch house stood. In spite of Selby's close attention to the bandit on the seat in front of him, he was conscious of the lovely scenery which they were passing. He could see that the stage was driving through a virgin, brown-carpeted, sweet-scented pine forest which extended up to the fine old ranch house. Then the driver, with a fine flourish, hauled the stage to a stop in a green square before the house. Dogs barked a welcome. A tall man, in shirt sleeves, with a dark, pointed beard and sharp eyes, walked down the broad steps. He wore leather top boots with spurs, and Ernest immediately took him to be John Hepford.

"What the hell?" the man on the ground called in a tone of surprise, staring at the inmates of the stage.

"Oh, Dad, I've been held up twice," cried Miss Hepford.

"Held up? What are you talking about? Is this one of your highwaymen?" he asked, gesturing toward Ernest and his prisoner.

"Hepford, we shore hev been held up twice," spoke up the driver wrathfully. "I took on two hombres at Holbrook. At Concha they'd a got thet bag of Miss Anne's if it hedn't been fer this here young cowboy. He fought them an' drove them off. Then back hyar by the pines this galoot piles on an' he did get the bag. But this gent hyar stopped him, as you see."

"Steady there, cowboy," said the rancher, coolly. "You've a fidgety finger, I see."

"Yes I have," replied Selby. "Here's the bag these fellows wanted so badly." And Ernest tossed it out to Hepford.

"I *told* you not to make me draw all that money," burst out the girl, as she climbed out.

"You come too, Mrs. Jones. We'll drive you to Springer later. I'll send some of the boys with this thief to the sheriff's office."

By the time the frightened Mrs. Jones had been helped out of the stage, several young cowhands had come running up in answer to the rancher's call.

"What's doin', boss?"

"Anne's been held up. You boys take this hombre

to Springer an' turn him over to Sheriff Walker."

The three cowpokes all boarded the stage at once and at different points.

"Been ridin' him hard, cowboy?" said one. "Wal, you c'n climb off. We'll do the rest."

Ernest pocketed his gun and jumped down off the stage. Here the driver came to his rescue. "Much obliged, cowboy. This is whar you git off. I heahed what you said to Sam Brooks....Don't forget your bags."

The young Iowan suddenly became aware of the fact that he was being examined by a pair of hypnotic green eyes.

"I want to apologize, Mr. Gunman," said Miss Hepford. "I thought it was a cowboy trick....I am Anne Hepford. This is my dad."

"What's your name?" queried the rancher.

"Ernest—Howard," stammered Ernest.

"From where?"

"Iowa."

"Did you follow my girl out heah?" he went on, his sharp, cold gaze fixed on Ernest.

"No sir," replied Selby stiffly. "I can't say that I care for your insinuation. Just the same, it was mighty lucky for you I happened to be on the stage."

"Shore." The rancher's voice lost its tone of suspicion. "I'm not overlooking that. Reckon you're looking for a job."

"Yes sir."

"Wal, hunt up Hawk Siebert and see if he'll take you on," concluded the rancher, waving his hand.

"Mr. Ernest Howard," added Anne sweetly, "you can tell Siebert that *I* said for him to give you a job."

CHAPTER

3

*S*ELBY picked up his bags and hurriedly departed in the direction indicated by Hepford. He passed the house, not daring to look up the high porch steps into the wide, open hall. Presently on a bypath that led to the bunkhouse he encountered a fine-looking giant of a cowboy whose eyes were like gimlets.

"Where can I find Hawk Siebert?" asked Ernest.

"Gawd only knows," drawled the tall cowpoke, and strode on. Ernest halted irresolute. He found it hard to understand the indifference, the distrust, not to say open antagonism of these Westerners. His instinct was to shake the dust from this inhospitable place. But his feet seemed already to have taken hold of soil that belonged to him. And perhaps even if that were not true, the strange fascination which the Hepford girl held for him would let him leave. Again he started on.

The young Iowan had begun to realize by this time that a tenderfoot cowboy did not cut much of a figure on a big ranch. This was precisely what he wanted, yet he reacted to the situation with the feelings of Ernest Selby. Perhaps when Anne Hepford found out who he really was, she would not be so snobbish. But it occurred to Ernest right then that when the time came there would not be much real pleasure in being noticed because he owned Red Rock Ranch. He did not know which he cared for less—her present snobbish attitude or the feeling of hatred and resentment she was sure to exhibit when she discovered who he really was.

A stable boy directed Ernest to the bunkhouse and said he would find Siebert there. Arriving at the long one-story structure he espied several young cowboys and an older man sitting on the porch.

"I'm hunting for Hawk Siebert," Selby announced.

"Heah you are. But I don't recollect ever doin' anythin' to you," replied the foreman dubiously. Ernest liked his face and eyes, even though they had distinct association with his first name.

"I'm asking for a job," said Ernest.

"Where?" queried Siebert, growing more attentive. And the other cowboys now became aware of the stranger's presence.

"Here—at Red Rock Ranch."

"What kind of a job?"

"Any kind."

"Cowpuncher, eh?"

"I'm not choosey."

"Hope you ain't one of them gun-totin' riders from Texas?"

"I'm from Iowa....Yes, I'm toting a gun."

At this juncture the tall, good-looking cowboy whom Ernest had encountered out in front arrived on the scene singing:

> Son-of-a-gun from Ioway
> He stoled my gurl-l away-y.

Hawk Siebert now took keener note of the job-seeker and after a moment, when the singer had clanked across the porch and into the bunkhouse, he asked: "Ride out here with the boss's daughter?"

"She was on the stage," replied Ernest.

"You any particular friend of her?"

"Me!—Never saw Miss Hepford before today."

"Wal, a day's a long time out heah in the West," remarked Siebert dryly.

Selby grasped a good deal from the foreman's last remarks, and he thanked his lucky stars that he had not introduced himself as Miss Hepford had ordered him to. Siebert ran a speculative and appreciative eye over the new applicant for work at Red Rock. Ernest had no fear on the score of his stature. The distant yet intent regard of the cowboys, however, made him begin to grow red under the collar.

"This one has been pretty long for me," admitted Ernest.

"You look like you've been in a scrap," observed Siebert.

"Yes. But nothing to speak of."

"Ahuh. Depends on how you look at it."

"Say, Hawk," called the cowboy who had gone inside. "Iowa is a plumb bad breedin' ground for tramps, grubline punchers, gun-throwers an' lady-killers who hire toughs to make a fake stage holdup."

Siebert paid no heed to this surprising sally.

"What's your name?"

"Ernest Howard."

"Wal, I'm not needin' a rider, but I might take on a feller who was handy all around."

"I'm certainly the fellow you want," said Ernest, with a smile.

"Diggin' fence-post holes, stretchin' barb' wire, pitchin' hay, doin' errands, an' sich as thet?" drawled the foreman.

Selby did not know then that for a cowboy to admit willingness to do these menial jobs on a ranch was to define his status as the lowest of the low.

"Such as that is apple pie for me," he replied, smiling. "I want a job, and I'm not particular." And he was not sure but that his eagerness and his smile went far with Hawk Siebert.

"You're on. Forty a month. Throw in with Ne-braskie Kemp, at the end of the house," concluded the foreman, pointing to an open door farther down the porch.

Ernest thanked him and turned back to fetch his baggage. One of the cowboys let out a wail. "Aw, Hawk, what'd you pick on me fer? Throw him in with Dude or Lunky." A yell went up from another cowboy, and before the Iowan got out of hearing his ears were burning. Between the redheaded Hepford girl and these cowboys, it began to look as though he were going to have a tough time of it here at Red Rock. Still, in spite of the young lady's haughty attitude and the cowpokes' evident dislike, the newcomer began to see interesting possibilities in acting as a hired hand on his own ranch.

Ernest made for the end of the bunkhouse, as he had been directed, and discovered the door of that room open, and a cherub-faced cowboy slamming things around in a petulant fashion.

"Are you Nebraskie Kemp?" asked Ernest, genially, with his most engaging smile.

"I shore am, wuss luck," replied the other.

"Say, but I'm lucky. I was afraid I'd draw that pretty singing cowboy for a bunkmate. You look like a human being."

"Wal, I ain't so blame shore I can return the compliment," returned Nebraskie gruffly, but he was studying his new bunkmate with big, bright blue eyes.

"See here. If I'm not welcome I'd rather sleep in the barn. That wasn't a very good crack you made to Siebert, after I left. 'What'd he want to pick on *you* fer?' I'm not a polecat. For that matter, how do you know who or what I am?"

"Reckon thet's the hell of it," agreed Nebraskie. "But I've got to take a chanct on you. So get down an' come in."

Ernest brought his bags inside and set them down. He thought it best to have a straight talk with this cowboy.

"I have to take the same chance on you, don't I?"

"Wal, come to think of thet, yes, you do," replied Nebraskie with a laugh.

"I'll lay my cards on the table. I'm a tenderfoot. Bad in need of a job—and a friend, besides. I'll probably be a lamb among wolves in this Red Rock outfit. But—how do you know I'm *not* worth sticking up for?"

"I don't. An' you give yourself away as no cowboy or Westerner ever did, when you let Siebert saddle you with a job no self-respectin' cowboy would. But heah a stranger is no good till he proves it ain't so."

"All right, I ask no more than that," replied the tenderfoot simply, and offered his hand.

The nonplussed Nebraskie took it reluctantly.

"You got a bad start, young feller. Whenever a puncher comes ridin' in *with* Miss Anne or *after* her—wal, he's throwin' a red flag in Dude Hyslip's face. An' Dude sort of runs the outfit, after Hawk."

"I'll bet Dude is that conceited singing cowboy," declared Ernest.

"Shore is. But don't let Dude hear you callin' him a singin' cowboy."

"Nebraskie, I didn't come with Miss Hepford or after her. Anybody can see that she's mighty easy to look at. But I came here to get a job. But I'm asking you not to tell Hyslip this. Let him think what he darn pleases. Only—if he keeps on singing that son-of-a-gun from Ioway song—there's going to be trouble."

"Ahuh. What'd you say your name was?"

"Ernest Howard," replied Ernest.

"Wal, your handle will be Ioway, shore as shootin', same as mine is Nebraskie....An', Ioway, you can bet your sweet life Dude will go on singin' thet song."

"Then I'll just plain have to lick him," asserted Ernest.

"You'll *what-t?*" exploded Nebraskie.

"I'll lick him. And don't you think I can't do it! He may be at home on a horse. But he walks as if his feet hurt. And I'm at home on the ground."

"Ioway, if you lick Dude Hyslip, by golly, there'd be some chanct of your lastin' heah at Red Rock."

"Don't worry. I'll last all right," said Ernest with a good-natured laugh.

"I kinda like you, doggone it," returned Nebraskie, peevishly. "Wal, you take the upstairs bunk an' throw your outfit around."

About ten minutes later, while Ernest was unpacking his smaller bag, the foreman, Siebert, entered. His eyes had more of the hawk-like quality even than before.

"Howard, do you mind my talkin' out plain before Nebraskie heah?" he queried.

"Not at all. Nebraskie is goin' to be my friend."

"Wal, if he is you're lucky....Already there's a story flyin' around. Dude Hyslip must have got it somewhere or made it up. What's this about you holdin' up three bandits on the stage?"

Selby had expected this and welcomed the inquisitive and not unkind query.

"It's straight goods," he declared, looking frankly at the foreman and the curious cowboy. "Listen. Here's how it happened." And Ernest told in detail the whole affair, not omitting a confession of his reason for not notifying a sheriff at Holbrook.

"So thet was it," replied Siebert, evidently convinced. "I reckon I believe you, Howard, but if you've jest pulled some fun be honest aboot it now."

"I've told the truth—on my honor," the tenderfoot declared, impulsively.

"Hawk, it ain't sense, but doggone it—I believe him," said Nebraskie.

"Wal, so do I. But we'll keep our traps shet aboot it.... Howard, as Hyslip told it, you hired some Holbrook loafer to make a bluff at robbin' Miss Hepford, so you could rescue her. Thet's been done before heah, so *she* says."

"Hyslip is a damned liar," replied Ernest hotly. "I told Nebraskie I'd lick Hyslip if he sang that Ioway song again. But he doesn't need to sing it. I'll go right out now—"

"Hold on, rooster," broke in Siebert persuasively. "It ain't the thing fer you to do pronto. Hyslip stands in an' if you want to hang on, why, you'll have to go slow.... Now as fer the holdup, I happen to know somethin' which I'll keep to tell Anne Hepford someday. Thet feller you fetched in the stage was Bud Miller, an' he shore is the genuine article."

"Why not let me take care of this ridiculous charge myself?" demanded Ernest.

"Wal, all in good time. You're shore a hothaided boy.... What do you say, Nebraskie?"

"Reckon I'd let it pass," replied Kemp thoughtfully. "Anyway nobody is goin' to believe you didn't come out heah to Red Rock after Anne."

*　　　*　　　*

Next morning at daylight the new hand went to work helping the Mexicans shingle one of the sheds. The cowboys rode by and Dude Hyslip sang, "Son-of-a-gun from Ioway" at the top of his lungs. At mealtimes they passed banter to and fro along with the food, the former of which was directed at Ernest, while of the latter he had to help himself.

That day served only as an initiation. The following one, and those succeeding would have been nightmares for Ernest Selby, except for the inward satisfaction he derived from working for himself and learning about the ranch, and for the disturbing fact that he had at least a glimpse of Anne Hepford every day.

Nothing escaped Ernest's eyes. The tricks the cowboys played upon him grew in proportion to his efforts to ignore them. Some of them were harmless and funny; others were neither. Ernest accepted everything with good grace. He could afford to be patient, not only because he was in no hurry to show his hand, but because of the redheaded girl. If she had been dazzling in ordinary traveling clothes, he feared to think of seeing her more formally dressed— say for the dance to be given at Springertown presently. Selby decided to go, if only to watch. That insufferable Dude Hyslip! Snatches of cowboy gossip acquainted Ernest with the belle of Red Rock.

The new hand did not get a chance to straddle a horse for over a week, and then his mount certainly was not one of the thoroughbreds he saw prancing in the pasture or kicking the bars of the corral. Ernest loved horses and he had to turn away his eyes, whenever the cowboys rode by where he was doing some menial job. He could not help being thrilled by the thought that every one of these beautiful horses belonged to him. What a jolt Mr. Dude Hyslip was going to get someday, when he discovered that the son-of-a-gun from Ioway was his boss!

But Ernest did not allow his infatuation and longing for Anne and his jealousy of Hyslip to interfere with the main issue—his duty to discover what was wrong with John Hepford's management of Red Rock.

Springertown lay several miles beyond Red Rock. It was the center of a group of ranches, and was larger than Selby had expected. He rode down the main street, taking in the unpainted, high, boardfront stores, the hitching rails, the saloons, and the people. It was Saturday and a busy day. Nebraskie had told him the cowboys had the afternoon off, but that privilege did not extend to hired hands, of whom Ernest was one.

The Iowan dismounted and tied his horse to a rail, feeling a wonderful satisfaction in the act. His errand was to leave an order at the Springer brothers' store and when that had been attended to, Ernest walked up and down the street, taking a look in the saloons, stopping to exchange amiable talk with a farmer here and a youngster there. But he gave the cowboys, especially the high-stepping ones, already tipsy, a wide berth. He couldn't help noticing that Steve Monell, Bones Magill, and Shep Davis, of the Red Rock outfit already were decidedly under the influence of liquor. By dark, according to Nebraskie, these cowboys would be whooping up the town.

In front of one of the stores he encountered a girl much too burdened with parcels for her slight

stature. She dropped a parcel, while putting her load
into a buckboard outside of the rail, and she climbed
up to the front seat without noticing her loss. Ernest
stepped out into the road and, recovering it, handed
it up with the remark: "Miss, you dropped something."

"Thanks," she replied, in confusion.

For a moment Ernest wondered where he had
seen her. Then he remembered the dark eyes. It was
Daisy Brooks. Here were two opportunities in one,
the Iowan thought, and not to be overlooked.

"I almost didn't recognize you," he said pleasantly, and he became aware that the bright dress and
hat made the difference. "I'm Ernest Howard. Didn't
I meet you that day I arrived on the stage and made
the acquaintance of your dad? He asked me to come
up to see him, but I haven't had a chance so far. Wish
you'd tell him that you saw me. Maybe I'll take that
job he offered me. They're sure killing me at Red
Rock."

"We heahed all aboot it," she said shyly.

"Oh, did you? Well then I don't need to bother
you with my complaints," replied Ernest, laughing.
"I didn't think I was the talk of the range—just yet."

"Cowboys usually are—when they go to Red
Rock," she said.

Ernest caught a glimpse of something deep and
furtive in the dark eyes before they dropped.

Then her father came to accost Ernest in his
bluff and hearty way.

"Wal, ketched you makin' up to my gal, eh?" he
said laughing, and stepped up heavily into the vehicle. "You're most as bad as Dude Hyslip."

"As a matter of fact, Mr. Brooks, I haven't been introduced to her. But you can't blame a fellow for talking to a pretty girl. I'm so darned lonesome for a human being to talk to—and seeing Miss Daisy made me remember how—how friendly you were to me on my way up from Holbrook."

"No offense, son. I was only teasin' Dais heah," he said, indicating the blushing girl. "Cain't you come fer dinner tomorrow? It's Sunday. Make a kick to Siebert. He'll let you off."

"I sure will. Much obliged," replied the younger man, but it was at Daisy that he looked.

Ernest bade them good-by and strolled on down the street, unaccountably annoyed with himself. Did the whole countryside imagine he had become a laborer at Red Rock only to be near its young mistress? He resented the idea, knowing it to be only half true. He was not overly vain, but it was certain that he had not made any impression whatever upon Anne Hepford. As a result of this encounter with the Brookses and the train of thought they had set into motion, Selby rode back to the ranch in a rather testy state of mind.

At the barn he met Hawk Siebert, the second time he had ever seen that busy individual alone.

"Can I have tomorrow off?" asked Ernest.

"Shore. An' why didn't you stay in town fer the dance tonight?" replied the foreman, good-naturedly, his keen eyes bent hard on his new hand.

"Dance nothing. That outfit of yours would run me out of the hall," declared Ernest bitterly.

"Like hob they would," returned Siebert. "Howard, you don't 'pear to be the runnin' kind. Reckon you haven't guessed it, but I'm onto the deal you been gettin' heah. It's the wust any admirer of Miss Anne's ever got.... Wal, you don't stand deuce-high with that young lady. An' you're shore a misfit with my cowboys. But you've made good with *me*, young feller. An' on Monday you take to ridin' the range."

CHAPTER
4

*O*N Sunday morning Selby manifested some interest in his personal appearance, the first time since his arrival at Red Rock, and it did not escape the keen eyes of Nebraskie.

"Huh! Ridin' in to church with Anne today?" he hazarded, in mingled surprise, curiosity and jealousy.

"Wouldn't you like to know?" taunted the Iowan.

"Wal, reckon it doesn't matter aboot me, but keep it from Dude. He's sore as a busted thumb this mawnin'. Anne dished him for the dance last night. She was shore steppin' high, wide an' handsome. If thet gurl ain't the meanest flirt in Arizonie I—I'll eat my shirt."

"Nebraskie!" ejaculated Ernest, as much in amazement at this revelation as resentment for the outrage to the object of his admiration.

"Aw, don't Nebraskie me. An' don't try to fool

me, either. Wasn't she askin' fer you last night?
Where's my new cowpuncher? . . . I oughtn't give you
a hunch, Ioway, but you let thet troublemaker alone."

Ernest went off in high dudgeon with Nebraskie,
at the same time walking on the clouds of hope. So
Miss Hepford had not forgotten him! Selby walked
all the way up to the Brooks' farm, a good five miles,
and never once thought of the distance.

Probably if it had not been for Nebraskie's
chance remark he might have been impressed by
Daisy Brooks. As it was he did only justice to the
occasion that plainly meant a great deal to her. The
tidy little cottage, the wholesome and savory dinner,
certainly attested to her ability as Sam Brooks'
housekeeper. Besides at any other time he might
have been more susceptible to Daisy's shy beauty.
The girl's eyes betrayed her, and once, when she
served him at table, and her hand touched his, she
turned away quickly, blushing furiously. But in con-
trast to the blooming rose of Red Rock she seemed
only a modest little cornflower.

After dinner Brooks took Selby out to show him
the ranch, and particularly the spring which watered
the valley, and in dry seasons wholly saved it for the
cattle. Ernest had never seen a spring like this. It was
a deep dark well roaring from under the mossy cliff,
a source of never failing abundance and fertility.

"I shore could do a lot with thet water if I
had some capital," asserted Brooks. "Mebbe someday—"

"Brooks, would you ever sell out—if you got
your price?" queried Ernest casually.

"Sell nothin'," retorted Sam. "Don't I know what

I've got? Someday I'll be a pardner of John Hepford's or the unlucky cowboy who finally lands Anne."

"Why unlucky?"

"Say, Howard, have you been at Red Rock all this while an' don't know thet yet?"

"I'm afraid I have."

"Wal, you're a mighty blind an' kindhearted boy thet's all I'll say."

Ernest tramped here and there with Brooks over the small ranch, expressing such keen interest that the rancher was plainly delighted, and as their friendship grew, he grew more loquacious. The talk turned eventually to Hepford and Red Rock Ranch. Sam's visitor did not betray that he was probably the only employee who did not know there was soon to be a big drive of cattle. Hepford, it appeared, sold many cattle, but only a few times during the last few years had he had one of these big drives. Selby was all curiosity, as befitted a tenderfoot. What was the difference between a small and a large drive? Brooks did not openly declare any irregularity about the latter, yet the intimation was unmistakable.

"Hepford sends bunches of two-year-olds to Holbrook," said Brooks. "But when he sells one of these big drives the cattle don't get to the railroad. They go out by way of Pine, down over the Blue Ridge, to the reservations. Government buyer named Jones. The last drive was a year ago in June. Funny aboot thet! Shore'd like to see the reports sent back to the owner, Selby."

"Sam, I heard Silas Selby was dead," said Ernest, looking down.

"What?—You don't say? Wal!—Where'd you heah thet?" exclaimed Brooks excitedly.

"It's known at the ranch. Siebert mentioned it— telling the cowboys they'd have to walk turkey if another owner showed up."

"Wal, I should smile. Walkin' turkey ain't the word. Walkin' off the ranch is what. Howard, reckon I don't need to tell you there're some mean punchers in thet outfit. Thet Dude Hyslip, for instance. Damn him! I'd like to hosswhip him, if no wuss."

"What'd he do, Sam?" inquired Ernest.

"He hurt Daisy's feelin's. She was sweet on Nebraskie Kemp till Dude cut him out. But Nebraskie was serious an' Dude only fast an' loose."

"Nebraskie! . . . Well! . . . Sam, I'll remember that when I lick Dude," said Ernest, soberly.

"Wal, I hope you do. You're a husky fellar. An' there's somethin', Howard. But be sure to pick a time when Hyslip ain't packin' a gun."

Brooks seemed upset by the news of the death of Selby and he grew thoughtful. Whereupon Ernest bade him good-by and started back on the long walk, glad for the solitude that would give him time to think.

When he arrived at the bunkhouse it still wanted an hour till sunset. Ernest unlocked his bag, took out the precious papers upon which hung so much, and hiding them inside his shirt he strolled off, and then climbed the slope to emerge on a wooded bluff—one of the red-stone cliffs. The view from there was superb, but at the moment Ernest had no eyes for the beauty of the valley. He read over all the legal papers, the correspondence, the yearly reports. Some of these dated back as far as a decade. It was noteworthy, however, that there was no report of the year in which Hepford had taken up the management of Red Rock. And more noteworthy still was the fact that the reports showed no evidence whatever of any big drives of cattle. Here in a nutshell was proof of how twenty thousand head of cattle had slowly dwindled to the present number of six thousand. Hepford obviously was merely a cattle thief. Ernest had not listened to Brooks and Siebert, and the cowboys without learning considerable about past and present rustling. There were cattle thieves of all degrees.

Hepford had probably calculated that he would never come into ownership of the ranch, but while he had the operation of it he would see to feathering his nest. The past ten years had not been lean ones on the range; quite the contrary, and twenty thousand head, counting for frequent sales of two-year-olds and the usual fall bunch of steers, should have still been around that figure, if not a greater number. So John Hepford had gotten rid of in the neighborhood of fifteen thousand head of cattle, and ought to have at least two hundred thousand dollars "salted away," as the cowboys called it.

But had he been able to hide his tracks or had he counted upon the great improbability of the invalid Selby ever again visiting Red Rock? If he was dishonest, as appeared most damningly evident, did Hawk Siebert deliberately shut his eyes to what must have been plain to any old cattleman? On the other hand, there was a likelihood that Siebert had never seen the reports sent east. Hepford himself probably had made them out. Ernest sat there on the bluff pondering, and the only conclusion he could come to was that he ought to set about trying to prevent this last drive of cattle. But before he declared himself he must have something that appeared to be wanting, and he could not say precisely what that was.

Monday dawned, a momentous day for Selby. He was thrown by three horses before he found one he could stay on, and this one he selected himself. On Monday mornings after a roistering week end the cowboys were a lote of soreheaded spiteful devils. Even their riotous mirth smacked of the sinister. Ernest had ample chance to pick the fight he wanted with Dude Hyslip, but waived it because the first horse that threw him jarred and weakened him considerably. So he contented himself by retaliating in loud voice: "Hyslip, you are a slick rider, but that lets you out. You're good-looking, too, but that only lets you in for some wild dreams which will never get you any place. Do you get my hunch? I'll bet a million dollars I get to see you fired off this ranch."

"Haw! Haw! Listen to him," burst out Hyslip jeeringly, though his handsome face flamed. "Why don't you offer to bet two bits, you poor tenderfoot hick from Ioway?"

"Look out you don't insult Iowa," declared the younger man. "And how do you know I haven't got a million?"

"Boys, he's gone batty," howled Hyslip, and the cowboys shared his glee.

Ernest shut up then, realizing he could force the

issue whenever he chose, and grimly faced what the day had had in store for him.

It had plenty. Riding the range on a hot dusty day in June would not have been any fun even if the cattle had been left out of reckoning. As it was, the new hand's first day of chasing steers exhausted him completely. That night he fell into bed and slept like a dead man. Nebraskie had to beat him in the morning to awaken him. The second day was even worse. The third was the same. After that the situation began to ease a little.

The job was to round up as many as possible of four-year-old steers each day, and drive them off the range up on the ranch. When Ernest naturally asked who was keeping tally on the number Nebraskie said: "Nobody at this end. Reckon Hepford has 'em counted all right when he sells."

Selby did not need to be told why the stock was not counted there on the ranch. Therefore he counted them himself, as nearly accurately as was possible. This was the flaw in Hepford's drives. They came but seldom, and no cowboy could or would remember how many head were driven in. Ernest verified this by asking casual questions now and then at mealtimes.

The end of June saw more than fifteen hundred head of four-year-old steers in the large pasture on Red Rock Ranch, ready for the drive. Selby heard Hepford say to Hawk Siebert: "That'll do till after the Fourth. Some of these go to Holbrook. Jones' outfit will come after the rest."

So, on the face of it, Hepford's mismanagement of stock was not so easy to unravel, after any con-

siderable time had passed. In the present case Ernest
had enough data, if the matter had to go to court,
which he greatly doubted.

Selby's left arm had been injured in a fall, and
he used that as an excuse to get permission to go to
Holbrook. He traveled on the stage, boarding it in
front of the ranch house, not at all regretful that Miss
Anne Hepford curiously watched him leave. Of late
she had actually noticed Ernest, for which little attention he found himself much elated. For Anne's
sake he had made up his mind that he would not
arrest Hepford, but he wanted what he considered
rightfully his own.

He found a lawyer in Holbrook to whom he entrusted the case. This lawyer, Jefford Smith, was a
Westerner and a catteman. His practice of law was
a side business, and had been taken up as a matter
of exigency for the county. Smith whistled long and
loud over Ernest's papers. "Plain as the nose on
your face," he said succinctly. "It beats the cele-
brated Presston butchering case all hollow. I happen to know Hepford has more money on interest
in Holbrook than has ever been paid Selby all together. Hepford's a director in the bank here. He
does considerable banking in Globe, too, and no
doubt other towns....Young man, you'll certainly
have him in a corner if you can prove your case. It
was right smart of you to come out here as an unknown cowboy to see for yourself. But go slow. Work
to get proofs. Be careful. If you get the proofs Hepford
will break his neck to compromise—to keep this
quiet, not to say buy his escape from jail."

Ernest felt a drumming in his ears and he required a good deep breath before he could speak. Presently he would hold the fate of Anne Hepford in his hands. At the moment he seemed to feel nothing but tenderness for the girl with the green eyes. He certainly did not wish to ruin her happiness, and more than ever he inclined to the dream of making the ranch really hers, along with himself. But he preferred to win her as Ernest Howard, cowboy from Iowa.

"You will keep this matter secret, of course," he said to the lawyer. "I'll remember your advice. I'll take time. There's no hurry."

"Very good. That'll be the wisest course. This is the West, an' possession is nine-tenths of the law. We must have proof," replied Smith.

Selby spent the night at Holbrook and caught the stage next morning. The hours did not drag. In fact such was his state of mind that he did not seem to have enough time to think. He wasted most of it in dreams. On the return trip he got off at Sam Brooks' lane. He was not a little surprised to meet Daisy at the gate. She had come to meet the stage to get things that had been ordered from Holbrook. Her rosy color and Ernest's confusion amused the stage driver, not to say the other passengers.

So it came about that Ernest walked up the lane with Daisy. He did not feel insensible to her charm and to the evident fact of her naïve pleasure in his company. Yet there was something not quite right, and before they had reached the cottage the vivacity that seemed now in her had changed to the quiet familiar wistfulness. A vague dissatisfaction with himself troubled the visitor. He could not get his mind off the compelling fact that someday he would be master of Red Rock.

When they reached the cottage Brooks beamed upon them so approvingly that again he felt uncomfortable.

"I've been to Holbrook," began the Iowan without preamble. "Afraid I—I'm in a peck of trouble. And I just wanted to ask you if you'd stand by me if I need help."

"Somethin' to do with Hepford?" queried Brooks, his eyes suddenly hard and light.

"Maybe. I've got a pretty good idea I'm going to lose my job. Would you take me on here?"

"Shore. An' ask no questions," replied the rancher warmly.

"Much obliged. It is good to know that I have one friend I can count on. Good day, Sam, I'm moseying along," concluded Ernest abruptly, and turned away.

He had not got far when he heard Daisy's voice. She had followed him down the path to the stile. Selby halted. He was uneasy in his mind, yet interested in what the girl wanted, despite his preoccupation. Her face was red when he turned and pale by the time she reached him.

"I—I couldn't say it before Dad—but you've got two friends," she said, bravely but falteringly.

"That's awfully good of you, Daisy. I'll remember it," he replied, and restrained an impulse to take her hand. Any fool could see what darkly eloquent and beautiful eyes she had.

"I'm sorry, Ernest. I—I think I know what trouble you mean," went on Daisy. "We drove down to the ranch yesterday, and I met Nebraskie. I—he—we used to be—well, Dad told you. I reckon Nebraskie doesn't hate you. But the other cowboys do, especially Dude Hyslip. Nebraskie said that when Anne gave it away she was going to the dance at Springer with you—why, Dude raved. . . . Ernest, the least you can expect is a—a fight. It's happened before aboot her. I—I wish you could see—well, never mind aboot that."

Ernest was dumbfounded over Daisy's words. Things evidently had happened during his absence. Then elation succeeded his amazement, and it was with difficulty that he concealed it.

"It's good of you to warn me, Daisy," he said gratefully. "Hope I'll see you at the dance."

"I reckon I'll go. Joe Springer asked me," she replied. "He's only a—a kid. It's going to be a big dance. . . . But I—I didn't run after you to say that."

"Daisy, what *do* you want to say?" queried Ernest gently, suddenly realizing what it had meant for her to tell him what she had. He took her hand.

"I—they—oh, darn it—don't let my cousin make a—a fool of you!" she exclaimed with sudden passion, and snatching free her hand she ran back up the lane.

"Well!" ejaculated Selby soberly. What was this that threatened his paradise? He could not unravel it. All the way down the valley trail he cudgeled his brains. Something was afoot, that seemed certain, and inimical to him. Daisy Brooks flashing out of her shy reticence was a surprise. He divined her sincerity. But what had that hint of hers meant?

Before he realized it he had arrived at the end of his walk. Sunset was gilding the red crags. He was tired out with travel and thought. As he came around the big barn he espied a pinto mustang standing before the bunkhouse porch. Suddenly Ernest halted, scarcely believing his eyes. Anne Hepford sat on the porch beside Nebraskie dangling her riding boots over the edge. She waved a gauntleted hand at him, called: "Hello, Iowa. Come heah pronto!"

CHAPTER
5

SELBY responded to Anne's gay summons as if it had been a trumpet call. Breathless, sombrero in hand, he reached her side, and quite forgot any sort of greeting to Nebraskie.

"Nebraskie said you'd be back on the stage. But you weren't—and I've waited all this time, " she announced reproachfully.

"I got off at Brooks'—and walked—down," replied Ernest.

"Strikes me you get off at Brooks' a lot," she shot at him, with a green flash of her eyes. It made the Iowan forget all about Daisy's recent warning. It did not, however, blind him to the fact of Nebraskie's displeasure.

"I—I've been there only a couple of times," he stammered, his face turning red. "Brooks is about the—only friend I have around here—unless Nebraskie—"

"Brooks? Bah, you mean *Daisy* Brooks. That's all right, only don't lie about it. My cousin is a sweet kid. The point heah is I hope you haven't asked her to the dance the night before the Fourth."

"No, I haven't," replied Ernest, and despite an effort to be nonchalant he seemed to himself to look and speak with school boy eagerness.

"I want you to take me," she said very sweetly, and if there had been any hope of Ernest's reacting sanely to that situation, it died before the smile she gave him.

"I—I'll be—delighted," he stammered.

"Thanks, Iowa," she replied with another smile. "It's late in the day, I know. But I really didn't expect to go to this dance. I've been coaxing Dad to let me go to Holbrook, for the big dance there. But he said, 'No.' He's shore cross these days....Please don't wear your cowboy boots."

"I won't—nor spurs, either," he said with a laugh of comprehension.

She slipped off the porch, and stood before them in all her lithe and supple beauty, and threw back her head with a taunting little laugh at Nebraskie. Then she mounted the pinto pony.

"Wednesday night, then—and oh, I nearly forgot. Come close," she said.

Selby stepped up to the pony. Anne leaned down till her sombrero brushed his ear. She put a hand on his arm. "If you want to tickle me sing that 'son-of-a-gun from Ioway' song where Dude can heah you."

"I'll do it," cried Ernest aloud.

She squeezed his arm, and straightened up in the saddle, with a gleam that was not all roguish in her eyes. Then she rode off.

Ernest watched her until she was out of sight. Many times had he done that same thing, but never with feelings such as possessed him now. Then he flopped on the porch floor beside the glowering Nebraskie, noting for the first time that individual's sour expression.

"Wal, Barnum was right. There's one born every minnit," drawled Nebraskie.

"Born!—What?"

"A sucker. An' if you ain't the biggest thet ever hit Red Rock I'll swaller my spurs. Gosh, but I'm disappointed in you, Ioway."

"I—I'm darned sorry, Nebraskie," replied Ernest, frankly puzzled. His bunkmate looked actually grieved. "I didn't know you liked me well enough to care a damn about me."

"Wal, I did. An' only this heah day I stuck up fer you, an' riled the outfit something scandalous."

"You did! Nebraskie! Honest now!"

"I swear I did. You can ask Hawk. An' he put in a word fer you, too. Sort of stumped Hyslip. Wal, we had it out. You'll have to lick Hyslip or you'll never last heah."

"Nebraskie, I'm going to last," said Selby slowly and emphatically, and he thrust out a hand. "You're the best hombre in the outfit and if you're my friend they can all go hang."

"Wal, I cottoned to you, Ioway," rejoined Nebraskie, as if confessing a terrible weakness, and he reluctantly shook hands. "You've shore been a real feller. But, aw! if you jest hadn't let this heah green-eyed hussy—"

"Nebraskie! Be careful—if you're a friend of mine," interrupted Ernest.

"Hell! It's *because* I am your friend thet I'm seein' red. I mean what I say aboot her. Do you savvy thet? She's made a sucker out of you. An' I shore did hope an' believe you'd be the one feller she couldn't work. But she does it to all of 'em.... Listen, Ioway, Anne Hepford hasn't any use fer us cowboys, except to play with. She's let Dude in for more than any one else. An' serves the conceited fool jest right. She was goin' to the dance in Holbrook with a feller from St. Louis. But the old man blocked thet. Then she had a fight with Dude. An' as all the rest of us fellers has a gurl for the dance—why, she picked on *you*. An' say, you was too easy!... Thet's what the argument was about heah in the bunkhouse last night. It seems Anne told Dude she was goin' to ask you, an' Dude was fit to be tied aboot it. Wal, I ups an' says, sarcastic-like, that Anne Hepford couldn't make no sucker out of *you*. We had it hot an' heavy. Thet's where Hawk Siebert put a word in for you. Hyslip laughed us down. 'What?' he bellered. 'Thet Ioway hick turn Anne down? Boys, you're loco. He'll break his neck eatin' out of her hand!'"

"So that's it," groaned Selby, chagrined. "I can't believe you, Nebraskie."

"Wal, Hawk an' me reckoned you would have the spunk to turn her down," returned Nebraskie. "An' I'm shore plumb disappointed in you."

Ernest got up. "I'm darn sorry," he said. "But

don't be *too* disappointed in me. I may fool you yet—
if there's any truth in what you say."

"Call me a liar now. *Me*, who stuck up fer you.
If thet ain't like a tenderfoot!" railed Nebraskie.

Sight of Dude Hyslip, with Bones Magill and
Lunky Pollard, coming along the short-cut path from
the barns, filled Selby with a most extraordinary satisfaction.

"Better sneak indoors," advised Nebraskie.

Ernest was in no state of mind to accept advice.
He waited till the three boon companions had arrived
at the porch, when he called out in a loud cheerful
voice with a pseudo-western accent.

"Howdy, boys. I'm back, and shore ararin' to go."

"We heah you," replied Bones sarcastically.
"Whar' you rarin' to go?"

"Why, golly—to the dance, of course."

Dude Hyslip looked sullen and dark, and the heat
of his face was not from the sun. He never even
glanced at Ernest, but sneered to his friends: "Wal,
he may be ararin' to dance, but he's liable to trip
himself up before he's through."

At that Nebraskie sauntered to the door of his
room, and looked back over his shoulder.

"Pretty strong talk, Dude, when the other feller's
only out of his haid an' funny."

"Nebraskie, you shot your chin off last night,"
snapped Hyslip. "You've declared yourself for Howard. An' thet queered you with the outfit. After the
Fourth, when this bunch of cattle is gone, you both
get fired."

"The hell you say!" retorted the usually mild

Nebraskie. "Wal, I reckon I couldn't be no wuss off then hangin' on heah."

Selby joined Nebraskie in the doorway. "You're right, Hyslip," he said cheerfully. "There's going to be some no-good punchers hitting the road out of Red Rock soon. *I* happen to know."

Then he went inside and began to sing in a fair tenor voice:

> The son-of-a-gun from Ioway
> He stole my gurl away.

Then he repeated the lines in higher, more piercing tones:

> *The son-of-a-gun from Ioway*
> *He stole my gurl away.*

Nebraskie had been petrified at the first stanza, but at the second he motioned to Ernest to stop. The third time the soloist departed from all musical rhythm to bawl at the top of his lungs.

> SON-OF-A-GUN FROM IOWAY
> HE STOLE MY GURL-L AWA-A-AY!

The Iowan doubled up with mirth. But the crack of a gun and crash of glass made that mirth short-lived. Nebraskie dove under the lower bunk. Ernest stood stock-still a moment, then as another shot came and a bullet tore through the door he squeezed in behind the built-in chimney. Bang! A third bullet spat through the window and passed through the flimsy wooden wall. At this point, Hyslip's comrades tried to stop the fusillade, but the enraged cowboy proceeded to empty his gun.

"Say, Howard, you'd better let that do for a while," he bellowed.

Nebraskie rolled out from under the bunk, scared and resentful. "An' now I'm dodgin' bullets fer you!"

"Nebraskie, before too long we'll have this shack to ourselves, and we won't have to be dodging bullets," said Selby.

"By gum, you *are* loco. Wal, fer Gawd's sake jest don't sing thet song no more."

"I am going to," declared Ernest. "And what's more, pard, when I catch that swelled-up pup without a gun I'll beat his handsome mug flat."

Whereupon Ernest again proceeded to sing the objectionable lines, this time not melodiously nor yet vociferously, but with bold emphasis. Blank silence followed this defiance. Apparently Hyslip had either been restrained by his friends or had passed out of hearing range.

Two days of brutal work followed, during which Ernest acted as though he were in a trance. Then the day of the dance arrived, sunny and hot. By this time the Iowan had persuaded himself that the doubts engendered by Daisy and Nebraskie were baseless. He had almost succeeded in silencing a still, small, unsatisfied voice. He must have been a sore trial to the patient Nebraskie on that warm summer day. About four o'clock, while he was lolling on his bunk, waiting for the tedious hours to pass, Nebraskie came in for about the tenth time that afternoon.

"Ioway, the fire's out," he announced.

"What fire?" queried Ernest, with a premonition of evil.

"Wal, I shore hate to tell you an' say I told you so. But your flame has gone up the flue. Anne's St. Louis gazaboo came an' they jest drove off to Springer. She was shore dressed fit to kill—or I reckon I should say *un*dressed. Never saw so much of Anne. She had a shawl on when she came out, but you bet she let it slip off so we could see her."

"St. Louis?—gazaboo!—shawl!" gasped Selby uncomprehendingly.

"Crawl under the bunk. Cain't you savvy when you're licked? Anne Hepford has dished you as everybody knowed she would—if she could git some other feller to take her to the dance."

Something within Ernest snapped. Nebraskie had imparted this news in a bitter tone, without looking at his friend.

The Iowan got up without a word and stalked out, and through the pines to the ranch house. His thoughts and emotions were in a whirl. He stamped up the high front steps of the porch, and knocked. The door was open and the hired girl bade him come in. He saw Mr. Hepford in the living room in earnest conversation with another man.

"Hello, it's Iowa. What do you want, cowboy?" said Hepford.

"I've called to ask Miss Anne about the dance tonight," replied Ernest.

"Anne's gone. She left a little while ago with

young Sinclair from St. Louis."

"Will she be back?"

"No. She was dressed for the dance. They're having dinner in town."

"Mr. Hepford, I expected to take Miss Anne to that dance. She asked me to go with her."

"Is that so? Sorry you're put out about it, Howard," replied Hepford somewhat testily. "Anne was just having herself a little fun. She's full of tricks, as all you cowboys should know. Certainly she never intended you to take her seriously."

"How would you take it, Mr. Hepford, if you were in my place?" asked Ernest bluntly.

Hepford laughed. "I'd just lay it to being a tenderfoot."

"But, Mr. Westerner, a tenderfoot can be a human being," retorted Ernest, and that was the first time he had allowed himself to speak his mind since he had come to Red Rock. How it stirred him! "You may tell your daughter that I fear she will have to take me seriously after all."

The tenderfoot followed his blunt speech with a dark and piercing glance at the startled Hepford, and stalked out of the house and down the steps.

His fool's paradise bubble had burst. And in that mocking moment he realized why he had never believed it could be real. He was sorely wounded, but not beyond repair. He had just been on the eve of falling in love with Anne Hepford. Now he realized that he had really only been dazzled by a pair of green eyes and a crown of red hair.

When he burst in upon Nebraskie like a whirlwind a little later, that worthy drawled: "Good! You look a little more like a man."

"Shut up, you crazy Nebraskie fool, or I'll wallop you one," yelled Iowa.

Then Ernest hurriedly packed a dark suit of clothes, a pair of black shoes and other accessories and strode out.

"Better pack your gun, too," called Nebraskie, after him. And receiving no reply, he added, "I'll see you at the dance, Ioway, an' I'll stick to you till hell freezes over."

Ernest could not resist such proof of loyalty, and he turned to call back: "Nebraskie, pard, you won't ever regret it."

It was three miles to Springer, but to Ernest it seemed only a short walk. But by the time he reached the town he had recovered his balance. What a complete jackass he had been!

Springer was decorated for the Fourth and the town appeared to be full of people. The stores were open, though it was past six o'clock, and small boys were still busy with firecrackers. He went to the town's only hotel and registered: Ernest Howard, Red Rock Ranch.

He went up to the room assigned him, and with considerable satisfaction he threw off the cowboy sombrero, shirt, overalls and boots. Then he applied himself as never before with razor, towel and wardrobe to his personal appearance.

CHAPTER
6

ERNEST had the grace to laugh at himself. VANITY had never been one of his besetting sins. But the truth was that he had not particularly relished Anne Hepford's taking him for a hick from the countryside of Iowa. Back home he had enjoyed a certain amount of popularity with the fair sex. And he guessed he would sooner or later derive some personal consolation from acquainting Miss Hepford with the truth. What a treat it would be to see her face when she realized *he* was Ernest Selby!

He went downstairs a little late. The hotel lobby was crowded. The Fourth of July ball had begun. Ernest, cool and serene, went into dinner. He felt like himself for the first time since he had landed in Holbrook. The dining room was half filled, but it was a large place for such a small town. His luck had changed. Almost immediately he saw Anne Hepford sitting at a nearby table in company with another girl and two young men. She wore a gown cut rather low and sleeveless for a young lady in a western village. But it enhanced her beauty beyond belief. He swallowed hard and thanked his lucky stars that he had found her out before he had seen her as she looked now.

Presently he was himself again and he began to look about him casually. Anne obviously did not recognize him at first glance, and this was balm to the Iowan's wounded soul. When her glance came his way again and she recognized him, he saw her eyes open wide in surprise. Then, blushing becomingly, she bowed to him. But Ernest might never have seen her before for all the sign he gave, and he did not look her way again.

Selby finished his dinner, went out, strolled up and down the short noisy street, took a peep into the dance hall where the young folks were gathering, and then went back to the hotel. The night was warm. He sat outside on the stoop for an hour and it was a pleasant hour. Finally Ernest went over to the dance, not at all disturbed that he had to go alone. As a matter of fact, he had a sense of pleasant anticipation. The dance was on, and the hall was noisy with the sound of music and laughter and dancing feet. He was stopped at the door by a man who sat at a table and demanded a dollar admission. Ernest would cheerfully have paid all the money he had with him.

"Packin' any hardware, stranger?" inquired the keen-eyed doorkeeper, and he slapped Ernest's hips.

Selby crowded his way into the hall. It was a barn-like structure, but rather prettily decorated with flags and evergreen boughs. The many wide-open windows gave plenty of ventilation on this hot July night. He walked around among the whirling dancers, and found a convenient point from where he could look on. One whole side of the hall opened upon a roofed porch, which led into a garden. The Iowan found a seat near the door.

From his point of vantage he could see that some of the girls were not only pretty but well dressed. The cowboys were conspicuous for their shiny faces, silly looks, plastered hair, flaming scarves and scraping boots. They danced like playful hippopotami.

Presently Ernest caught sight of Anne and her partner. He was not a bad dancer, though he held her too tightly. She was stunning to look at and grace itself. On a wild impulse Ernest conceived a wild idea. He would ask her to dance.

So when that waltz ended and the couples trooped to the chairs that lined the walls Ernest singled Anne out and approached her. She saw him coming, and her embarrassment was obvious. He made her a gallant bow and asked her if he might have the honor of one dance.

"Iowa, why didn't you speak to me over at the hotel?" she asked bluntly.

"You didn't recognize me—out of my cowboy clothes—and besides you—"

"I know I didn't. And I hardly do now," she interposed with shining eyes. "Yes, I'll give you a dance. The second after this."

Selby murmured his thanks, plainly aware of the

surprised scrutiny of her partner, and went back to his post. The next dance was a Virginia reel, which afforded him the opportunity to view the dancers to better advantage. Dude Hyslip was one of them, and Ernest had to confess he made a fine figure on the dance floor. But his face was too red, his mirth too gay, his hands too free, and his boots too lively. Dude had evidently been overfree with the bottle. In the set Hyslip dominated with his boisterousness, dancing with a slim girl in white, and she stood out rather markedly by her modest grace. Presently Ernest was surprised to recognize in her the very girl he had been looking for—Daisy Brooks. For the rest of that dance and through the intermission, during which he strolled about, and the following dance he scarcely saw anyone but Daisy. Several times he believed he had caught her eye, only to be disappointed. He was quick to observe that the shyness that became her so well seemed even more evident in the dance hall.

The next dance was a waltz, and when the fiddles started up the Iowan nerved himself as for an ordeal. Anne was in a corner of the hall, surrounded by admirers and friends, whom Ernest noticed only vaguely.

"My dance, Miss Hepford? . . ." he said, looking steadily into her eyes. He read there what he surely had never beheld in those green orbs before.

"I've remembered, Iowa," she replied, as she stood up.

He felt her start of delighted surprise as he swept her out onto the dance floor. Ernest was a natural dancer, and if ever he strove to surpass himself it was then, with the redheaded girl with the low-cut dress clasped tightly in his arms.

"Oh—Iowa! Yore a wonderful dancer," she whispered, and looked up at him with eyes alight.

"So I've been told by girls in St. Louis, Des Moines, Peoria, and plenty of other hick towns. But it didn't help my horseback riding much," he replied casually, without looking at her.

"Don't spoil it by bragging.... But I'm wondering about you," she said, a bit unsteadily.

Ernest gazed down at her then and saw her face like a flower pressed against his shoulder. Through her long lashes he caught the expression of her eyes and in that instant almost, his desire for revenge suffered an eclipse. Gradually she gave herself wholly to the enjoyment of the dance.

It was just as well that the music ceased then. Through a wideopen door moonlight beckoned. He led Anne out into the soft night air, under the silver radiance, which seemed caught and held by her hair.

"Anne, you treated me rather shabbily, didn't you?" he asked somewhat stiffly.

She came out of her dreamy abstraction. "I played you a dirty trick. I'm sorry. I did it more to annoy Dude Hyslip than to be with Sinclair. Fact is I'm not a bit crazy aboot him, I confess.... And doggone the luck, I *do* like you. I'd rather dance with you than any fellow hyah. Somehow you seem sort of different tonight.... You'll dance with me again?"

"Sure. I'll be delighted," replied Ernest hesitantly. He did not know what to make of this green-eyed girl, except that she was bewitching. Her allurement was real, irresistible. She had many moods and sides. When had he ever seen her pensive, sincere, regretful? But was she not merely acting? That thought added to his bitterness. He would see. Presently as they entered a patch of shadow under the moon-blanched trees he slipped his arm around her, boldly yet fearfully, knowing that it was his doubt that actuated him. To his surprise she leaned toward him rather than pulling away. And at last they appeared to be alone.

"Anne, all this time you've known I loved you, haven't you?" he asked, speaking aloud the thought he had meant to hide.

"I'm afraid I have," she said with a little laugh.

"And you've been—just playing?" he went on bitterly.

"Reckon so—aboot. But you wouldn't let me alone."

"I'm to blame there—that's sure. But still— Anne, you've been pretty low-down mean to me, as Nebraskie says."

"I've been nothing of the kind," she retorted. "Can I help it if you run after me—like the rest of them?"

"Oh, be honest! A man can forgive a girl anything but dishonesty."

"Oh, Iowa, I *cain't* be honest, even with myself, let alone any man," she confessed with surprising candor.

"What do you mean?"

She shook her shining head. To do her justice, he felt, she was not coquetting with him now. She turned her face away. He noticed her quick breathing. Suddenly he responded to an impulse, born of passion, yet of deliberate scorn as well. He took her in his arms and drew her round against his breast.

"Heah now—cowboy—you're going just too far," she exclaimed, with a catch in her breath. She pushed with her hands against his chest, but not enough to break his hold. He himself might be wholly mad, he thought, but it was not deviltry that he saw in her eyes.

"This is not far—for *you* to be," he said.

"I've not allowed any cowboy to go so far," she returned with spirit.

"What a beautiful green-eyed liar!"

"Iowa!"

She appeared to be more surprised than either angered or hurt. Ernest clasped her close, showered her eyes, her cheeks, and then her lips with kisses. He was not so far gone himself that he was not conscious of her momentary yielding. She was soft, pliant in his arms. Her eyes closed. Her head lay back on his shoulder. It was he who first awakened out of that seductive moment. Laughter and approaching footsteps caused him to release her, to shake her a little.

She laughed. "Iowa, you're shore an amazin' cowboy tonight.... I deserved that. But don't you tell."

"What do you take me for?" he asked. "I'm not the kind that will kiss and tell."

"I shore haven't got you figured at all. Let's get away before somebody sees us out here."

They walked back along the moonlit path in silence. Ernest was aflame now and knew that his wits were scattering. If she were only not such a flirt! They passed other couples, wholly intent upon themselves.

"Iowa," she said presently. "I believe you when you said you'd not tell."

"Thank you," he replied stiffly. "If I needed any assurance of your shallowness that remark would serve."

At the steps she turned to regard him curiously.

"You're a new one to me tonight. But I'll have you know, mister, that I'm not a shallow. I'm plenty deep. You've made me feel it—out heah. I'm not accustomed to let cowpunchers hug and kiss me. I'm afraid I let *you*. I never raised a finger.... So there, Mister Ernest Howard!"

She ran up the steps and left him standing in the moonlight, a victim of conflicting thoughts and emotions.

It was only after some moments that Ernest could compose himself sufficiently for coherent reasoning. He realized he had gone too far. He had stepped over the precipice. To hold Anne in his arms, to feel her grow soft and lax, to kiss her unrebuked— that had been weakness. Whatever she was he had now fallen madly in love with her. But what of her singular actions and words? She had confessed her insincerity, her meanness—then had made strangely sweet amends. He had to admit—she had been a brazen flirt, but she had found that when she was alone with him she liked him, perhaps. Ernest dared not think of the implication that it carried. Had he really some power over Anne Hepford? Something had gone amiss. His calculation had fallen short of this hour. He wiped his wet brow and shook his head slowly. It looked as though he had jumped out of the frying pan into the fire. Only one thing could he be sure of—her charm, her physical attraction, which he had been unable to resist.

Ernest turned back from the porch and walked into the garden again. He wanted to get out in the open, where the night breeze could cool his blood. He avoided dancers and turned aside on another path, to come upon a shadow-enclosed bench. He saw a slim figure in white almost enveloped by a tall one in black. Then a familiar drawling voice: "Wal, Dais, you shore cain't come that with me."

"No you—you—" panted the girl, struggling with her escort.

Ernest had only to take a few quick steps to be upon them. With one powerful hand on each he pushed them apart, and faced Hyslip.

"Wal, if it ain't Ioway!" ejaculated the cowboy in good-humored surprise. Then the meaning of the situation reached him. "See heah, you dressed-up hick—"

Then Ernest, with all the might of a hundred and seventy pounds of bone and muscle, plus the incalculable energy and spirit behind them, leaped upon Hyslip. He struck him flush on the chin. Hyslip catapulted backward, broke the back rail of the bench, crashed to the ground and lay still.

"There—you dude cowboy!" muttered the Iowan with infinite satisfaction.

Then he turned to Daisy. She had sunk down on the seat, and her eyes appeared unnaturally large and dark in her pale face. "Oh, it's—you, Iowa.... That was—the—" she started to say, almost sobbing.

But she did not conclude her sentence.

"Come on, Daisy. Let's walk," he replied, and helped her up. They walked out into the moonlight, and away from that part of the garden. "Perhaps we'd better go in," he said, on second thought. "Hyslip may come to, and get ugly.... Can I have a dance with you, Daisy?"

"Yes, indeed," she replied gladly. "My partner, Nebraskie, isn't much on dancing tonight. He's drinking and quarrelsome. That one with Dude was my last—Iowa, I—I had to look at you three times before I recognized you. Oh, you're so different! Everybody seems to be noticing you—I watched you dance with Anne."

Her shy naïveté elicited the welcome fact that to her he was still Ernest Howard, though somehow transformed. They fell in with the dancers. Daisy was so slim, so light that he scarcely felt her body next to his, and for this reason, perhaps, held her a little closer. She did not talk while the music was playing. Afterward out on the porch she said: "You're the best dancer I ever had."

"Thanks. Daisy, I want to confess something," he began. "Anne Hepford made a fool out of me. I didn't listen to you—or Nebraskie—and—well, I've let myself in for something I may not know how to handle."

"Never mind, Iowa. It's all right—" she replied sympathetically.

"No, it isn't all right—yet," he persisted. "I want you to know I already see my mistake and my—my weakness. Anne is—well, a wonderful creature, but not for me."

"Good heavens, Iowa!" she ejaculated. "You didn't really hope you—she'd be serious. She just can't be serious—with any man."

"I've forgotten now. I had a lot of fool ideas. And I'm furious when I think what a jackass I was, letting her play with me."

Ernest danced again with her, and afterward promenaded around, the cynosure of all eyes. Daisy was radiant. Her eyes shone like stars. He sat at her left during the intermission and paid her marked attention. Then after another dance he took her to an open window. She sat on a chair close to his and looked up at the moon.

"Daisy, I'm afraid Dude Hyslip has a way with him," began Ernest.

"Iowa—don't *you* blame me too," she entreated. "Nebraskie is bad enough."

"Oh, I see. Nebraskie is jealous. He's in love with you, isn't he?"

She averted her face, and when Ernest gently drew it around he was surprised to discover not shyness, as he had expected, but tears.

"Daisy! What is it?"

"I—I might tell you sometime. But not now—not here," she whispered.

"I'm Nebraskie's friend. I want to be yours, too."

"I know. Nebraskie swears by you. But lately he's been accusing you of—of running after me."

"Humph! The cantankerous cowpoke! I could do worse. I have done worse. . . . Be frank with me, Daisy. Aren't you and Nebraskie pretty sweet on each other?"

"We were—till Dude—" she replied hesitantly.

"But, Iowa, I won't tell you any more now. If you really are my friend get me out of here. Find Nebraskie. He must take me home. And you'd better come too. Dude Hyslip has shot up more than one dance hall."

"Has he? Well, I'm not anxious to have him use me for a target again. He did that the other day. But, Daisy, I have a feeling that he's going to lose his job presently."

"I thought he stood in strong with Hepford. Even if he didn't, though, my cousin would keep him on the ranch. . . . Ernest, please take me out of here."

"Sure. I don't blame you for wanting to leave. We'll get your hat and coat. Then I'll find Nebraskie."

To Ernest's relief they did not encounter Hyslip or Anne, but they ran into unexpected embarrassment in the person of Nebraskie Kemp.

*N*EBRASKIE'S boyish face was brick-red and sullen. His usually big wide-open blue eyes burned with an unnatural fire. He squared himself in front of Ernest and Daisy, his hands on his hips, and regarded them as though they were two very guilty persons.

"Come on, pard, let's get out of here," said Selby.

"Huh! You ain't no pard of mine, Iowa Howard. You're a snake in th' grass, just as I thought you was when I first seen you," replied Kemp in a bitter voice. Certain it was that he arrested attention from others besides the two he confronted.

"Hold on with such crazy talk, cowboy. You've been looking at red liquor," retorted Ernest sharply.

"Nebraskie, you're drunk. Come out this very minute—or I'll ask Ioway to take me home," said Daisy in distress. She placed a nervous hand on Kemp as if she feared he might strike his friend. There appeared to be some justification for her action.

"I'm gonna sock you on yer—han'some mug," muttered Nebraskie in a thick voice.

Selby laughed. To see the usually good-natured Nebraskie so pugnacious was funny, though evidently the scene was painful for Daisy. He laid powerful hold of Nebraskie. "Grab him, Daisy. We'll drag him out."

They did so, amid the laughter of the bystanders. It required considerable effort to pull and lead Kemp out into the street, along which they hurried him. When they reached the park he broke loose from them.

"We're gonna fight it out—right here," declared the cowboy.

"All right, if you've got to fight. But what's it all about?" returned Ernest patiently.

"You're second han'some galoot to steal my gurl."

"Shut up, you big fool!" cried Daisy hotly.

"S'there. She's swearin' at me," said Kemp, jerking a lax hand toward Daisy.

Ernest swept a glance about them, glad to find that the street was deserted. He placed a friendly hand on Kemp's shoulder.

"Pard, I'm your friend and Daisy's friend."

"Ahuh. Yore shore hers. Mebbe her sweetheart, I seen you dancin'. Huggin' her pure shameful . . . Aw, damn the wimmen anyhow. All same. It takes the han'some fellers to win them. . . . Ho'ard, I gotta sock you one. I hate t'do it."

"I'd hate to have you, Nebraskie. I'm losing my

patience, cowboy. Here's Daisy wanting to go home and you acting like a coyote.... Hold on, there!—Be careful."

Kemp swung a slow arm, which Daisy caught and clung to.

"Nebraskie, if you hit Iowa I—I'll never speak to you again," she protested tearfully. "You're accusing your best friend. Why, not half an hour ago he—he knocked Dude Hyslip stiff for—for insulting me."

"Whash thet aboot Hyslip?" demanded Kemp furiously. "You didn't look at him again?"

"Yes—I did. I—I danced with him," confessed Daisy. "I know I promised you. But I couldn't help it. He asked me right before Anne and—and others. He didn't wait—just waltzed me out on the floor. Afterward—"

"My Gawd—whadda you think of thet!" exclaimed Nebraskie, with a tragic gesture to Selby. "Wimmen are jest no good."

Ernest began to realize that there was more to this than just a drunken cowboy's absurd jealousy. Daisy began to cry. This evidently was more than Nebraskie could take.

"Dais, don't you go blubberin'. I cain't stand thet. Let Ho'ard take you home. An' I'll go get pretty-faced drunk."

"No—no. I want to get you away from town. If you meet Hyslip—"

"Ahuh. So you're feared I'll take a shot at him, an' not with my fist, either? What'd he do? Tell me—or I'll go after him anyhow."

Here Daisy broke down. "Oh, Iowa—can't you—do—anything? People are—coming—I—I can't stand this. I want to—go home."

Ernest nodded grimly and began dragging Kemp along the street, at no slow pace, using words as blunt and forceful as his actions. Every once in a while the cowboy would rebel and try to halt, talking incoherently, but they forced him on. In this manner they traversed several blocks. The night air, sweeping down from the mountains, was cold and keen. Daisy drew her coat closer around her throat. She looked white in the moonlight. She had ceased weeping. Ernest thought she looked very sad and troubled. Again he wondered. Finally they reached the corral.

"Nebraskie, you make up with Daisy while I fetch the horses," said Ernest.

"Make up nuthin'," growled Kemp. "Never no more. I've been a sucker too often."

"Say, you locoed range rider," exploded Selby, "I've a notion to slam you the same as I did Dude Hyslip."

"Slam! Whadda you mean?"

"Well, Daisy told you once. I knocked him stiff."

"An' why for?"

"I went out in the garden and presently heard a girl cry out. It was Daisy. She was on that bench with Hyslip. He was trying to pull her to him, and she was resisting—or something—so I yanked her away from him—and slugged him one....Look at my fist....All swelled up!"

Nebraskie gazed from the swollen hand up into Ernest's face, and then at Daisy. He was recovering somewhat from the effect of the liquor he had imbibed.

"Dais, if you went out there with him—"

"I told you how it happened—I didn't want to go—he just rustled me along. He's strong. I didn't want to scream. What could I do? . . . But when he tried to—to come it over me again I screamed."

"Honest now, Dais?"

"Yes, honest. I cross my heart."

"It just come aboot natural—thet you got took out in the garden—when you didn't want to go?"

"Oh, I am a—a little fool!" cried the girl bitterly. "I *could* have avoided it. But I—I was out of my haid. Dude always does that to me."

"Now you're talkin', Dais," returned Kemp grimly. "This shore ain't no time to keep things to yourself, as you did before. I want it straight. Reckon I can forgive you fer lettin' yourself in fer thet little walk in the moonlight. But if Dude laid a hand on you—against your wish—"

Here Kemp took the girl by the shoulders and shook her, and bent down to peer into her face.

"Nebraskie—don't—you're hurting me," she faltered.

"Never mind Ernest. If he's my friend, as you both swear, I don't care if he knows aboot us. . . . Now you tell me—"

"Sure I'm your friend," interrupted Selby. "But, Nebraskie, doggone it, I don't like the way you're treating Daisy."

"Wal, you can lump it, then."

"You're drunk, man!"

"No, I ain't drunk no more. Leastways not very drunk."

As this appeared to be evident Ernest made no further effort to interfere. His sympathy went out to

Daisy, but even a more sentimental person than himself could have seen that the girl appeared guilty of something. Nebraskie, however, let go of her.

"I'll wrangle the hosses," he said, and strode away.

Ernest watched his lithe form move away in the moonlight, across the dark side of the corral, where the fence and trees cast deep shadows. Then he turned to Daisy.

"What does this all mean, Daisy?" he asked gravely. "Has Nebraskie a right to speak to you that way—to bully you, as he did?"

"Oh, yes. He has the right to beat me—and I wish he would," she replied, in bitter self-contempt.

"Daisy Brooks! How can you talk that way?"

"It's true. I've treated Nebraskie as low-down as—as I don't know what," she went on hurriedly. "He's the best boy ever.... We were engaged, Ernest. Then—then Dude Hyslip came between us.... And I broke it off."

"Well then, how comes that air of proprietorship Nebraskie showed so rudely?"

"Oh, he hasn't broken off, even if I have. Nebraskie sticks to me, even when I'm not worth it."

"Nonsense. Of course you're worth it—you're not the kind of girl you're trying to make yourself out to be! Do you still care for Nebraskie?"

"Do I? Oh, that's what hurts so. I do. More than ever!"

"Fine! Now be honest with him, Daisy. Absolutely honest. Then it'll all come right."

"I'm afraid I cain't be. I would if I wasn't sure he'd kill Dude."

"*Kill* Dude? . . . Good Heavens! Daisy, are you serious?"

"I shore am," she replied.

"Then—there's evidently a good deal more to this than a—mere lover's tiff?"

Her answer to that was silence, almost pitiful silence, but it was enough to confirm Ernest's fears. He felt intensely sorry for this defenseless girl.

"Do you want to tell me any more?" he asked gently, taking her hand.

"Not now. But I will sometime."

At this juncture the clip-clop of hoofs broke in upon their whispered conversation, and a moment later dark forms appeared out of the gloom. Nebraskie came up leading three horses.

"Like to never found your nag," said Kemp, handing out a rope end. Ernest took it, and searched along the fence for his saddle. Presently he returned to the gate, to find Daisy leaning white-faced and silent against the fence, while Nebraskie hitched the team to the buckboard.

"Ioway, tie your hoss behind, an' drive Dais home, will you?" he queried. "I'll fetch your clothes from the hotel."

"Why sure. But I think you ought to go with us," replied Ernest.

"I've a job on hand," he said, and completing the harnessing he threw the reins up into the buckboard. His face looked dark under his wide-brimmed sombrero. He waited expectantly. Presently Daisy came slowly away from the fence.

"Nebraskie, you take me home."

"Climb up, gurl. Ioway will take care of you."

"Please don't stay."

"Look heah, Dais. It's aboot come to a show-down. I was sore at you. But I'm gettin' over thet. Same as I'm gettin' sober. If you want to know, I won't drink no more. Reckon I'd best be clear-haided for what I've got to do. I've had enough of Hyslip's lordin' it over you."

"What are you going to do, Nebraskie?" she asked quietly.

"Wal, thet depends on Dude. If he draws on me—okay. But if he shows yellow, as I reckon, I'll jest beat hell out of him fer good an' all."

"Dude is a coward. He'll never meet you, for all his reputation as a gun-fighter. I'm not afraid of that. But I know your fiery temper. You might have good intentions, but when you meet him you will do something rash. Please don't stay, Nebraskie, for my sake."

Ernest added his solicitation to that of Daisy's. She was composed now, though evidently under a severe strain. The cowboy wavered as he looked down upon her.

"Reckon I cain't go far wrong," he said. "Ye won't tell me nothin', so I'll jest have to take things for granted."

"What things?"

"Thet I've good reason to lick Dude, if no wuss."

"You have good reason, Nebraskie. But for my sake, my reputation, don't do it."

"Ahuh. So you're fessin' up. Come on, Dais. Out with it. I'll think more of you an' so will Ioway."

The girl seemed greatly distressed. Yet she answered bravely: "Nebraskie, he can wind me round his little finger, *when* he gets with me. But only then.

Away from him I hate him. I hate him. You've got to believe me."

"You do?...Dais, this is shore the seriousest moment you and me ever lived."

"I do. I hate him," she declared darkly. "He's made a—a toy out of me. He comes out home and gets round Dad with a bottle of liquor. You know Dad's weakness. And then he—he makes a play for me."

"But, Dais, if you're square you could hide from the skunk," protested the cowboy.

"I have hid, many a time. But some other times I cain't give him the slip....And when he gets *hold* of me I—I—"

"Then you love him, huh?"

"No! No!...Maybe I did, right at first. But not after. Only that doesn't make any difference. I'm like a bird with a snake, I guess, and he knows it. That is what he comes for. Oh, it's shameful."

"Ahuh....Wal, Dais Brooks, suppose you tell your true feelin's aboot *me*."

"I've never changed, Nebraskie. Despite it all I— I cared more and more—and now—"

She faltered at the end, nearly weeping again. Nebraskie snatched her to his breast and held her close. His sombrero slipped back, as he raised his head in the moonlight. His face shone.

"Pard, you heah her?" he asked his friend triumphantly.

"Yes, I heard, Nebraskie. And I guess that makes everything all right, doesn't it?" replied Ernest with relief.

Nebraskie bent his head over the slight form in

his arms. "Dais, I'm shore thankin' you fer bein' honest. Reckon I don't quite understand, but thet's no matter. You're only a kid. Make me a promise an' I'll keep away from Hyslip."

"Yes—anything," whispered the girl.

"Be true to me from now on."

"Oh, Nebraskie, I swear I will."

He shyly kissed her cheek, and with that, lifted her up on the seat of the buckboard. Then he held out a hand to Ernest.

"Reckon I haven't been much of a pard tonight, Ioway. But heah you are, from now on."

"Nebraskie, I'm downright glad, for both your sakes," replied Ernest, coming to grips with that proffered hand. "For myself, too. I'm going to need friends."

"Wal, you've got two, anyhow," said Kemp with a laugh. "Dais, our pard heah has trouble of his own. Heart trouble, most like ours!"

"I'm afraid I saw it coming," replied the girl regretfully. "Oh, we're all tangled up in—in life."

Nebraskie clambered up into the buckboard while Ernest mounted his horse. Then they started off on their long ride back to Red Rock. Ernest trotted behind the buckboard. Soon they were beyond the outskirts of town, out into the country. And then the ride became pleasant to the Iowan. The exercise warmed his blood. The night was still, cold, frosty, and clear as a bell, with a soaring full moon blanching the rangeland. The mournful wail of a coyote floated down from the hills. At first Ernest had not liked these desert beasts. But now he felt they were part of this lonely land. As they made their way along the road the far-off cries came only at long intervals. Jack-rabbits like gray streaks crossed the road. Gradually the flat cedared country gave way to the encroaching pass through to the dark rugged foothills. Far beyond them the pale peaks stood up. These too were coming to have an inexplicable effect upon Ernest.

Presently he turned his eyes toward the buck-board rattling and jouncing ahead of him. Nebraskie had his free arm around Daisy and she was leaning against him until their forms seemed merged into one. The sight thrilled the Iowan, but at the same moment gave him a peculiar pang.

Only an hour or two before, he had held the beautiful form of Anne Hepford in his arms. A wave of emotion passed over him. He found it difficult to remember intelligently. Still, how could he have any reason or sense where Anne was concerned? He wanted to recall clearly, to analyze her reaction to his wild impulse, to find something tangible to sub-stantiate his absurd conviction that Anne had been surprised by his ardor and forced for once into sin-cerity. But that could be only his wild hope. He re-alized he was in a bad enough situation, without Anne Hepford really and truly having responded to him in one weak moment. If that were true, if in spite of her brazen coquetry, her scorn of him as a crude cowboy, if the yielding she had betrayed were genuine and for him, then indeed his plight would be desperate. For he knew that he could never resist her. He would be always waylaying her, to force a repetition of that tumultuous moment in the garden.

Vainly Ernest regretted his going to the dance. He had committed himself. It was too late. Passionately he denied being really in love with Anne. But he knew that he was. Whatever he had been before that mad moment he could not recall: now he was caught in the toils of passion, infinitely worse than he had ever been before, and for a woman he knew he could not trust. The realization fetched the hot stinging blood of shame to his cheek. It hurt his pride, his vanity. He had continually to fight down a clamoring championship of Anne. To invent excuses for her! To delude himself with a belief that deep down, in her heart, she was really good!

Ernest rode on through the night, a prey to conflicting emotions. Nebraskie waited at the turn of the road. They had reached Red Rock. The stars were paling. Dawn was not far off. The coyotes had ceased wailing. The moon had gone down behind the mountain.

"Most daylight, pard," said Nebraskie in a low voice. "Hell of a Fourth, huh? The wust and happiest I ever lived through! . . . Dais is asleep. Poor kid! She's had to stand a lot. Men are no good, Ioway. . . . I'll be back early in the mawnin'. Lay low till I come. Reckon Dude will be ugly. So long, pard."

"So long, pard," echoed Ernest, sitting his horse. He was learning things and the things he had learned that night brought him closer to this friend of his. He watched Nebraskie gaze down at the little head sagging on his shoulder, and a lump came up in his throat. The cowboy drove on up the road, to disappear among the cedars. Ernest headed his horse for the ranch corrals.

CHAPTER
8

*A*LL next day cowboys kept trailing back to the ranch, each betraying more or less the effect of a hilarious Fourth. Dude Hyslip did not show up at all, nor did several of the visiting riders, who had come from over the Blue Mountains to take charge of the big drive of cattle Hepford was starting on Monday. Late in the afternoon Nebraskie was still asleep in his bunk.

Ernest had not slept a wink and his face showed the effect of both physical and mental fatigue. He was restless, nervous, watchful, and spent a good deal of his time on the bunkhouse porch. Toward sundown Siebert, the foreman, encountered him there.

"Hey, Ioway, the Fourth is past an' you still packin' hardware," he commented in surprise, his hawk eyes taking Ernest in from gun to face.

"Sure boss, but there are a lot of things that are

not over yet," replied Ernest, endeavoring to grin.

"What, for instance?"

"Trouble."

"Iowa, I'll bet ten pesos you're the galoot who blacked Dude's eye," replied Siebert, as if suddenly enlightened.

"Can't say. I haven't seen his eye. But I sure pasted him hard enough to black both his eyes, only I had an idea it was his chin I connected with." He looked down at his still-swollen hand.

"I'd a-gambled on it. You son-of-a-gun. Tickles me powerful deep," replied Hawk. "I reckoned mebbe Nebraskie did it. Wal, Ioway, go put up your six-shooter—Dude was awful drunk last night. Raved an' roamed around, lookin' for the feller who hit him. Funny part of it is he doesn't know."

"What? He called me by name, before I busted him," said Ernest incredulously.

"Wal, by gosh, he's forgot. An' if you don't give yourself away no one'll be any the wiser. Hope you didn't tell anyone else?"

"Only Nebraskie."

"Wal, we can keep him quiet. So put your gun away."

"Hawk, don't you honestly think I ought to pack my gun from now on, and practice throwing it and shooting whenever I get a chance?"

"Aw, Ioway, I hoped I'd have one decent cowboy on this ranch," declared Siebert regretfully. "I took a shine to you."

"I am decent, boss. And I've sure obeyed you— taken your advice in everything. You're my only friend around here, outside of Nebraskie."

"Wal, if you put it thet way I'm up a stump," acknowledged the foreman resignedly. "I reckon trouble is brewin'."

"You're dead right, boss. But I can't confide in you. Not all *my* trouble," said the Iowan soberly.

"I peeped in at the dance last night. Seen you dancin' with the dazzlin' Anne. Ioway, you've shore gone the way of all the others, and it's a doggone shame."

"Which way is that, boss?"

"Plumb loco."

"I'm sorry it was so plain."

"Ioway, had you been drinkin'?"

"Nary a drop. Whatever addled my brains didn't need any stimulant to help it along."

"I savvy. Damn! Like your cool way of takin' it, though.... Ioway, have you any kin—anybody who cares anythin' for you?"

"Nope. I'm all alone in the world," lied Ernest with a straight face.

"Boy, I hate to see you goin' to the bad this way. For that girl will drive you to drink shore as shootin'. An' you're the kind who won't last out heah."

"She will *not*," declared Ernest passionately, and he felt the hot blood flush his cheek. In that denial he was also answering his second accusing self.

"Shore she will. If ever there was a girl mad to take the scalps of men Anne Hepford is the one. Why, Ioway, she's even made eyes at *me*, many a time. But I'm a cute old fox. I been hit a couple of times, years ago."

"Ahuh. But, Hawk, aren't you speakin' disrespectfully of our employer's daughter?"

"Reckon I am, Ioway. An' I shore wouldn't talk this away to everybody. But I like you powerful well, an' I still have an idea mebbe I can steer you a little straighter. An' heah I'm goin' to give you a hunch. Things are not so good between me an' Hepford. I'm leavin' presently, an' when I pull out, I'd like to take you an' Nebraskie with me."

"Thanks, Hawk. That's good of you. I'm surprised, though. What's wrong between you an' the rancher?"

"I jest don't like the way he runs cattle," replied Siebert tersely.

"Ahuh. Well, I don't know much about cattle. But, to come back to the girl, aren't you a little hard on her?"

"Wal, I'm darned if I know," rejoined Siebert. "Mebbe she's got some good in her. You know what I mean, Ioway. But the way she dresses—or undresses I ought to say—an' flirts with the boys—it's shore scandalous. Why, I used to dandle thet girl on my knee, when I first came to Red Rock. It seems long ago, but it ain't. Even then she could cock them green eyes at a feller. She's the kind thet goes to your haid. I just hope you ain't serious, Ioway. If you are—go to her like a man an' ask her to marry you. It sounds plumb crazy, but do it. She told me onct thet all the boys made turrible love to her, but none of them asked her to marry him. Funny thet."

"Humph. They didn't dare. They knew darn well she wasn't serious."

"Shore, an' thet's why she couldn't take them serious. Mebbe she is not so black as she's painted. 'Fore you know it you'll hev me stickin' up for her.

Anyhow thet's how I'd tackle Anne. It'd be somethin' new to her. An' *quién sabe*, you can never tell aboot a woman."

"Maybe I'll take your hunch, Hawk. It's sort of fascinating."

"Wal, do it now. I just came from the house. She's on the porch in the hammock. The old man is with Anderson, thet buyer from over the mountains. They're havin' a session, believe me. Hepford fired me out pronto. Take my hunch, Ioway, an' go *now*."

Ernest leaped up as if he had been propelled by a catapult. What persuaded him to take Hank Siebert's advice he had no idea, but it was instant and overpowering.

"Hawk, here goes," he said, and stalked off.

"I'll be waitin'," called Siebert, after him.

Ernest took that walk to the ranch house like a man in a trance. He weighed nothing. He just wanted to see. What he liked most about the idea was the fact that it would place him in a different position from the other cowboys who adored Anne, but knew that the situation was hopeless.

The late afternoon was losing its heat. Shafts of sunset gold shone low down through the pines. An eagle was soaring above the red crags. But the Iowan was completely unconscious of these things. He reached the house. The front and left side of the angled porch were unoccupied. Ernest mounted the steps noiselessly. The door was open. From within came Hepford's caustic voice. "That's my price, Anderson. And you drive the stock."

Ernest walked round to the left wing of the porch, where he espied Anne lying in a hammock under the generous shade of the pines that grew close to that side of the house. He approached, to find her asleep, and most appealing in that unguarded moment. The instant he gazed down upon her, to realize her charm anew, and strangely different, he realized that he had made another blunder. At that moment he had an irresistible desire to kiss her eyes open. She wore white, which brought out the beauty of her gold-tinged skin and the glorious red hair. Her position in the abandon of sleep was not as modest as it might have been. Ernest, catching his breath, hastened to awaken her.

Then, suddenly, he was gazing down into wide, sleepy green eyes. They blinked. The sleepiness gave place to lazy wonderment.

"Why, hello, Iowa. How long have you been heah?"

"Just a—second," replied Ernest, swallowing hard. Removing his sombrero he sat down on the rustic chair that faced the hammock. The amazing fact seemed to be that she was neither offended nor scornful nor amused by his presence. Perhaps she was not yet quite fully awake. Then a sudden feeling of coolness and dignity and poise came over Ernest, he had no idea from where. "Anne, I've come to apologize for my conduct last night and to explain," he heard himself saying.

"Oh, you have. Well, that's interesting," she drawled. But the faint color which streamed into her cheeks denied the indifference of her words. Ernest had never seen Anne Hepford as she was then, and for the first time since he had known her he looked at her without suspicion.

"I was not drunk," he went on. "I just gave way to the overpowering love I felt for you. You didn't know that. Neither did I, then. But you must realize that I meant no insult. I was not trifling, or taking advantage of the moment. I apologize for my violence....And I ask you to marry me."

She stared. The color in her face deepened to pink. Her eyes opened wider, to become singularly beautiful, with the thought and emotion that darkened them.

"Ernest Howard!" she murmured.

"It's a shock, I know. But I'm not apologizing for that or my presumption. Only for the way I acted last night."

"You—love me, Iowa?"

"I'm afraid I do," he replied, through tightening lips, for only then had he wholly realized the hopeless fact and nature of his infatuation.

"And you ask me to marry you?" she went on, lingering almost dreamily over the words.

"I sure do."

Then she underwent a subtle transformation which turned her in a twinkling into the Anne Hepford he knew.

"You crazy cowboy! If Dad heard you he'd throw you off the porch," she replied, swinging her feet to the porch floor, with a gay little laugh.

"I daresay. But what's your answer, Anne?"

"Are you plumb loco, Iowa? To imagine I might marry you, an odd-job cowboy at forty dollars per!"

"My financial condition is not the point," he replied with dignity. "I asked you because I owed it to you and to myself. Probably you can't understand that."

"I understand you're the most surprising cowboy who ever rode a grub-line into Red Rock Ranch. And that's a compliment, Ioway."

"Thank you for that, anyway," replied Ernest rising. "Good afternoon, Anne. I'll not annoy you further."

"Who said you annoyed me? Sit down, Iowa. I want to ask you something." Her eyes were shining and only the part he had elected to play kept him from surrendering completely to them. He did not take the chair at her invitation, but remained standing, gazing down upon her. "Tell me, did you fight with Dude Hyslip last night?"

"No."

"Doggone!" she exclaimed with genuine regret. "I hoped it was you who did. Someone gave him the most beautiful black eye. Oh, he was a sight."

"Well, I gave him the black eye all right, but there was no fight. Only two blows struck. The one when I hit him and the other when he hit the ground."

"Iowa! I *knew* you did it. And I knew why, too."

"Did you?" queried Ernest, who plainly saw that she knew nothing of the kind.

"It was because of *me*. You were out there in the garden. I'll bet you followed us. Dude was half drunk, you know. You must have seen him get gay with me. Oh, he was nasty. And when I ran off you must have jumped out to let him have it."

"Very well, if you know all about what happened, why ask me?"

"No reason, now I'm sure you did it. . . . Except,

Iowa—you may kiss me if you wish." She held out an unwavering hand. He caught no other sign of feeling, except the swell of her breast, but she was wonderful then. The thrill that vibrated through Ernest's veins warned him of the peril of that moment. Something warned him that this was no moment for Ernest Selby to yield to Anne Hepford. In the sharp spiritual conflict which he suffered then he made some amends for the deceit he had perpetrated upon her.

"You're generous, Anne," he replied, striving to quell his emotion. "But I certainly wouldn't jeopardize your good name a second time. Last night was enough. I didn't come for more of the same. I came to propose marriage. But I can see, Anne, that's something that doesn't interest you."

"Iowa, you're right. And I'm a darned fool. Thank you again."

"Don't mention it. So long. I'll go now," replied Ernest, as he bowed and backed away.

"Iowa—you—" But she did not conclude her speech. The Iowan believed that he saw her bite her tongue. Her great eyes were blazing, too, if not with pique then Selby was completely wrong in his deduction. He turned to go round the angle of the porch. "Iowa—" she called after him roguishly, "all the same that offer stands."

Ernest felt that he wanted to run. He did step off the porch and down the lane at a swift stride. Once in the grove he slowed down. "Whew! That was a close shave," he whispered. "What a girl!...I'm worse off than ever. But I'm glad—by thunder I am! If Anne Hepford is not an utterly heartless coquette that will make her think."

By the time he arrived at the bunkhouse, where Siebert awaited him on the porch, he was outwardly composed.

"How aboot it, cowboy? Any luck?" queried the genial foreman, with a flash of his hawk eyes.

"Nope. Guess I was lucky to get away alive," replied Ernest fervently.

"Say, Ioway, you didn't really ask Anne, did you?" continued Siebert, incredulously.

"I sure did. Got laughed at for my pains. But, Hawk, I'm glad you put me up to it. Honest I am. It was an experience I'll never forget."

"Ahuh. Say, Ioway, you got me guessin'. There's somethin' queer aboot you."

Here Nebraskie appeared in the doorway of the bunkhouse. His ruddy face wore a warm smile and his big blue eyes looked fondly upon Ernest.

"Whatthehell's goin' on around heah?" he demanded. "What you been askin' Anne Hepford an' why you totin' thet six-shooter?"

Siebert laughed shortly, as he stepped off the porch. "Ioway, you've got a rep to live up to now. Reckon I'll send you over tomorrow with Anderson's outfit."

"Sure, I'd like that," replied Selby, quickly.

"Boss, my pard cain't go nowheres without me. Savvy?"

"All right, I'll send you both. Anderson is short of riders. They won't be back, an' thet drive starts soon as it's light enough to see in the mawnin'."

"Fine, Hawk. It ain't a bad idee," called Nebraskie, as the foreman sauntered away. "Jest as well for us to be scarce around heah. How long can we take?"

"Wal, three days goin' an' two comin' back," returned the foreman.

Whereupon Nebraskie wrestled and pummeled Ernest into their small lodging room, after which he closed the door.

"Pard, I lay in heah an' heerd every word you an' Hawk said," he announced.

"What of that, Nebraskie?" asked Ernest, with a sheepish grin.

"You amazin' son-of-a-gun! You most perfiderous strange galoot! I cain't savvy you atall. But, my Gawd, how I admire you!"

It flashed through Ernest's mind then that he was in line to return any and every sentiment Nebraskie might have for him. "I'm sure glad we're real friends at last," said the Iowan with deep conviction.

"Set down, doggone you," ordered Nebraskie, pushing his friend down upon the bunk. "Ioway, you've been an' gone an' done it. You braced thet green-eyed redhaid an' ast her to marry you."

"I did, Nebraskie, so help me Heaven," rejoined Ernest, weakly.

"Good Lord! . . . An' what fer?"

"I—I don't know."

"You fell in love with her, same as me with Dais?"

"Something like that, I guess."

"Aw, don't try to fool me. You love her real an' true. I seen it."

"All right, then."

"Pard, you love her turrible?"

"Yes, turrible."

"Wal, thet's tough. Blast the luck anyhow. . . . Ioway, I'm gonna give you a hunch. If you wasn't a no-good tenderfoot would-be cowpuncher without a hoss or a dollar Anne Hepford would shine up to you. I got a hunch!"

"Bah! You idiot!"

"Wal, I seen it. You cain't fool me aboot wimmen. Thet was how I seen through Dais's case with Hyslip. Lord knows she was quiet aboot it—the little mouse. I've seen Anne lookin' at you when you didn't know. An' it was in her eyes. Them bootiful betrayin' eyes of hers. Hell no, she's never guessed it—yet!"

"Nebraskie, you can dream if you want to. But that's no hunch. And even if it was, I'll tell you something! I wouldn't *have* Anne Hepford, unless she loved me for what I really am—a no-good tenderfoot—a would-be cowpuncher, without a horse or a dollar."

"Pard, thet's onreasonable. Wimmen don't love men fer nuthin'. But come to figger it out, you've got a lot. You're damn near as good lookin' as Dude Hyslip. Dais says you're manlier, an' not so pretty. An' pard, you're smart. There ain't no use thinkin' otherwise. You've got a haid on you. No bad habits. An' you're young. You'll be a big rancher someday. Anne could do a heap wuss, an' you can bet yore last peso I'm gonna tell her."

"Pard, I'm afraid we are two love-sick hombres," returned Iowa, gazing at his simple but eloquent champion with affection.

"Shore, we're sick all right," agreed Nebraskie, making a wry face. "Let's throw some grub together an' then hit the hay. It's three A.M. fer us tomorrer."

Two days later, about the same sunset hour, Ernest Selby was squatting before a campfire with

Nebraskie and the Anderson outfit, in Bull Tank Park, halfway across the Blue Mountains.

Hard as the riding had been, the Iowan's appreciation had steadily mounted for this Arizona wilderness and the outdoor life he was leading. He was growing used to the saddle and fond of his horse, slow old nag that he was. Anderson's cowboys were civil but distant. There were none to laugh at Ernest or ridicule his efforts or to play tricks on him, wherefore the trip grew more and more enjoyable. During those last few hours he and Nebraskie had become as close as brothers. "Wal, Ernie, you shore give me a helluva pain, but aside from all pertainin' to range-ridin' you are a guy to pin to," Nebraskie had said more than once. And Ernest would make reply: "Doggone it, Nebraskie, I wasn't born in a manger, but why can't I learn your cowboy tricks?"

"Far as gurls are concerned you can give us cards an' spades," Nebraskie had grinned. But loyal as he was he would not look upon Ernest's awkwardness in the saddle with anything but ill-concealed disgust.

Anderson had ridden with his outfit. He was foreman for the big cattle company across the range, and he struck Ernest as being a hard-faced, shifty-eyed, taciturn boss. He never spoke to the Red Rock boys, except to give them an order, which was sure to be for the worst possible task. Nebraskie complained a good deal, and gave vent to considerable profanity, but his companion seemed to be singularly content. In fact, except when his thoughts reverted to Anne Hepford, he appeared carefree and happy. The ruse which had brought him to Red Rock was succeeding even better than he had dared hope. Almost he believed himself what others thought him—a tenderfoot cowboy at loose ends instead of Ernest Selby, owner of Red Rock. Almost he did not want the inevitable revelation to come. He tried to put it out of his mind as much as possible. He was learning many things that as owner of a ranch he could hardly have discovered in any other way. And he was on the track of Hepford's elusive machinations.

Out in the park the cattle were bawling. The air was drowsy and warm, and thunder muttered over the ramparts of the Blue Mountains. The peaks were hidden in black clouds. Low down in the west the gold and purple lights of sunset burned. Night was coming and a cool breeze edged down from the green slopes. Coyotes were calling from the foothills.

"Aboot time fer Baldy, Dot an' Mex to rustle in," observed one of the riders. "Boss, who're you sendin' out on watch?"

"Fix thet up among yourselves next watches. You can put Hepford's punchers on guard at three," replied Anderson.

"Looks like a storm," spoke up another rider. "Them cattle are none too quiet as it is. Might stampede."

"Shore, if we have thunder an' lightnin'," was the reply. "But I reckon we won't get none heah."

Ernest and Nebraskie, having heard their orders, moved away from the fire to the spruce tree where they had unrolled their beds. Nebraskie sat on his tarpaulin to kick off his boots.

"Pard, I ain't stuck on this heah Anderson or his outfit. Air you?"

"Aw, they're all right," replied Ernest. "That boy Lee is a real good chap."

"Wal, Lee is sorta human, I'll agree. But the rest are N.G.... Ernie, you're new to the range. You don't get underneath. Things are what they look to you. But a real cowpuncher like your Uncle Dudley—he sees through all these heah tight-lipped fellers."

"I suppose I am a dumbhead, Nebraskie," admitted Selby, laughing. "It's up to you to coach me."

"You shore air a curious cuss. An' I reckon I like you the better fer thet. If you was experienced an' curious you'd find this stock deal a little queer."

"Queer? What do you mean, pardner?" asked the Iowan. "What's wrong with it?" He was somewhat shy about this way of addressing Nebraskie. He saved it for emergencies. Nebraskie was always visibly and pleasantly responsive to that appellation.

"Wal, ask yourself this. Why does Hepford want to make this long drive with a big herd—most fifteen hundred haid, I'd say—when he could sell at Springertown for forty dollars a haid, or forty-five at the railroad? He cain't get thet price over heah. Course I don't know thet, but I'd gamble on it. Then why this round-about way of sellin' his stock?"

"It *is* queer if you are figuring right," replied Ernest thoughtfully. "But there seem to be lots of funny things about ranching."

"My figgerin' is mostly pretty good," observed Nebraskie sagely. "My father was a rancher. I've lived all my life with cattle. An' if I had enough money to start a herd—even a few hundred haid—I could shore make a success of cattle raisin' an' sellin'. But hell, I cain't raise enough money to buy Dais a ring."

"You will someday, Nebraskie. Or I'll lend it to you."

"Huh! You forty dollar fence-post digger! But doggone you, if you did strike it rich, I'll bet you'd stake me at that!"

"I sure would, pard. But what's your angle on Hepford's selling over here, if he could get more in town?"

"I've got my idee. More'n ever now since I tried to feel out Hawk Siebert the other day. Hawk shore gave me a funny look. But he didn't say nuthin'."

"Ranchers help one another now and then, don't they?" asked Ernest.

"Shore they do. But this is the sixth big drive Hepford has made over heah since I joined his outfit. An' you can bet your chaps he ain't helpin' nobody but himself."

"Well, what's your idee, pard?" continued Ernest soberly.

"I reckon Hepford is workin' a trick as old as rustlin'. Only it's safer. Many a foreman has got a start for himself workin' thet dodge. It's coverin' sales, an' it's plumb easy to do if the owner of the ranch isn't aboot."

"Covering sales? Just what is that?"

"Wal, it means sellin' so many cattle, an' reportin' considerably less to haidquarters. Shore Hepford has to report to somebody. Down east, I've heard."

"Oh, I see," replied Ernest dubiously, as if he did not see. "But how would this—this sort of thing make it easy to be crooked? For that's what it amounts to."

"Wal, it's hard to trace an' check up. An' after considerable time it couldn't ever be checked. For instance, I was on two of them drives over heah, years ago, an' I'll be darned if I can remember how many cattle was in the herds. Now suppose I had to testify in court, if I'd do such a thing. I shore couldn't swear there was two hundred haid or a thousand haid in them particular herds. An' most cowpunchers would be wuss off than me. Do you savvy now, Ernie?"

"It's clearing up. If your surmise is correct Hepford will sell this bunch, send in a report of so many less than he actually did sell, and pocket the difference in cash."

"Exactly. An' I'll tell you if a foreman wanted to work such deals an' not be a hawg—to be satisfied with a little profit—he could never be ketched."

"Ahuh. Is Hepford that kind of a foreman?"

"I couldn't swear to thet. Strikes me he's pretty high-handed. He's well-heeled, I've heerd say. Fifteen years he's run this ranch since Brooks had it. An' the big boss has never been heah. I reckon there won't be much left of Red Rock when he does come."

Ernest bent over his boots to hide his face, and laboriously pulled them off.

"Nebraskie, let's make a count of this herd, just for fun," he suggested.

"Shore, I'm game. But it'd be risky tellin'. They shoot fellers out heah for thet. . . . It wouldn't have no point, though, onless you got the figgers Hepford reports."

"I suppose not. All the same we could satisfy ourselves."

"Siebert is goin' to take you an' me with him, when he leaves. Be tough on you, Ernie, to say good-by to the green-eyed girl. Huh?"

"It'll be terrible, pard."

"Air you thet bad over her?"

"I couldn't be worse."

Nebraskie sighed and maintained a thoughtful silence, during which he rolled and lighted a cigarette. Finally he said: "Love is a turrible disease. Sometimes I feel like a sick cow thet has eat too much larkspur. But I always get over it. Thet's the blessin' hid in love, Ernie. You always get over it, an' ready fer another attack right away."

"Could you ever love any girl but Daisy?"

"I don't feel like it now. But I know damn well I could."

"Then you shouldn't blame her for kicking over the traces."

"Wal, I won't blame her next time," replied Nebraskie gruffly, "but I'll spank the everlastin' daylights out of her."

"Fine! That's an original idea. How'd it do for me to try the same on Anne?"

Nebraskie whooped under her breath. "Glory, it'd be grand! An' it might work bootiful, Ernie. Wimmen are so blamed oncertain. I'm afraid, though, Anne would jest turn around and lambaste you back. An' she's husky.... Nope, you gotta use strategee with that un. But be straight as an arrowweed, Ernie."

"She's not so honest. I can testify to that all right."

"Don't you fool yourself. Thet gurl *is* honest. Not in her flirtin' ways, of course. No purty gurl is thet. She'd jest naturally lead on a hundred fellers an' fool 'em all, an' laugh. Thet's wimmen's privilege, they seem to reckon. But I'll bet you—if Hepford is even a little shady—Anne isn't wise to it."

"Nebraskie, I'm glad you think that," said Ernest warmly, as he folded his coat for a pillow. "Cause when Anne and I are married I couldn't invite you to our house, if you'd ever entertained any suspicions of her."

"Aw, you locoed gent, go to sleep," declared Nebraskie disgustedly. "Dream of love an' Anne an' a big ranch, an' lots of other guff. An' at three A.M. when I have to kick you in the slats to get you up then you'll know you're only a low-down poverty-stricken cowpoke."

Ernest laughed, but could not take his friend's advice. His mind was active with a number of things. Night had fallen. The threat of storm had passed. White stars shone through the dark boughs above where he lay. The summer heat had blown away on the wings of the nightwind. The cattle were quiet once more, but coyotes still called plaintively in the distance. A deep booming bay of a wolf rang out. Ernest had mistaken that once for the bay of a hound. It sent the cold shivers up his spine. The wind appeared to be laden with the aroma of pine from the stands of pines in the foothills. Dark forms of big-sombreroed cowboys crossed and recrossed between him and the flickering campfire. Their voices were low and now and then one yawned.

It was all marvelously real and enticing to the

tenderfoot from Iowa. He felt sure he could still be happy in this country, even if Anne Hepford broke his heart, if that was what she had set out to do. He suddenly made up his mind that he would postpone taking over the ranch as long as he possibly could. Just so he could continue to live in his fool's paradise a little longer! Then the old baffling hopes, doubts, conjectures, misgivings assailed him again, as was inevitable when the image of Anne Hepford returned to his consciousness. His happy moments were not these.

From Anne, however, his thoughts drifted to her father, and to Nebraskie's shrewd observations, and lastly to the actual fact that he was on one of those questionable cattle drives, about which the few cowboys and stock men aware of them had personal opinions which they did not air. He had to keep his wits about him if he were to prevent the ruin of the ranch his uncle had bequeathed him.

What would the next few weeks bring forth? Before the snow fell there surely were bound to be great changes at Red Rock. Ernest thought that he would like to retain Hawk Siebert, and of course Nebraskie. How was Nebraskie's love affair going to turn out? For that matter how was his own? And then he was right back where he had started with thoughts of the beauty, the strong charm, the doubtful virtues, the unlimited possibilities of Anne Hepford.

CHAPTER
9

A rude hard object, with a rotary movement and a jingle to it, violently disrupted Ernest from his dreams.

"Roll out, you Ioway greenhorn," called Nebraskie's drawling voice. "Wake up an' see how you like it in the cold dark mawnin'."

Selby roused himself, but he did not enjoy the shock to his sensibilities, nor the cloudy darkness, nor the icy air. He pulled on his boots and his coat and gloves, but he could not find his sombrero.

"Did'y swipe m-m-my hat?" he queried, his teeth chattering.

"Quiet! If you wake thet outfit they'll kill you," warned Nebraskie. "Pard, your haidgear must be under the chiffoneer."

Ernest vouchsafed no reply to that facetious

sally. He found his sombrero where the wind had blown it.

"Say, I'd like a cup of hot coffee and a biscuit," he said, forgetting the fact that he had experienced this dreary dawn business twice before.

"Haw! Haw!" laughed Nebraskie, low and scornful. "Th' deuce you say. Wal, I'd like some hot cakes an' maple surrup, an' some big fat fresh—Aw, what's eatin' you? Get out heah an' raise hair on your chest."

Not long after that Ernest found himself alone, out in the wide gray park, where spectral forms of cattle were revealed motionless in the dusk of early morning. His beat was on the protected side. Nebraskie had generously seen to that. Nevertheless the wind pierced right through him. Dismounting he led his horse to and fro. The cattle appeared to be huddled together and quiet. No stars shone. Ernest had neglected to fetch a warm coat or even a slicker. And for a while he was pretty miserable. Yet still his enthusiasm, though dampened, stayed with him, even though he had never been so cold in his life.

An hour dragged by. Then a faint paleness appeared in the east. The day was dawning. Nebraskie saw it too. From far across the park came a cowboy song. Not a cheerful rollicking song, but a sad lament of a cowboy's unrequited love.

In another hour day had broken, and Ernest thrilled to the glory of an Arizona sunrise. It burst slowly over the endless range, as if unwilling to unfold all its beauty at once. Rose and pink limned the horizon. A vast, clear, golden span of light followed the appearance of the blazing sun. Then the shadows stole away. The crisp air was full of a fresh sweetness and songs of birds and the lowing of cattle.

Nebraskie and Ernest were the last two called to breakfast, and they had to be satisfied with the last and least of the food, too. By the time they had made away with what was left the herd was in motion. They followed and soon caught up with the hindmost riders. The park proved to be the head of a magnificent valley, gray with bleached grass and dotted with green clumps of trees. Mountains rose beyond and it was easy to see why they had been called the Blue Range. Ernest espied a ranch not many miles down and calculated that the drive did not have many more hours to go. Across the wide valley a winding road, white in the sunlight, led south into a pass through the mountains. Beyond that range he knew lay another and different cattle country.

Soon sun and heat and dust, not to count hard riding, made the Iowan forget everything save the weariness of the hour. He wondered why he and Nebraskie were kept on the outskirts of the scattering herd. But he was sure of one thing, and that was that when the cattle had been driven through wide gates into an immense fenced pasture he had not been given any chance to ascertain their number. Moreover he was sure that Nebraskie had had no better opportunity.

The drive ended late in the afternoon. It was none too soon for Ernest. He fell in with Nebraskie and rode up to the ranch houses, which contrasted markedly with those of Red Rock. The buildings were old, gray, and weather-beaten; the cowboy quarters consisted of a couple of dingy log cabins, the courtyards and corrals were dry, devoid of green. There was no running water in sight. Nebraskie vouchsafed that it was a big ranch, but no place for two Romeos.

"Wal, we're aboot as welcome heah as two snowballs in Hades," he continued. "But, doggone it, they ought at least to feed us."

"Sure we'll stay all night?" asked Ernest eagerly.

"Boy, we will sleep out under the stars again, an' don't you forget thet. Suits me better, too. We'll hang around an' let our hosses rest, then pull out after dark sometime."

Ernest took his cue from Nebraskie, and gave no evidence that he noticed the aloofness of the Anderson outfit. The exception was the cowboy Lee, who appeared to be friendly and agreeable. There never had been any love lost between Red Rock and Blue Valley, Lee remarked dryly, with a significant little laugh.

"I wouldn't know. I'm new on this range," said Selby with a smile.

"So I seen," drawled Lee.

"First big drive I was ever in," the tenderfoot continued, with enthusiasm. "Must have been over two thousand head."

"Laws, cowpuncher, you're missin' it by a mile," replied Lee.

"Gosh, pard," put in Nebraskie, who was sitting with them against the corral fence that fronted on the cabins, "I'd shore hate to ride fer you, if you ever get to be a rancher."

"How many do you figger?" asked Lee.

"Wal, I wouldn't say. I never had one doggone chance to see the herd bunched."

"Fifteen hundred eighty-six haid exactly," declared Lee. "I heered Baldy tell thet to Anderson. Dot's count was fifteen sixty-two. But Baldy's count will take the money, you can lay to that."

Ernest dropped his head, as had become his habit when he did not trust his eyes. "Gosh, it'd be great to own that many cattle."

"Lee, who's the heavy-set guy in the boiled shirt, talkin' to Anderson an' Mr. Wilkins?" asked Nebraskie, indicating the group of dusty-booted men in front of the ranch house.

"Buyer from Mariposa, so I heered. Didn't ketch his name. He was heah once before. Reckon Wilkins will make a quick turnover of most of this stock we drove in."

Ernest entered no more into the conversation. His thoughts were running rampant again, and his resentment against Hepford waxed hot. He had wit enough, however, to listen to all that was said within his hearing, especially when they were called to supper, which was served to the riders in a big kitchen of the ranch house. The cook was a Mexican and the food good. Ernest had felt starved for three days. Nebraskie, too, made away with a prodigious amount of hearty food.

After the meal Lee bade them good-by, saying he had a girl, and they were left to themselves. Selby suggested that they stroll round the ranch house. The front proved to be little more prepossessing than the rear. There was no porch. The door to the living room stood open. In the dusk Ernest could not see inside, but he could hear voices.

"Nebraskie, I've an idea I'd like to slip up there and listen," he said without shame.

"What fer?"

"I don't know. Guess you just made me curious."

"Wal, it's too durn light yet. Wait till it's dark. But take a good look aboot, so you'll know the lay of the land. I'm sorta curious, too—"

They sauntered back to the corral, leisurely packed their pack mule, and saddled their horses. Meanwhile dusk fell. The log cabins grew indistinct. They led their horses down the lane to the open country.

"Better slip off your boots," advised Nebraskie. "Be careful. Run like hell if they see or heah you. This isn't no healthy place for a eavesdroppin' Red Rock puncher."

"You can bet I won't be caught," replied Ernest.

Bootless and hatless he stole stealthily down the lane, eyes and ears vigilant, slipped through the fence before he got to the corrals, and with the lay of the ground well fixed in mind he worked his way around to the front of the house. Here he felt reasonably safe. A bright light streamed from the living-room door, and also from a window which Ernest had not observed before. As there were no stars shining the night was dark. It was very still, however, and he had to make sure there were no persons outside. Gradually he drew into the deep shadow of the house. Then he sank to hands and knees and crawled up to the open window. Now that he was there it seemed a senseless risk. Yet, he felt urged to do it. He tried to hold his breath while he listened.

"I could have laughed in his face when he gave me thet old stall about rustlin'," Anderson was saying.

"Nothin' to laugh at," came a gruff reply. "Plenty of rustlers heahaboots."

"Shore. But you know what I mean," went on Anderson. "Hepford was tryin' to plant in my mind a loss thet really doesn't exist, thet is, from rustlin' causes."

"How about this man Siebert?" This query came from a third person, one with deep chest and hoarse voice. That would be from the Mariposa buyer.

"Lay off him," retorted Anderson sharply. "I didn't like the way he looked at me. An' he shore wasn't half civil, even before Hepford."

"Sharp cattleman, Siebert. I've heard of him."

"Anderson, you've nothin' to worry about," said Wilkins. "If there *is* any crooked work goin' on we shore ain't implicated. Our deals are above board. We buy cattle from Hepford. Yes. What if we do get them for less than he could sell in Mariposa, or in Holbrook?"

"I don't know aboot thet, John," returned Anderson. "We might get into court. I never was satisfied aboot Hepford till this last talk with him. He's shore a slick one. An' he proposed to make another an' last drive, in October."

"The devil he did!"

"I shouldn't have been surprised," went on the foreman. "When I was in Springer I heard rumors about Red Rock. Hepford has let the ranch run down. He never owned it. An' I'm of the opinion he shore doesn't own the stock. He'd been there years before I came to Arizona. Now I reckon there has been, or will be soon, a change of ownership. You can gamble Hepford is goin' to clear out."

"Aha. That sort of deal has been worked before in Arizona. Well, it's an ill wind that blows nobody good. My conscience is clear about buyin' in this stock. I reckon, though, I'll turn down the October deal."

"Why, man? What do you care? Some other cattle dealer will profit by it, if you don't."

"It seems different, now we're on to Hepford."

"I may be entirely wrong. Hepford makes enemies instead of friends. Maybe he has reasons for not sellin' in Holbrook or shippin' east....Hello—what the hell?"

A harsh voice had startled Anderson, as it had paralyzed Ernest where he lay so absorbed in this colloquy that he had not heard the approach of a man.

"You sneakin' coyote!" rang out a harsh voice. A powerful hand dragged Ernest to his feet. Then something hard was shoved into the middle of his back. "Put up your paws, cowboy....Now march in there!"

With that peremptory order the eavesdropper was jerked out of his trance and he lost no time in putting up his hands. He had been caught in the act. And he was passing from astonishment to fear when he was shoved across the threshold into the presence of three men as much astounded as he. Being forced to confront them, however, had the effect of restoring his presence of mind.

"What's this mean, Baldy?" bellowed his foreman.

"Damned if I know, boss," replied the burly individual behind Ernest. He had a dry drawling voice, somewhat like Hawk Siebert's. "I was smokin' down the lane an' I see this feller slippin' along like a shadder. So I follered him. Lost him out heah in the dark, but I moseyed around till I come on him. Layin' out there under the winder, listenin' to beat hell!"

"Well!" ejaculated the rancher, Wilkins, his open countenance darkening.

The third member of that company, the stout buyer from Mariposa, had turned decidedly pale.

"Say," snapped Anderson, suddenly, "it's one of the punchers from Red Rock. I had two. Helped us drive. They called him Iowa."

"Put down your gun, Baldy," interposed the rancher, with a gesture. And he bent a pair of piercing black eyes upon Ernest. When that cold hard pressure no longer was felt against his back, Selby felt better. "Young man, what's your name?"

"Ernest Howard," he replied, looking his interrogator straight in the eye.

"Where are you from?"

"Iowa."

"You ride for Hepford?"

"Yes, sir."

"You're certainly not drunk. And you don't look like a thief. . . . What do you mean—spyin' that way under my window?"

"No harm, sir. I guess I was just curious," returned Ernest with a disarming smile.

"Curious. What about?"

"About you Westerners." Here Ernest had made

up his mind that he had better resort to subterfuge. "I haven't been treated well at Red Rock. I'm sort of looking for a new job."

"Well, we don't want any cowboys of your curious stripe round here," returned the rancher coldly.

The Mariposa buyer pointed with fingers in which a cigar shook. "Have you gentlemen observed that this visitor is in his stocking feet?"

"No, I hadn't."

"Wal, by gum!"

"Pussyfootin' it, huh?"

A moment's silence ensued. The expressive glances of the three observers before him were not lost upon Ernest. But though the situation was embarrassing it did not alarm him. In the last analysis he had the best of them. None of these men could have any intimation that he was personally interested in the sale of the Red Rock cattle.

"Boss, I reckon I'd better lock him up an' let him explain to the sheriff," said Anderson.

"Probably you had."

Here Ernest dropped his hands and vigorously protested that they would do nothing of the kind. He had made up his mind to bolt through the door, if anyone made a further move to detain him.

"Wal, my curious tenderfoot, I shore will lock you up, an' hawg-tie you in the bargain," drawled the rider who had captured Ernest.

"*Hey in thar! Don't move—nobody!*" came an angry but businesslike voice through the window. Ernest recognized it with a start. It was Nebraskie.

THE DUDE RANGER • 121

The others stiffened and their eyes seemed hung on compass needles.

"Drop your gun on the floor, Baldy. . . . Quick, you cattlerustlin' skunk, or I'll blow your arm off!"

The voice was all-convincing. Baldy promptly dropped his gun.

"Now, Ioway, you come on out heah."

Ernest lost no time recrossing that threshold. From the steps he espied Nebraskie's face gleaming in the light from the window.

"Baldy," he continued in a biting tone, "pullin' a gun on a tenderfoot ain't to yore credit. This heah boy ain't no thief an' he ain't no sneak. He's jest a nosey boy from Ioway. Reckon if anythin' made him curious it was yore onhospitality. You shore was behavin' pretty mean and miserly to two hands who helped you make your drive."

"Mean, hell!" exploded Baldy hotly. "You cain't lay thet to me without a kick."

"Wal, lay it to Anderson then. . . . An' see heah, Mr. Wilkins, I reckon this little play of Baldy's will just about ruin relations between your outfit an' ours."

"I'll see that Hepford fires you both," retorted Wilkins, angrily.

"Wal, go ahaid. But you gotta rustle or we'll beat you to it."

Selby ran off into the darkness, halting some rods distant to wait for Nebraskie. He heard the laugh of hoarse derision, then heavy thud of boots.

"You snoopin' punchers!" yelled Anderson from the door. "Don't ever show up round heah again."

"Go to blazes, you crooked foreman," bawled Nebraskie.

Ernest saw sudden red spurts of fire. A gun banged. Then another bang! Bang-bang! Bullets struck the ground, to whine past where he was standing. His heart stopped—then gave a great throb of relief as Nebraskie's dark figure loomed up, moving fast. The cowboy's language was incoherent, though evidently profane.

"This way, Nebraskie," called Ernest.

More shots rang out from the ranch house as Nebraskie joined him. Two assuredly came from a double-barreled shotgun. And a rain of lead pellets all around him lent wings to Ernest's bootless feet. He reached the lane ahead of Nebraskie and sped down it to the open gate, where he halted to find and pull on his boots. He heard the horses whinny. Then Nebraskie came lumbering up, panting like a blacksmith's bellows.

"I'm—full—of shot!" panted Nebraskie wheezingly.

"Aw no, pard. You didn't get hit!" protested Ernest hopefully, as he leaped up to peer at his comrade.

"Thet—shotgun—peppered me—shore enough —anyhow, Ioway!—I follered you—cause I was— afeared you'd—do somethin' loco.—You damn near —landed in jail."

"Don't let that worry you, pard," rejoined Ernest quickly. "I'm obliged to you for coming, though. But if you're shot—"

"It ain't nuthin'. I've been shot before. Only never from *behind*. Haw! Haw! Thet's what I get—fer runnin'. By thunder—I'm liable—to do some real shoot-in'—over this heah deal.—You shore played hell, though, with your eavesdroppin' notion, Ernie Howard.—Hop your hoss."

Ernest had to cinch up his saddle, which caused him to fall behind Nebraskie, who rode off at a brisk trot, leading the pack-mule, but soon caught up with him. They made good time for several miles, until they struck the grade.

"Hosses tired," said Nebraskie. "We'll go on to the brook up heah aways, then camp....Doggone, Ernie, it'll be all over the range that we got shoved an' shot out of Blue Valley."

"What if it does?"

"You're a cool cuss. Sometimes I wonder if you're all there above your eyes."

"We'll get fired—that's sure," agreed Ernest regretfully.

"Now I'm just wonderin'. Mebbe Wilkins would blow on us. But Anderson will hold him up....What'd you heah?"

After a moment's consideration Ernest concluded that Nebraskie's opinion would be valuable, so he carefully repeated the conversation of the cattlemen, as it had occurred, word for word.

"Wal, I guess little ole Nebraskie wasn't figgerin' close," ejaculated the cowboy with satisfaction. "Io-way, our boss is as crooked as a rail fence."

"Looks that way. But how can we prove it?"

"Lord, puncher, whadda you want to prove it fer? No mix of ourn. Onless you want to use *thet* to fetch your redhaided lass to her knees. Haw! Haw!"

"Nebraskie! Do you think I'm as low-down as

that?" flashed Ernest indignantly.

"All's fair in love. Pard, it ain't a bad idee, come to look it over. You might save Anne from disgrace, instead of fetchin' it down on her haid."

"How so?"

"Wal, I ain't figgered thet out. It jest popped into my mind. Lemme see now....Fust, get the showdown on Hepford's dealin'. Then tell the gurl. Then both of you scare him into gettin' away from Red Rock before somebody from the East comes down heah an' ruins him. If you love Anne as bad as you seem to think, go ahaid. It's pretty, if I say so myself."

"Nebraskie, you're a regular Machiavelli," declared Ernest admiringly.

"Who'n hell is he?" asked the cowboy suspiciously.

"Pard, I wouldn't care to win Anne that way," replied Ernest firmly.

"See heah, young feller, what difference does it make *how* you win a woman, so long as you get her?"

Whatever Nebraskie's philosophy, at times it was unanswerable. As they rode on into the night Ernest fell to revolving the situation in his mind. Whatever the angle from which he viewed it, he could see that things would soon come to a head. But the actual winning of Anne Hepford's hand had no place in his calculation. In the first place it seemed preposterous: in the second, he did not feel sure that he wanted her now. He had bitter misgivings about the girl. He could overlook her father's undoubted perfidy; he could forgive her vanity, her coquetry; but if she had gone too far with other boys, as rumor had it, then she was not the girl he wanted to love permanently. Love, however, he had discovered, did not seem to come to one's beck and call. One loved because he could not help it.

"I better stay away from her," he soliloquized aloud.

"What's thet?" inquired Nebraskie.

"Gosh, I was talking to myself."

"Wal, reckon you was tellin' the truth then.... Heah's the brook, Ioway. I smelled the water before I heerd it. We'll turn off into them cedars, hobble the hosses, an' snooze till daylight."

CHAPTER
10

SEVERAL times during the night Ernest awoke, each time with a vague sense of pleasure over the events of the previous evening. He had been held up by a cowman with a gun; he had been shot at; he knew what the whistle of lead sounded like. And there was the prospect that a posse of trackers might take the trail in the morning.

Certain it was that Ernest arose before break of day, and he had the horses in shortly. While he was building a fire Nebraskie awoke. He sat up. When with a wry face he tenderly felt the hindermost parts of his anatomy, and exclaimed, "Doggone if I don't reckon some of them shots went in. You gotta pick 'em out when we get home."

"Rustle, you lazy hombre," sang out his camp-mate cheerfully. "The day's busted and we may find we're tracked."

"Lordy, but you're a romantic gazabo," drawled Nebraskie. "Strange Anne doesn't fall haid over heels in love with you. At that I'll gamble she will."

"Nebraskie, for heaven's sake, give me a chance to forget that girl," Selby burst out in right-eous wrath.

"Misery loves company, pard.... Where the devil air we?—Aw, I savvy. Wal, it's a tough old world."

All Nebraskie had to do to be fully dressed was to don his sombrero. He rolled his bed, tied it and gave it a toss. Then without washing face or hands he set to peeling potatoes in their only basin. Ernest noted the omission.

"Wash your hands, anyway," he advised. "You're trailing with me now."

"Wall, I'll be durned!" ejaculated Nebraskie, star-ing. "You're getting mighty particular." Then he emp-tied the potatoes out of the basin and made for the brook, whistling a cowboy tune.

For breakfast they had fried potatoes, hot coffee, and hard biscuits, which they soaked in their tin cups. Then Nebraskie strapped the pack-saddle on the mule, while Ernest washed and dried the utensils. A few minutes later they were mounted and riding out of the cedars to meet the red glow of sunrise. Having surmounted the grade they traveled at a brisk trot. Nebraskie never thought to look back over his shoul-der, but Ernest did, more than once. No dust puffs appeared back down the long pass. Before the sun got hot they had entered the forest, taking a trail far to the left of the cattle road.

"Ioway, we can ride in tonight late if we want," said Nebraskie, breaking a long silence.

"What's the hurry?" objected Ernest. "We have two days. And then Siebert is sending me to Holbrook for a load of grain."

"Haulin' grain is apple pie," returned Nebraskie. "All day an' night in town. Stores to loaf in an' gurls to see....Say, I tell you what. You can take a letter over to Dais fer me. Will you, pard?"

"Sure. And make her kiss me to get it," replied Selby, teasingly.

"Ernie, please don't fool with my gurl. She's only a kid. An' you're a handsome, fascinatin' devil, you know. Why, you'd have it all over Dude if you wanted to be thet kind."

"Very well, then. I'll try to resist temptation. But I'm sorry I didn't see Daisy first."

"So'm I. Then I wouldn't be in so helluva much trouble."

"Trouble? Say, Nebraskie, you've no trouble compared to mine."

"Didn't you heah Dais confess what hold thet pretty-faced skunk had on her?"

"I heard, and to be honest it worries me. I'll talk to Daisy. We've just got to keep her out of Hyslip's clutches. He's a smooth brute."

"Funny, but most wimmen seem to like brutes."

"No, they don't," denied Ernest with considerable emphasis.

"I can be somethin' of a brute myself," vouchsafed Nebraskie. "An' tryin' thet with Anne wouldn't hurt your cause none neither."

Selby also denied that sentiment vigorously, until he suddenly remembered how his one and only act of violence toward Anne had brought such surprising and unforgettable results. Maybe Nebraskie was right. But that one commission of rudeness of his had left him ashamed, if it had not Anne. Somehow Nebraskie's simple uncouth words had the power to stir him mightily. And when he admitted that, he realized he was acknowledging that he would repeat his violent conduct toward Anne Hepford, if he ever got the chance.

They rode on, up the shady trail, under gray beetling crags, and down through canyons where water splashed melodiously, and all was cool, fresh, sweet, fragrant. Then they rode over a dry pass where the yellow pines grew wide apart and deer flashed like red ghosts through the aisles. From the pass the trail led up over the red cliffs, from which their glance swept down over the red rocks below to the wide green ranch sleeping in the sun.

Ernest reined in his horse and stared out over the park floor. Yes, he loved Red Rock Ranch. His feeling for it had stolen upon him gradually. He wanted to work there all his life. But what of Anne? Could he be happy there without her? His answer was a dogged one, fruit of his pain, and it had to do with a hope and surety that there must be another lovely girl somewhere, perhaps with red hair and lively green eyes, one who was as true as Anne Hepford was shallow. In his heart he knew very well that there was only one redheaded girl for him.

At sunset they camped at Agua d'Ora Spring,

which up to the present, was the wildest and most beautiful spot Ernest had ever seen.

"What's it named from?" he asked.

"Wal, some say a Mexican found gold heah. An' others thet it's named from the color of the water," replied Nebraskie.

"Not so far from the ranch, is it?"

"Aboot a mile, if you jump off the cliff. Three mebbe by trail."

"Gosh, then it's on Hepford's—I mean on Red Rock land?"

"Shore. It belongs to the ranch."

"Then why in the name of common sense didn't Hepford pipe water down to the house and bunkhouse and barns?"

"Big expense, an' Hepford ain't interested in improvin' the land. The fact is, Ioway, these foremen an' superintendents jest work for their own interests."

"Nebraskie, if I—if I owned that ranch the first thing I'd do would be run this wonderful cold water down there."

"Ump-umm. Scuse me, pard, fer disagreein'. The first thing you'd do would be to go lopin' to your knees before the read-headed lady. Wal, it'd be a cinch you'd get her then. Haw! Haw!"

Wherewith Ernest threw the first article he could get his hands on, which happened to be a can of milk. It hit Nebraskie, who wheeled quickly, presenting that part of his anatomy where the shot from the rancher's gun had landed. He forthwith was treated to some extremely robust language. The two partners wound up with roars of laughter which must have shocked a peaceful-minded Gila monster dozing in the dust.

They had supper, unrolled their beds, haltered the horses with a nosebag of grain, after which tasks they climbed up and out on the rim of the cliff that overlooked the valley. Twilight lay shadowy and mysterious beneath them. The slope was a deep blue. Across on the other side, the red crags stood up, sunset-flushed and unbelievably beautiful. The silence was profound. Ernest could not detect a single sound, except the excited beating of his heart. The sweet solitude of that height settled upon him like a restful mantle. He resolved to come to this place often—to give it a name for himself alone. But no felicitous one suggested itself to him.

"Mighty nice rondevoo fer lovers," Nebraskie remarked sentimentally.

"Pard, you're right. But never the time and the place and the loved one all together!"

"Thet ain't the gurl's fault."

This cowboy certainly expressed a lot of pertinent and thought-provoking ideas. But at the moment Ernest wanted to watch and feel and dream, so he shut up Nebraskie by the sad prophecy that neither Daisy nor Anne were for them.

He was roused from his reverie by Nebraskie's call from the darkness behind: "Hey, what you gonna do—moon out there all night?" Reluctantly he clambered back to join his comrade, and was soon snug under his blankets, no longer inclined to resist sleep.

Next morning Nebraskie had the laugh on him, for the cowboy was up, and when he rolled out of his blankets there stood the horses saddled, coffee was steaming on the fire, and the bacon was sizzling.

"Mawnin' kid," drawled Nebraskie. "Wake up an' heah the birds. Roll your bed an' get outside some provender. An' we'll rustle down to find out what gazabo has made love to Anne last."

"Joy-killer!" was the reply.

They were halfway down the zigzag trail by the time the sun rose over the eastern foothills. And they got in just as Jeff, the cook, was calling the outfit to breakfast.

"Pard, take your time slippin' the pack an' saddle, while I get a line on Hyslip," said Nebraskie, when they halted before their door in the bunkhouse.

"Uhuh," grunted Selby. He was beginning to sense a protective thoughtfulness in his comrade and it made him feel warm deep inside. Of late Nebraskie seemed to have greatly matured. No longer was he the rollicking carefree rider! Perhaps trouble had brought out the latent strength of his character. It struck Ernest anew that Nebraskie would make a bad enemy. He leisurely slipped the saddles and turned the horses loose in the corral. When he came back Nebraskie was waiting for him.

"Reckon nuthin' to make you feel worried," said that worthy. "But the outfit's sore as a boil. Hawk has a long face. I'll bet two bits Hepford has been razzin' them plenty."

They went in to breakfast, and straddled the long bench to face some of the cowboys on the other side of the wooden table. Ernest shouted a cheery good morning to everybody. Shep Davis and Steve Monell replied, as did the foreman Siebert. But Hyslip, with his cronies, Lunky Pollard and Bones Magill never even batted an eye. Hyslip could not very well have batted one of his eyes, for it appeared to be hidden in a large black swelling. The regularity of that handsome face had been sadly marred. The Iowan felt a satisfaction that he was sure his expression betrayed, so he bent low over his plate.

"Lordy, Nebraskie, but this outfit is sure plumb glad to have us back," he observed, above the noise of the clattering dishes.

"Shore we're glad," returned Shep. "We haven't seen a smilin' face fer days."

Hawk Siebert fixed his penetrating gaze upon Ernest.

"You can hitch up the big wagon an' rustle fer Holbrook right after breakfast. I'll give you an order on Babbitt."

"Fine, boss. I sure am de-lighted. It'll be great to see town again. All the stores—and all the pretty girls."

"Haw! Haw!" laughed Hyslip humorlessly, without looking up. It was a cold, exaggerated laugh, full of contempt. It brought that quick flash of heat into Ernest's veins. Some of the other cowboys gave him a laugh, too, though not insultingly.

"Nebraskie, what you think about that?" inquired his friend.

"Pretty raw. But you've only got yourself to blame. Keep your cheery trap shet."

"Come back sort of cocky, didn't you?" said Siebert shrewdly. "What happened over at Blue?"

"We got shot at and chased off the ranch," replied Selby laconically, acting upon the cue he and Nebraskie had agreed upon.

"Say, tenderfoot, you're plumb loco," accused the foreman. "What's he talking aboot, Nebraskie?"

"Fact, boss. An' if you don't believe it I can show you some black and blue shot marks on my legs."

"Shot marks! From a shotgun?"

"Shore. An' before thet we heerd the real old Colt slugs zippin' along. You know thet sound, Hawk."

Hawk leaned forward. All the other cowboys were now intensely interested.

"What fer? Who shot at you? Why?"

"All fer nuthin', boss," replied Nebraskie coolly. "Anderson an' his outfit was mean as hell to us all the way across. An' once we got there why they didn't even ast us to set down an' eat."

That sort of thing, in the hospitable range country, was to cowmen a heinous omission. More than one muttered curse struck Ernest's ear.

"Well, what'd *you* expect?" cut in Hyslip significantly.

"Dude, I'll do the questionin'. You keep still," said Siebert sharply. "Go on, Nebraskie."

"Wal, Ioway an' me busted into the kitchen anyway an' set down. They had to feed us. Afterward we was walkin' around the ranch, smokin' an' talkin' aboot our gurls—which my pard shore likes to do— an' we goes by the open door of the ranch house. Ioway stopped to listen, an' course I did too.... Wal, we get ketched an' it was either run or flash guns. So we run.... Did they shoot at us? Wal, I should snicker to snort they did."

Siebert banged the table till the cups jumped

and clanged. His keen eyes had little dancing flecks in them, like hot sparks. But that show of feeling did not hide his surprise and curiosity.

"Nebraskie, what'd you hear them talkin' aboot?" he queried.

"Wal, boss," drawled the cowboy, "if you scuse me, thet's our bizness. It concerns Mr. Hepford, an' when he gets wind of our little fracas an' is aboot to fire us—then we may tell *him*."

Ernest detected a slight gray shade stealing under Siebert's tan. It made the blood surge through his veins. So the foreman was not blind to Hepford's dereliction after all. Perhaps he was a party to it. This occasioned Ernest keen regret. He liked Siebert and did not want to lose him.

"Aw, I see," returned Hawk slowly, and he certainly controlled whatever it was that had actuated him. "Wal, if it's none of my bizness, I've no more to say."

But half an hour later he pushed open the door of Ernest's bunkhouse and, entered, then closed it behind him.

"Where's Nebraskie?"

"Wrangling the horses."

"Ioway, suppose you lay the cairds on the table," began Siebert brusquely.

"What cards, boss?" inquired Ernest innocently.

"Them cairds Nebraskie was braggin' aboot."

"Hawk, you've been a good friend to me and I like you," rejoined Ernest, sparring for time to gauge the foreman, and to think how to meet this situation.

That speech made Siebert sit down abruptly on

the bunk. He was plainly perturbed. Ernest concealed his surprise.

"Shore I've been your friend, more'n you know. I've kept you on heah, when the outfit was agin it. An' I'm shore goin' to take you an' Nebraskie with me, as I told you boys once before."

"Where we going?"

"I don't know yet, but it'll be some miles from this range, believe me."

"Ahuh. Why are you takin' us, Hawk?"

"Wal, you're two good boys. I like you. An' there's bad blood heah. There'll be some spilled if you hang on."

"You mean Hyslip and his pards are against us?"

"I should smile. Only yesterday Dude swore I had to fire you or he an' Bones an' Lunky would quit."

"What'd you say, Hawk?"

"I told him to go to hell. No use fer me to fire *him*, Ioway. Hepford would take him right back."

"That so? He likes him a lot, then?"

"No, it's not thet. Dude has a hold on the rancher."

"Through Anne, you mean?"

"I wasn't alludin' to thet hold, if there is one."

Right there Ernest had an inspiration to unmask his battery. With his gaze hard on the foreman he shot the query: "And you're leaving Red Rock soon because Hepford is crooked?"

The shot went home. But Siebert was an old hand on the range. With certainty that Ernest really knew something he overcame his slight perturbation.

"Where'd you ever get thet idee, cowboy?" he

asked, coolly, and then with a smile he began rolling a cigarette.

"Nebraskie told me."

"Hell you say!....So you're two bright cow-punchers? I told the boss he was makin' a big mistake on this last Wilkins cattle drive. He cussed me an' told me to run the outfit an' not him."

"Hepford sure did make a mistake with that drive. And a bigger one to let Nebraskie and me go on it."

"Ahuh....Wal, what'd you heah over there?"

"You ask Nebraskie after I'm gone. If he wants to tell you it's all right with me."

"Ioway, I'm glad you're listenin' to Nebraskie. He's no fool. An' he knows cowmen. You're skatin' on thin ice, if you're figgerin' on scarin' Hepford or workin' him. Once he got wise—an' he's quick-witted, he'd shoot you before you got two words out. An' fer thet matter your words wouldn't have much weight against his."

"Thanks, Hawk. I appreciate your advice. *I'm* sure not making any mistakes....How thin is the ice you're skatin' on?"

Ernest had launched this last question like a flash. But Hawk never batted an eye. He gazed admiringly at his green hand.

"Now I know why I took a shine to you. I jest sorta felt you was no ordinary clodhopper of a cowpuncher. Reckon you an' Nebraskie an' me had better rustle away from Red Rock, while our health is good."

"What's the hurry, Hawk? It's just getting interesting."

"Wal, too damn interestin'.... Ioway, the ice under me ain't even froze yet."

"Hawk, don't tell me you're in with Hepford on this queer cattle dealing," said Ernest, his hand going to the older man's shoulder. That gesture and his look proved something to Siebert.

"No, by Gawd, I'm not," he said in a tone that suggested the words had been damned up in him too long. "I've only been on to Hepford fer a couple of years. An' he's begun to suspect me. Shore, if the new owner of Red Rock would drop in on us sudden like, Hepford would implicate me. An' Ioway, I'd have a hell of a time provin' otherwise. I don't believe I'd even risk goin' into court."

"What'd you do, Hawk?"

"Wal, I've throwed a gun before this to keep out of goin' to jail. An' I could do thet again."

"Hawk, whatever kept you stayin' on here, after you were sure Hepford was not strictly a rancher you could respect?"

Siebert laughed, though the red came up in his swarthy cheeks.

"Ioway, I was an old fool. Like all the rest, I was sweet on Anne!"

"For heaven's sake! Not you, really?"

"Shore. Anne wasn't above bein' nice to me, if there was no other ride aboot. She was just a tyke when I came, but when she was sixteen, then.... Don't look so blame disgusted. I got over it, Ioway. An' then I jest stuck on heah."

"Like Red Rock much?" went on Ernest, stepping to the window to look out.

"Awful much, Ioway. But we got to go, jest the same."

Ernest turned round, once more composed and sure of himself.

"I hope we won't have to leave right off. I'd like to see Anne a couple of more times."

"Lord, what thet redhaid has got to answer for!" ejaculated Siebert fervently.

"Hawk, do you think—she's absolutely no good?" asked Ernest, his voice breaking.

"Anne's all right. Jest boy-crazy. If she ever finds the right feller an' gets jarred into knowin' it, wal, she'll be as big an' true a woman as this heah West."

"I'd like mighty well to be that fellow you speak of," replied Ernest with a sigh. "But to come back to our senses, Hawk....Nebraskie and I talked round our campfire. Just two speculating cowboys, who'd happened on an irregularity. Now just between ourselves, how could Hepford ever be apprehended on whatever slick deals he's making?"

"Wal, I doubt if we could ever *prove* anythin'," replied the foreman dubiously. "These court proceedin's aboot cattle most always go up in smoke. Talk is cheap. If one witness swears there was two hundred haid of stock sold or stole an' another witness swears there wasn't, where does the court get off? But I'll allow if we could compare the report of this drive Hepford sends back East to the figures we know *right now* it'd be mighty ticklish for Hepford. He'd sweat blood. On the other hand if weeks an' months went by an' then we compared notes on this last drive, wal, it wouldn't phase him none at all. He's sold a dozen bunches of cattle this summer."

"Humph, he's sure a track-covering hombre," the Iowan replied.

Nebraskie came tramping in, his eyes bright.

"Get outa heah, you confabin' road agents. I gotta write to my gurl. Ernie, you're elected to be mail-carrier fer Anne, too. She sent word down by Jeff fer you to call to take her letters. An' aboot some errands, too."

"Anne!"

"Thet's what I said. Don't look as if I'd punched you one in the gizzard."

Siebert laughed and went out. Then Ernest, while Nebraskie sat at the window writing, proceeded speedily into the task of changing, washing and shaving. He put on a new shirt and bright tie, and after brushing his hair again he dashed out to leap off the porch. Siebert was standing talking to some of the cowboys, among whom were Davis and Hyslip.

"Hey, Shep, what is it Miss Hepford wants me to do for her?" he called casually, as if he were used to being a courier for that young lady.

"Mail letters an' do some tradin' in town. All of which is a hunch fer you to fetch back a box of candy," replied Shep, who was not without a sense of humor. Ernest heard Hyslip muttering a curse. Never had he covered the distance to the ranch house in such short time. As he turned out of the pines he espied Anne sitting on the steps. His heart leaped. But he did not look up until he stood in front of her. He smiled as he bade her good morning, as if there had never been anything in his mind but glad thoughts about her.

"Mawnin', Iowa," she replied, as if sight of him made her thoughtful. "You look fresh and rosy for an overworked cowboy."

"Oh, I'm fine. Had a good trip. That's wonderful country. Did you ever see Agua d'Oro Spring?"

"Yes, but not for a long time. It is beautiful up there. I'd like to ride up to the spring again sometime. We'll go someday, when dad's away."

"I know I'm not one of his favorite riders," replied Ernest dryly.

"You shore are not. But you're mine," she said, with a bewildering smile. Then she beckoned to him to come up the high steps. "I wish you would mail these for me. Fetch any letters for me at the post office, of course. Never mind any others. Dad is fussy aboot his mail. He's going in himself next week. And here's a list of things I'd like you to buy. All written out on a list with money enclosed."

Ernest received the packet of letters, and the thick envelope, tinglingly conscious of the fact that Anne's cool fingers touched his and were not hastily removed.

"Anything more?" he asked, looking up at her.

"Well, is there? You're going to town," she drawled, her eyes holding his. There did not seem to be any help for it, Ernest groaned to himself.

"I'll see—if there is," he rejoined lamely. Why could he not be bold? The truth was that most of the time when he confronted Anne he was exactly what she took him for.

"Don't you go dallying after my cousin Daisy," she warned.

"But I must deliver a letter to her from Nebraskie."

"Is he still moon-eyed over her?"

"I'm afraid so. No wonder. She's very pretty and sweet."

"Yes, I saw how you appreciated that at the dance the other night," she said petulantly, and she flushed. This strange creature could not abide the least turning from her altar.

"Well, I'm not ashamed of it," declared Ernest stoutly.

"You should be—after the way you treated me. The more I think of that the angrier I get."

"I apologized to you and tried to explain."

"To be shore you did, and that'd have made it less—less unforgivable—if I could trust you. Iowa, I believe you are trifling with my young affections."

Her eyes were full of mischief, and laughter, too, which robbed her remark of its seriousness. Ernest had the wit to laugh in her face.

"*Your* young affections! Golly, that's a good one."

"What do you mean, sir?" she demanded, instantly suspicious and proud. "I'll have you know there's a vast difference between the mooing of a lot of cowboys and *my* affections."

"I hope so. Well, anyway, *I* didn't moo at you," he returned, with a glance as full of mischief as hers had been.

"You bet you didn't, you Iowa rail splitter. Look heah!" She rolled up the loose sleeve of her jacket to expose a beautiful arm, round and firm, the opal whiteness of which was marred by black and blue marks. "You did that?"

"No!...Oh, I couldn't have been *that* rough," he protested. "You've got me mixed up with some other—"

"Ernest Howard! Say you don't mean that— you can't believe it!" Her words, passionate and ringing as they were, did not convince Ernest, because somehow he had convinced himself that everything she said was insincere. But her eyes convinced him this time. They were big, wrathful, indignant.

"I'm sorry—I don't believe it," replied Ernest hastily.

"You're the only cowboy who'd dare insult me," she declared, her lips trembling. "That's what I get for—for not fighting you....You believe *any* cowboy can take liberties with me."

"I did," said Ernest deliberately, his eyes meeting hers.

"Yet you asked me to marry you," she went on, in wonder and scorn. "Shore I should think you wouldn't want a girl who'd been that free with other men."

"I wouldn't. But I could forgive you and forget it."

"Well sir, you're as mistaken aboot me as I was aboot you," she retorted.

"What'd you take me for, Miss Hepford?" he asked gravely. "That meeting of ours in Holbrook you're referring to, I know."

"I took you for a tenderfoot country jake, masquerading as a cowboy."

"And you were perfectly right."

"Well, anyway, you're frank aboot it," she rejoined, and again she betrayed her increasing interest in him. And again this strange man from Iowa had won a round. It required no great perspicacity for anyone to see that Anne had been little used to cowboys of any cultivation. "What did you take *me* for, that day?"

"A wonderful western girl, frank and democratic, free as the winds of her ranges, sincere as she was beautiful."

"Humph! You shore didn't show any of that opinion....And after you got to Red Rock—to see things going on—to heah these towhaids talk—what'd you take me for *then*?"

"An insatiable coquette! Vain as a peacock! Dead set to make every male in sight crawl at her feet! Not particular about preserving her charms for the *one* lover who might come to awaken the best in her!... A lovely thoroughbred who didn't need to be brazen and calculating to make men kneel!...A young woman going wrong!"

While Ernest delivered this scathing speech he saw the wave of scarlet rising from neck to temple, and blazing green eyes transfixing him.

"I'll never forgive you. I have the very sight of you," she cried, and leaping up almost inarticulate with fury, and graceful as a panther, she ran into the house.

So agitated was Ernest that he took the wrong way round the ranch house, thus doubling the distance back to the corrals, where the wagon would be waiting. That was just as well, for he would avoid meeting the cowboys. He did not care to be seen just then. His heart was throbbing in his breast. His face was wet with perspiration and clammily cold, yet his blood felt on fire. His anger had gotten the better of his good sense. How furious Anne had been—and how beautiful in her fury! Never forgive him—hate him! If looks could have killed he would not now be striding there under the pines. Well, now he had told her the truth, and now he had come to the end of his little romance. He tried to persuade himself that he was glad. But it was a sorry persuasion.

Ernest reached the big wagon and mounted to the high seat, where he unwound the reins from the brake. Nebraskie came running, with the awkward gait of a bowlegged cowboy unused to such exertion.

"Heah's my letter, pard," he said, handing a soiled envelope up. "Give it to Dais on your way out an' fetch her a box of candy on your way in. Savvy, old man?"

"Sure do. I'll put some good words in for you, too, Nebraskie."

"Good.—Say, you look kinda pale round the gills. Ahuh, I'm on. Jest seen Anne!—Cheer up, pard. There are other fish in the sea if we don't land her. Red-haired ones, too. Good luck, an' rustle back."

The five miles up the valley to where the Brooks' road branched off passed all too quickly for Ernest, so full was his mind, so varied and bewil-

dering his thoughts. Before he reached the end of
the lane he espied Daisy, who, at sight of him, came
bounding across the yard. Ernest halted to hide the
letter behind his back. What a pretty little thing she
was! Her eyes, like those of a fawn, dark, soft, vel-
vety, just now eager instead of melancholy, were altogether lovely.

"Hello, Iowa. I saw you coming," she said
brightly. "Going to town?"

"Yes, Dais, and I've got something for you. Guess
what."

"I'm a poor guesser."

"It's an important letter from Nebraskie. What'll
you give for it?"

"What do you want?"

"Well, I couldn't possibly take less than a kiss.
Would the letter be worth that to you?"

"I reckon, considering the messenger," she replied with a blush. Daisy, too, then had a little of
coquetry in her.

"Thanks," said Ernest, with a gay laugh, as he
delivered the letter. "I'll collect my toll after I see
Nebraskie."

"You'll never get it then," she returned, just as
gaily. "Goodby, Iowa."

He plodded down the lane and from his wagon
seat espied Daisy sitting on the fence. She waved the
letter. Ernest waved back. "Sweet kid. And she cares
for Nebraskie—the lucky son-of-a-gun. But she
would have let me kiss her! Doggone the women!
They're beyond me, too!"

CHAPTER

11

SELBY drove until dusk and halted at a grove of cedars where there were grass and water. It was the habit of teamsters and cattlemen, driving to town, to stop at convenient ranches along the road. The latch string was always out. But Ernest preferred to be alone; he did not want to talk the small talk of the range. If he had been given double the time it would not have been long enough for him to think. No other young man, he felt sure, ever before had found himself in such a baffling, heartbreaking yet exciting predicament.

He unhitched the team and fed the horses their grain. His next task was to start a little fire, and then to open the pack Siebert had instructed the cook to put in the wagon. The result was that he ate an ample supper and fared very satisfactorily indeed. Shortly afterward he unrolled his bed in the wagon, but he was not yet ready to go to sleep.

Darkness had settled down over the desert and it was very still. The air had not yet cooled off. Ernest sat down before his little fire of cedar sticks. He liked this being alone, on his own responsibility as a common teamster. "Any Iowa farmer should be able to drive a team of hosses," Siebert had remarked. The smell of cedar smoke was pleasant, but it was irritating to the eyes. As he sat there, listening to the tinkle of water over stones and the occasional thump of a hoof, presently there came a sighing through the cedars. His little fire was fanned red and sparks flew. The warm drowsy air appeared to rise and in its place came a cool wind out of the hills. Climbing into the wagon box Ernest pulled off his boots and stretched on his bed. The whole canopy of sky above was a glittering spiderweb of stars.

He tried to put off sleep as long as he could, but at last he succumbed to it. When he awakened the sky was gray-blue and vacant. He seemed to have slept only a moment. He sat up. The east was ruddy low down along the black-knobbed horizon. The cool freshness and fragrance of the desert air was the most exhilarating thing he had ever experienced. The problems that had harassed him last night seemed to have faded away. Life was rich, sweet, promising. The West seemed to unfold around him, new, glorious, all-sufficing. He leaped out to his tasks.

About midday on the third day out from Red Rock Ernest drove into town, and found with help of inquiry the store where he was to purchase what Siebert had sent him for. The wagon was soon loaded. Then Ernest drove back to the corrals on the outskirts, unhitched, watered and fed the horses, after which tasks he repaired to town again.

His next move was to call upon the lawyer Smith, who received him with great interest. They had an hour's colloquy, the upshot of which was that Smith agreed to write to Ernest's lawyer back home, and instruct him to send an urgent request to Hepford for a report of all cattle sales up to date, and of all other necessary details important to the new owner, who would soon be out to take over the ranch.

After that decision, Ernest, feeling at once elated, and yet strangely regretful, went to the hotel where he wrote some necessary letters to his people at home, who would assuredly be wondering what had become of him. And he was careful to instruct them to address him as Ernest Howard for the present. How curious that would make them!

Then he sallied forth to make Anne's purchases. In the envelope there were forty dollars in paper money, and a formidable list of articles, the dry goods part of which made Ernest's hair stand up. Perhaps he could find a girl clerk who would understand. And what puzzled him most was the last item on the list, if such it could be called. Below the last written word Anne had left a space, then a well-defined dash, and opposite it a question mark.

"What the dickens did she mean by that?" he asked himself.

After a little Ernest correlated those thought-provoking marks with Anne's reply when he had asked her if there was anything more he could do for her. "Well, is there? You're going to town." What a very significant reply. Transparent as crystal! He laughed. But she had written the list and made her remark before he had offended her so grievously. Nevertheless he would comply with her desires, in spite of the fact that she now cordially hated him.

Of all the embarrassing jobs Ernest had ever had imposed upon him this one of Anne's was the worst. He had an armful of bundles before he got to the dry goods store, and there, of course, his luck was to be accosted by a wholesome-looking, flaxen-haired western girl, who immediately took him for what he was—a tenderfoot. Her eyes betrayed her convictions. The first hour was the worst. This western girl clerk did not exactly make fun of him, and when friends of hers dropped in she was decent enough not to give her customer away, but all the same she was deriving an immense amount of amusement from the situation. Finally Ernest grew desperate. He asked: "Is there a dance in town tonight?"

"I—I don't know," she replied, surprised.

"I'm sorry. I'd sure like to ask you to go. Reckon I've seen all the girls in town, but you're the prettiest."

She blushed furiously, and from that moment Ernest had the better of the situation. When he paid the bill and gathered up the additional bundles the girl roguishly said: "There *is* a dance Saturday night."

"Gosh, I'm sorry I can't be here," he replied, and went out, satisfied that he had turned the tables. He carried his load out to the wagon and stowed the packages carefully under the seat. Then he hurried back to finish his purchases. Anne's money was all gone: indeed he had been compelled to use some of his own to pay for what she had ordered. Nebraskie had never thought to give Ernest any for the candy he was to buy for Daisy. In the third store Ernest found two enormous boxes of chocolates, wrapped in fancy colored paper and tied with scarlet ribbons. He bought them both, had them carefully wrapped, and treading on air he carried these back to the wagon and stowed them away with the other things, all of which he covered with a canvas.

It was not yet late in the afternoon. He had accomplished his duties fairly speedily, all things considered. So he decided to walk up town, and around a little, have supper there, and then drive out after sundown.

At the corner Ernest encountered two cowboys about his age, and they greeted him with the friendly loquaciousness of the range.

"Teamster for Hepford of Red Rock. I'm driving out tonight," said Ernest, accounting for himself.

"Punch any cows?"

"I've been punching at 'em, but haven't hit any yet."

"Nasty outfit down there, so I've heerd. Rider named Hyslip, cock of the walk," spoke up the second cowboy. "He's from Texas. Thet's where I hail from, too."

Ernest was interested then, and he sat down with the cowboys, talking freely himself, and asking casual questions in turn. He tried to find out something about Hyslip's past.

"Wal, stranger, you'd learn somethin' aboot Hyslip if you'd run down to Milford, or the Brazos, an' ast any range riders down theah," replied the Texan, somewhat curtly.

Ernest was learning that inquisitiveness was risky. He walked up town with these boys, but left them when they entered a saloon. Then he strolled about and talked with whom he could. He overheard a scrap of conversation between two rugged visitors, evidently cattlemen, one in a buckboard and the other on horseback. They had halted to greet each other opposite where Ernest happened to be walking along the sidewalk. He stopped and leaned against a post.

"I get forty-eight a head, on the hoof," the horseman was saying.

"Best price this year. Cattle goin' up, at thet rate," said the other.

"Fall roundup ought to fetch good money. An' it will if the pesky rustlers don't beat us to it."

"Thet so? Wal, there ain't much stealin' up our way. For thet matter there ain't much stock, which may account fer it. Right smart drift of cattle over in the Blues, I heerd. Some rustlin', too."

"Fine grazin' country down there. Wal, good day, Sam. Remember me to your folks."

The two ranchers separated, going in opposite directions. Ernest leaned thoughtfully against the post. He was a rancher and he was losing stock. Rustlers had to be considered. It was a risk of cattle raising. But the term rustlers always confused him. They were cattle thieves, to put it baldly. Still he had gathered that some rustlers were cattlemen, operating ranches; others were individual cowboys, stealing from their employers; a few were out-and-out robbers, roving the ranges, raiding in a small way here and there. He wondered if Hepford could be called a rustler, but he decided not. That worthy was a shrewd, calculating, long-armed thief. He vowed he would set his heel down long before the proposed October drive could be accomplished. Then he remembered Anne. If he brought her father to justice, would that not disgrace, if not ruin her?

The thought militated against Ernest's present state of vague enjoyment. He decided to bring his lounging about town to an end. Returning to the corral he caught his horses, watered them at the trough, hitched up and drove out of town, just as dusk was falling. The road was down hill, enabling him to travel four or five miles an hour. He placed a goodly number behind him before he made camp for the night. Next day he drove fourteen hours, with a couple of rests, but as the road was bad his mileage did not mount up considerably. The following day, early in the afternoon, from the top of the long hill that looked off into beautiful Red Rock Valley he espied a buckboard, drawn by black horses he knew, coming toward him.

The first thought that flashed into Ernest's mind was disconcerting. Hepford would be absent from the ranch and he could see Anne alone. Instantly he discarded the idea. He should not, he would not, he did not want to see Anne alone. Then he muttered to himself in disgust: "Bah! I don't know my own mind two minutes running."

He halted the team at a wide place in the road to let Hepford drive by. The rancher's driver was a

Mexican lad, who at a word from his employer, reined in the horses.

"Hello, Howard. You're making a quick trip. Siebert didn't expect you until late tomorrow," said Hepford, with an appraising look at the team. Ernest was glad that the animals showed they had not been driven too fast.

"I didn't stay long in town, sir. And I've been coming easy, camping wherever I happened to be. Driving early and late."

"Any mail for me?"

"No, sir. I was instructed to call only for Miss Anne's mail," replied Ernest.

"Quite right. And you'd better rustle along with it."

Selby's reply was drowned by the pounding hoofs of the spirited blacks and the crunching of gravel. Away Hepford sped, leaving Ernest prey again to the insidious temptation which confronted him when he returned to Red Rock.

The thoughts of Anne were so persistent and persuasive that he drove by the Brooks' lane before he remembered that he had a package for Daisy. He halted the team, wound the reins round the brake handle, and securing the box of candy, he jumped off the wagon and strode down the lane toward Daisy's ranch house.

Again his thoughts were pleasant. He would try the same trick, hiding behind his back what he had fetched, and demand the same toll. He was not so very sure now that he would not only exact it but collect it, too.

Someone had left the bars of the gate down.

Ernest's quick eye spied fresh horseshoe tracks in the sand. A rider had gone in there not many hours before, and he had not come out. Perhaps it had been Nebraskie. Then down by the brook, in a clump of cedars, Ernest saw a white pinto mustang. He could have recognized that calico-marked pony a mile away. Dude Hyslip's!

Ernest did not like this at all. He hastened his stride but gone were his former pleasant anticipations. Daisy, no doubt, was in no wise to blame, but he would have to take her to task about it anyhow. She had no business trusting herself alone with that handsome deceiving scoundrel!

The living-room door was open. Ernest rapped and then called out. He got no reply, so he stepped across the threshold. At first glance he thought the room was empty. Then he heard stentorian breathing. He entered. The room did not have its usual neat appearance. It reeked of raw whiskey. On the table lay two empty bottles, and beside them a third bottle stood upright. It was half full of liquor. The Iowan's eyes swept the room. Behind him on the floor lay Brooks, plainly in a drunken stupor.

Ernest wanted to kick him, but he took out his concern and wrath in a vigorous shaking. Brooks grunted and mumbled.

"You damned hog!—Where's Daisy?" he asked anxiously.

This demand elicited no more from the prostrate rancher than had the shaking. Ernest left off in disgust, and called aloud for Daisy. There were only three rooms in the house. He peered into the kitchen, which was vacant, with the outside door wide open.

The third room had a curtain over the doorway. Ernest called again, then peeped in. Indeed this tiny, colorful, and tidy little place could be no one's but Daisy's. It spoke of her. But it too was empty. He strode outdoors to look around. She might have gone down to Red Rock. No! Ernest refused to deceive himself. The very air seemed heavy with suspense and suggestion.

He found himself imitating the habit of cowboys, who always looked on the ground for tracks. He could not find any in front of the house, except his own, and the broad imprint of Brooks' boot. Then he went around back. In the bare ground near the kitchen door he espied small sharp tracks, made by the heels of a cowboy boot. He got down to examine them. Hyslip! as surely as that pinto mustang was Hyslip's. That heel track showed the impress of the heart-shaped piece of metal which Hyslip had nailed onto his boots. He was noted all over the range for that trademark. The cowboys used the fact as a stock subject for badinage. Ernest grimly ascertained the direction of the boot tracks and started following them.

He was annoyed with Daisy for having allowed herself to walk out along the brookside or the woods with Hyslip. To be sure, the brute was quite capable of taking her by force away from the house. Ernest felt his wrath slowly mount, particularly for Hyslip. He argued that this certainly was his business, as he was Nebraskie's friend, and Nebraskie's happiness, if not his honor, was threatened.

Ernest had been over the ground more than once with Brooks. He well remembered it, by reason of its beauty. The cedars and junipers along the bank made a delightful shade. But Daisy was not to be seen near the house. He went on, around and above the big spring hole, where the water roared out from under the gray, lichened cliff, and up to the pine knoll. There, coming suddenly out of the covert into a sylvan glade, amber-mossed and flower-dotted, he espied the two he was seeking.

Ernest confronted them. Daisy sat on a mossy rock. She uttered a faint cry of dismay at the sight of him. The paleness of her pretty face was marred by several dirty marks. Her hair had come undone and one white shoulder gleamed through a wide rent in her blouse. But telltale as these evidences were, it was her eyes that told the whole story.

A single glance at Hyslip was enough. His handsome face was hot and streaked with perspiration. His jaw sagged. With a curse of disgust at his failure he turned his back on Ernest.

"Daisy, here's the candy Nebraskie asked me to fetch," spoke up Ernest, extending the box to her. But she made no move to take it, though she murmured thanks. The Iowan dropped the parcel. He was angry and just a little disgusted with this girl who could be one thing with Nebraskie and quite another with this good-looking but dissipated lout. The look on Daisy's face made him sick with doubt, with sorrow, with disappointment. He felt like turning on his heel and leaving her there with the cowboy. But for his friend's sake, he made one more attempt to bring her to her senses.

"Daisy, you've broken your word to Nebraskie," said Ernest gently.

She nodded her pretty dishevelled head.

"You—you ought to be ashamed!" he continued. It was a ridiculous speech, for no girl could have manifested deeper shame.

"Ernest—I—I couldn't help—it," she faltered, wringing her hands. "When he came—I wouldn't see him. I went in the kitchen. He and Dad got to drinking....I—I should have run—but I didn't think of that—in time....He came in the kitchen—grabbed me—packed me up heah....Oh, Ernest—what could I *do*?"

Ernest felt a tigerish leap of every fighting instinct in his blood. He slammed a hard hand on Hyslip's shoulder and spun him round.

"If I had my gun I'd shoot you like the yellow dog you are," he declared coldly.

"Bah! You wouldn't shoot a coyote. You meddlin' tenderfoot. Get out of heah."

Hyslip's expression of surprise at the way things had turned out was changing to anger.

"Like hob I will. You're going to be told something, Dude Hyslip. And then—"

"What business is this of yours?" interrupted the red-faced Hyslip, hotly.

"Nebraskie is my best friend."

"What of thet? If Daisy loves me better than she does him?"

Ernest seemed to sink inwardly. "Well, friend or not, if that's true, I've no call to interfere. But I don't believe it."

"Wal, ask her, you Ioway hayseed."

Ernest turned to Daisy. He did not need to ask the question. Her face was flaming, her eyes were distended with misery and terror. "Once he—he had some kind—of power over me," she panted. "But I—I never loved—him....And I hate—hate him now! Oh, Ernest, I'm glad you came in time...."

"You hear that, Hyslip?" snapped Ernest.

"Aw, thet's talk. She's jest out of her haid. Why, when I was packin' her up heah—kissin' her—she kissed me back....What you got to say about thet, Dais Brooks?"

"Did you kiss him, Daisy?" asked Ernest quietly.

She dropped her head. "I—I—reckon I did.... I—I told you—he had some kind of power—over me."

Ernest concerned himself no more with her. He thought he understood the situation now. And he let himself go. He had always wanted a chance to get at Hyslip.

"Dude, the handsome! The lady-killing cow-puncher! You're sure a fine specimen of a man. My God, but you are a cowardly skunk!"

"Howard, I won't take much more from you," returned Hyslip, his face flushing even more deeply. "I'm shore makin' allowances fer your natural feelin's."

"You'll take a hell of a lot more from me, Dude Hyslip," retorted Ernest. "But before I cuss you as you deserve and give you the licking you deserve—I want to tell you as man to man that your treatment of this girl was too cowardly to let you go unpunished. When they hear about it on the range, they'll chase you back to Texas with dogs."

"Aw, it wasn't no such thing. She likes to be mauled an' hurt. Same as other girls."

"Good God! What a fine speech for a man to make! But you're not a man. You're just a big hunk of bones and meat thrown together with a pleasing effect. You please the eyes of women and you think that entitles you to take what you can get."

"Wal, I know what I know," returned Hyslip doggedly, and he seemed to be surprised with himself that he had done nothing to defend himself against the bitter attack.

"You pick on a slip of a girl like Daisy, who has no more strength than a kitten. What'd you get when you tried the same thing on Anne Hepford?"

This was only a random shot of Ernest's, but it brought the dusky red to Hyslip's handsome face.

"What'd you get?" went on Selby, following up his advantage relentlessly. "I know what you got. Anne *told* me! I had the laugh on you, Dude Hyslip. And you bet I know what you'll get if you ever lay another hand on her again. What's more *you* know, too."

Hyslip glared in slow acceptance of a disconcerting fact. No doubt the excitement of his affair with Daisy, whatever that had been, and the argument with Ernest, had tended to sober him. For the probability was that he had been somewhat under the influence of liquor. The Iowan's last thrust in particular silenced him. Sight of Hyslip's face made his accuser long to pound it into a bloody pulp. But for his insatiable passion to tell the truth to this conceited cowboy, he would have leaped at him long ago.

"You're a liar!" ejaculated Hyslip, in gathering fury.

"How'd I know if Anne hadn't told me?" queried Ernest.

"Prove thet—you—you—" burst out Hyslip, in jealous shame and rage. It was plain to see that Selby had hit upon the cowboy's . . . sorest spot—his vanity.

Ernest now was determined to sting this pompous cowboy—to abase him in his own sight!

"All thet's nothin'," returned Hyslip when Selby had completed his dressing-down. "Whadda I care for your mouthin'? . . . Prove thet aboot Anne Hepford—or I'll choke it out of you."

"Aha! That sticks in your craw, eh? Well, what do you say to *this*?" Ernest leaned toward the livid-lipped cowboy. "It was *I* who gave you the black eye for trying to force your vile lovemaking on Daisy once before—that night at the dance. It was *I*. And *I* told Anne. . . . And *she* was to tickled she . . . well, I wish you could have heard her laugh. . . ."

Hyslip leaped up as if he had been spurred.

"So thet was what she meant this mawnin'!" he ejaculated, in utter amazement and chagrin. Then rage followed, riotous and ungovernable. "Blast you, Howard! An' it was *you* hit me? . . . An' it's *you* she—"

He choked and the brown hand he extended shook in the excess of his agitation.

"You bet it was I," snapped Ernest. "And if I don't—Nebraskie will kill you!"

"Talkin' of killin', huh?" rasped Hyslip.

Absence of a gun belt and holster had deceived Ernest. Quick as lightning he leaped to pinion Hyslip's arm to his side.

"Daisy, grab his gun!" yelled Ernest hoarsely.

Daisy turned, her face white, her hands flying. She tore at Hyslip's right hand that clutched the gun handle.

"You damn little cat! I'll fix you fer this," raged Hyslip, straining to free himself.

"Bite him, Dais—bite him!" cried Ernest, twisting Hyslip's arm with all his strength. The cowboy could not break that binding hold on his right arm, but he began to kick Ernest with his left foot. Daisy was dragged to her knees. Then suddenly Hyslip let out a strangled yell. "Agghh!"

Daisy fell away from him then. But she had the gun.

"Run with it, Dais. Run!" ordered Ernest.

But Daisy was not of the running kind. She flung the gun far from her. Ernest saw it turn over and over in the air, gleaming blue in the sunlight, and disappear over the cliff. Releasing Hyslip he leaped up. The cowboy, his face working malignantly, was holding out a bloody hand.

"Dais Brooks, I'll treat you low-down proper next time," he ground out between clenched teeth.

"Dude, there'll never be any next time," sang out Ernest, and he swung with every ounce of strength and fury in him. He had punched a sandbag for years and he had hit many a fellow, in boxing as well as in earnest. He could hit when he wanted to and where he wanted to. And this blow landed on Hyslip's still discolored eye. The cowboy went hurtling over the mossy stones, to alight on his back and slide half his length. He bawled like a half-grown bull. Scrambling to his knees he bounded from them erect and flaming.

Already an egg-shaped lump was appearing over his eye.

"Ho! Look at your pretty eye, Dude!...Now for the other," shouted Ernest, with a wild laugh. This encounter seemed to have unleashed a devil in him.

But Hyslip parried that blow, and then they went at it hammer and tongs. Selby ordinarily would have ducked and blocked the cowboy's blows. Such was his anger, however, that he seemed not to want to avoid them. He took them gladly. All he desired was to beat his adversary as speedily as possible. This precluded science, the advantage he had over the cowboy, but it made for a stand-up, battering fight.

It was Hyslip who gave ground first. Twice he went sprawling headlong, to jump up bloody-faced but still savage. A third time, under a sledgehammer blow, he crashed against a pine tree, which saved him from falling. This blow, Ernest could see, was probably the crucial one. His confidence had been somewhat weakened by Hyslip's show of strength. But now he felt sure he could best the cowboy and soon have him at his mercy.

Hyslip ceased fighting in a manly give-and-take fashion. He crouched and rushed in, endeavoring to close with Ernest, who banged at his face with right and left. Hyslip plunged to get the Iowan's legs and tried desperately to trip him. But Ernest kicked free and eluded the bearish onslaught.

It came again. Ernest, whose blows now were losing force, could not stem the charge. He backed away, and thus they fought all over the glade, under the pines, down to the edge of the knoll where it sloped down to the spring-hole.

Suddenly Hyslip reached down to snatch up a dead tree branch. He swung it with all his strength. It struck Selby square on the head and cracked to bits. By good fortune it was a piece of rotten wood. If it had been solid, that blow would have meant the end of his opponent. One thing it served, however, and that was to revive Ernest. Instead of backing from Hyslip's onslaught he met it with a rain of blows under which the cowboy had to give way. He staggered for a moment and then fell heavily.

"All—right.... Fight—your way!" panted Ernest, and he pounced upon the falling Hyslip, flattening him to the earth.

Daisy's high-pitched voice rose almost in a scream: "Beat him—smash him—kill him!"

That wild appeal from gentle Daisy Brooks goaded Ernest into a last infuriated attack. The struggle now degenerated into a threshing, rolling, wrestling, tearing bearfight. It ended with the collapse of Hyslip on the edge of the brushy slope, where the Iowan, on his knees, smashed his fist again and again into the raw red visage before his eyes until Hyslip's body went limp and slid down over the steep bank. He crashed through the brush and landed on the rocks below with a thud.

Ernest slid forward, too, from his knees, and lay spent and half blinded by blood and sweat. Daisy knelt by him, crying out in her fright, trying to raise him, tugging at his shoulders. Presently Ernest sat up.

"I'm licked—Dais," he said in a sobbing whisper.

"No, no! It's Dude who's licked.... Oh, Ernest, but you gave it to him. I believe he's daid, he lit so hard.... And I shore hope he is."

"So—do I. Where is he? Let's—go see."

The Iowan staggered to his feet and started down the slope over which Hyslip's body had hurtled through the brush, but Daisy led him around to a path, and then down to the spring hole. Hyslip lay with his boots in the water and his handsome head on the rocks. His curly blond mane, stained by blood, stuck damply to his head. He was breathing heavily.

"He's not dead, Daisy. And I guess I'm glad," said Ernest with relief, and bending over Hyslip he lifted each arm and each leg to see if any bones were broken. Evidently the cowboy was only stunned.

"Gosh, I must be a pretty mess myself!" ejaculated Selby. His vest had been ripped almost in half and his shirt was bloodied and torn to ribbons. Ernest threw them into the bushes. His hands were bruised and bleeding.

"Dais, I can't see my face," he said ruefully, "but I'll bet it's a sight."

"Oh, Ernest—it is!" she replied, tears streaming down her cheeks. "But you saved your eyes.... That cut on your lip—let me take care of it! Oh, you've got as many cuts as lumps."

She wet her handkerchief in the brook and washed his face. Ernest noted grimly that the handkerchief came away red. He gave Daisy his scarf, and allowed her gently to bathe and wipe his face.

"That'll do, Dais. Thanks. Now let's rustle out of this," he said presently, and took the girl's arm and started to lead her away. They had scarcely taken a step when Ernest espied Hyslip's gun lying on the bank. It had rolled almost into the water. Selby picked it up and stuck it in his pocket.

"He would have shot you," whispered Daisy.

"Reckon he would. . . . Let him lie where he is. I'll chase his horse home. And he can walk back—if he's able. You bar yourself in the house—and never let this hombre come near you again. You'd better take Hyslip's gun. Can you use it?"

"Yes, Ernest," she said, trying to keep pace with his rapid steps, "but I won't need it."

"Don't tell your dad about this," he said.

"I won't, Ernest."

They had gotten halfway to the house when Ernest remembered the box of candy. Asking Daisy to wait, he hurried to fetch it. As he reached the place where he had dropped the box, he had a chance to see how the little sylvan glade had been plowed up by the recent struggle. The sound of groaning came from the brookside below. Then he picked up Nebraskie's gift and returned to Daisy's side.

"Here's the candy Nebraskie had me buy for you."

She took the package and murmured her thanks.

After a deep look into her eyes the Iowan said: "Dais, whatever happened between you and Hyslip up there—is our secret. Let's keep it."

"No, Ernest. I shall tell Nebraskie," she replied, without the slightest hesitation.

"No—don't. He'll kill Hyslip," he pleaded.

"I cain't let that fear stop me. I must tell him. It wouldn't be fair. . . . Shore he'll never forgive me again. But that's no matter. . . . You must try to prevent his killing Hyslip."

"I'll try, Dais. But Nebraskie is a stubborn devil,

when he's mad. Let's not risk it. What he doesn't know won't hurt him. Let's keep the whole thing secret."

"But Ernest dear, you don't seem to see it's a question aboot my honor," she remonstrated gently. She was inflexible.

Selby felt a lump in his throat. He had a protective and strong desire to take her in his arms. This girl might need protection, but not pity.

"Whatever you decide, count me on your side," he told her with feeling. "I've got to rustle now. Reckon you needn't have any more fear of Hyslip. Not soon, anyway. But keep locked in till your father comes to. . . . I'll take that bottle of whiskey. It's evidence we might need."

Selby hurried into the living room to secure the bottle and did so without a glance at Brooks.

"Tell Nebraskie not to fail to come up heah tonight," said Daisy, almost entreatingly. "If I had to wait long before telling him—I—I might lose my nerve."

"I'll send him, Dais. You won't have to wait long. It's getting late," returned Ernest hurriedly. "Keep a stiff lip, now. Good-by till I see you again. That won't be long."

The Iowan broke from her and almost ran out to the lane, slowing up only when he jolted the gun out of his pocket. With this and the bottle of whiskey in his hands he strode rapidly on to the wagon, his mind gradually working out of its whirl. From the wagon seat he glanced back. Daisy had gone in. The door of the house was shut.

CHAPTER
12

*N*EVER had that five miles from Brooks' farm to Hepford's house seemed so long to Ernest. The horses were tired, and he did not urge them because he wanted to get in late. So he timed his arrival at dusk, when the cowboys would be at supper.

As luck would have it when he drove past the corrals no one was in sight. Jumping down he quickly deposited his bedroll and Anne's bundles on the grass, and was hurrying to the bunkhouse, with his coat concealing the gun and bottle and the box of chocolates, when Siebert and Nebraskie came out of the messroom and espied him.

"Hey, you regular ole bull-whacker," called Nebraskie, gladly. "You shore come ahummin'."

"Quick trip, Ioway. I'm pleased," added Siebert

from behind Nebraskie, who had straddled the intervening distance.

Ernest waited for them, gazing beyond to see if any one else had come out. Nebraskie reached him, hand outstretched, then suddenly jerked up.

"Fer the luv of luvin'!" he ejaculated.

"Come inside. You, too, Hawk."

"What the hell?" queried the foreman.

They followed him into the room, where there was still light enough, at least near the window, for them to take a quick note of his appearance.

"Pard!" exclaimed Nebraskie sharply.

"Ioway, you've been fightin'," put in Siebert, in the same tone.

The Iowan laughed. This was not so bad. He had not anticipated any thrill in meeting them. But there was something warm and friendly and stirring in their eyes and voices.

"My Gawd, man, you're all bunged up," went on Nebraskie.

Before replying Selby took a glance into the little shaving mirror. One was sufficient. Then he laid all except the gun on the table.

"Hyslip's gun! I know thet bone handle," spoke up Siebert.

"Shore thet's the Dude's. . . . Ernie, I hope to die if you ain't ended your tenderfoot days heah on this range."

Ernest handed the gun to Siebert.

"Hyslip tried to draw on me," he began, striving to keep his breath. "I—I got it away from him—and then we fought."

"You don't say? Wal, doggone me!" returned the foreman, beaming.

"What fer?" demanded Nebraskie joyfully, as he pounded the Iowan's back.

"Ouch. Let go. I'm all sore. . . . Listen now, I got off at Brooks' lane to take your box of candy up to Daisy. I found the house open. Brooks lay drunk on the floor. Two empty bottles and this one—half full— stood on the table. Daisy was nowhere to be seen. But I forgot to tell you I'd seen Hyslip's pinto tied among the trees. . . . He ought to be here now. I chased him home. . . . Well, I surprised Hyslip with Daisy. She looked pretty upset. I took her to task for being up there alone with him. She told me—well, Nebraskie, what she'll tell you when you go up there tonight. So I cussed him, taunted him. Finally, in our wrangle, I admitted I had given him that black eye at the dance. He was plenty mad. Then I—I made a slight allusion to Anne Hepford—how that little punch of mine had tickled her."

"Pard, you shore was courtin' death," burst out Nebraskie, smacking his fist. "If you didn't finish that snake, then I shore as hell will!"

"Ioway, you're comin' plumb through," avowed the cool foreman. "But don't keep us waitin'!"

"He clapped his hand on his gun," continued Selby. "I grabbed him round the body, pinning his arm. Then I yelled for Daisy to get his gun. We had hell for a little. Hyslip was killing mad. Daisy bit his hand to make him let go of the gun. Oh, she's one game kid all right! She got it and then I soaked Mr. Hyslip right on that bum eye. . . . After that we had it out—no holds barred. I was too angry and too over-confident. He walloped me pretty bad, before I knocked him off the bank down on those rocks where the spring comes out. Thought I'd killed him at first. But we went down and found he was alive, all right. He's lying right there yet."

"An' Dais?" queried Nebraskie hoarsely.

"She braced up. We went back to the house. I told her to lock herself in. And she asked me to send you up pronto. She wants to tell you in her own words what happened."

"I'll go as soon as I can fork a hoss," said Nebraskie icily.

"Wait," called Ernest, as Nebraskie lunged for the door. "The thing for you to do right now is to think of Daisy."

"I am, pard, honest to Gawd," replied Nebraskie huskily.

"No gun slingin', Nebraskie," added Siebert, "unless Hyslip should corner you. It'd go hard with you if you killed him. No one to prove it was an even break. An' Hepford makin' a favorite of Dude. It would ruin the gurl's good name, to say nothin' aboot breakin' her heart. Use your head, cowboy."

"I will, Hawk. An' I promise you, Ioway." Then he dashed out the door into the gathering darkness.

"Gosh, how white he was!" exclaimed Ernest, aghast. "Hawk, will he keep his word?"

"Reckon so, onless it's not reasonable to. Depends on Hyslip. An' from what you say he's in no shape to meet anybody, much less Nebraskie."

"Not tonight, that's sure. But I'm worried, Hawk."

"Wal, so'm I. It's shore a bad mess."

"Please get some of the boys to unload the grain and look after the horses," said Ernest, remembering the important end of his trip. "I must hurry up with Anne's mail and bundles."

"Better let me take them. She cain't miss seein' how you're bunged up."

"Let you? Like hob I will," laughed Ernest, and stripping a blanket off Nebraskie's bed he hurried outside.

It was dark enough to prevent him from being seen by the cowboys, if any happened along, and he did not care if Anne discovered his disfigurement. Spreading the blanket he piled the numerous bundles on it, laughing under his breath as he came to the five-pound box of chocolates. He bet she would eat them, even if she did hate him. Then twisting the ends of the blanket he lifted the burden over his shoulder and strode off, relieved that he had encountered no one. With Anne's father and Hyslip both absent there was very little chance of his meeting anyone at the house. The burden was heavy and he was tired. Nevertheless, he did not rest until he reached the porch steps. The big house was dark, except for a lighted lamp in the room to the right of the hallway. The wide door stood open.

"Hoo-oo," called Ernest, and waited. Presently he heard light footsteps.

"Who's there?"

It was Anne's voice and it affected Ernest so powerfully that he hesitated, thinking the while what a silly ass he was.

"Nobody but your pack-horse and mail-carrier," replied Ernest.

"What!" Anne's white form emerged from the dark. She came out on the porch. "Mail-carrier? . . . It cain't be Iowa?"

"Yes, all that's left of him," he replied ruefully, and lifting his improvised sack he carried it up to deposit it on the porch.

"You blessed cowboy! To get back two days ahaid! Oh, I'm so glad I—I could almost hug you!"

Ernest could hardly believe his ears. Only a few days before she had told him she hated him. And now—well, he had not expected any such reception as this.

"Don't do it. I might break in two."

"Your voice is weak—you had a hard trip? I suppose you camped along the road so you could make long drives, just to please me?"

"Yes, I made pretty fast time—that is, till this afternoon, when I got delayed."

"Thank you, Ernest," she said, and her tone and use of his first name made his heart pound. He was of the opinion that he had better be hurrying away while everything was peaceful. Surely she had forgotten she hated him!

"Can I carry these inside for you?"

"Yes, do please."

She accompanied him into the hall, where some of the bundles spilled out of the blanket. Whereupon Ernest let the rest down, and sliding the blanket out from under them he pitched it out upon the porch. Then picking up the box of candy, his rashly intended gift, from the floor, he quickly hid it behind his back.

"What's that you're hiding, Ernest?" she asked quickly, noticing his action. She stepped closer to him. In the half gloom of the hallway her green eyes looked black. Ernest had a sudden conviction that there was little to fear in those wide dark eyes.

"Oh, just something. What—what'll you give me for it?" he asked audaciously. What had worked with Daisy might have a like effect upon Anne Hepford.

"Give you for it? Why, isn't it mine?"

"Hardly. Not yet. Not until I give it to you—if I do."

"Ernest Howard!—Just heah him—What is it? Please."

"Box of chocolates....Five pounds....Fresh from Kansas City," announced Ernest teasingly.

"For me?" she clapped her hands.

"No one else—providing—"

"You dear," she interrupted excitedly. "What would you like me to give you for it?"

He had been laughing, but now he stood silent as her face loomed close—closer—her eyes big, haunting. Then with a little laugh she put cool lips to his cheek, tantalizingly close to his lips.

"Ernest, what's the matter with your face?" she queried breathlessly.

He could not find a quick answer. It was not the fact of her discovery that something appeared amiss, but the tone of her voice, the way she spoke that made him remain mute.

She stepped to the light which came from the room to the right of the hall, and looked at the hand that she had removed from her lips.

"Ah! Blood!—I knew it tasted funny. Sort of salty. Ernest, how'd you cut your face?"

"Well, I might have fallen off the wagon, only I

didn't," rejoined Ernest, trying to be funny.

"Cowboy, have you been drinking?"

"No, I haven't," answered Ernest, quick to catch the note of unconscious regret in her question.

She peered closer. "You look different to me.... Come heah."

He could not avoid her grasp, and as she took no gentle hold of his skinned hands he winced perceptibly and jerked them free. That spurred her to resolute action. Seizing his arm she dragged him into the lighted room. There one look at his face made her cry out.

"Oh, mercy!...Why, Iowa—your face is all bruised and swollen....And you're bleeding."

"Ahuh," replied Ernest, glad that his sight was not impaired by disfigurement. This was the first time he had ever seen her in a simple and modest white dress. At the dance her gown had both dazzled and repelled him.

"You've had another fight," she asserted, her eyes lighting up.

"Sure have," he drawled.

"Dude Hyslip!"

"Yes."

"Oh—Iowa!—you're a perfect sight! Tomorrow you will shore be unrecognizable....Let's see your hands. Don't act so touchy....Turn them over. I want to see the back of them."

His hands presented a sorry spectacle. They were skinned, swollen, and red as raw meat.

"Oh, Ernest, why did you let him lick you?" she exclaimed. Tears stood in her dark eyes. She did not realize that she was tenderly holding his hands within the palms of hers.

"I'm afraid he did," replied Ernest, truthfully enough.

"Damn him! He's bigger than you. Taller anyway."

That moment was a desperately sweet one for Ernest. He could scarcely believe his eyes and ears. Footsteps in the back of the house brought him back to reality.

"Anne, please let's go outside. I don't mind you seeing me all bunged up, but I'd rather—"

"There's no one heah to see you," she interposed. "That's only Maria. I wish you'd let me fix up those bleeding cuts. I reckon you're too proud. You'll feel easier."

She led him out, her arm locked in his, and around the wide porch to the far corner, where in the dim shadow the big box hammock swung. She pushed him down into the seat amid the cushions and then quietly sat beside him.

"Now, tell me all aboot it," she whispered.

"I'd rather not, Anne," he said, looking off into the night.

"But you must. Shore you fought aboot me?"

"Well, your name precipitated the battle. We were jawing each other. I happened to remember how tickled you were when I told you I was the fellow who blacked his eye. So I threw that in his teeth."

"Ernest, you foolish boy! It's a wonder he didn't kill you."

"He tried. It's easy to see he's crazy in love with you. He went for his gun—"

Anne suddenly cried out in alarm, and then threw her arms round his neck. He sat perfectly still. Surprise and fear trembled in her voice; and if he were not in such an emotional turmoil, he would have found something sweet and moving in her actions.

"Oh, Ernest! I didn't guess it was so—so serious," she said, shuddering. "Hyslip has shot more than one man. He killed a cowboy in Winslow. That's nothing out heah, but somehow—in connection with—with you it stops my heart."

"It was worth the beating and skinning I got—if you—if you—you're sorry."

"Sorry! Shore, I'm sick aboot it and plain furious. I hate that Dude Hyslip. If Dad won't fire him I—I'll run him off the ranch myself."

Ernest imagined now that he surely must be dreaming. He was making up these kind and loyal words in his own imagination. And the touch of her arm, round his neck and soft and cool on his fevered cheek—that must be the stuff dreams are made on. Still that cool arm appeared to press ever so little closer. Her head now was almost on his shoulder, and she was trying to see his face in the darkness.

"What happened—when he tried to throw his gun?" she asked in a tremulous whisper.

Ernest suddenly realized that he had been led into a quandary. He could not betray Daisy's part in the adventure. Anne would find out eventually, still it should not come from him. On the other hand he no longer wanted to lie to Anne. She seemed to be transforming, developing in his estimation. He tried to think of her as he once had—as cruel and fickle and insincere. Suddenly he had to admit to himself that she really liked him—yes, that she was concerned about his welfare, that she was being gentle and sweet and unselfish. Yet in the back of his mind he was wondering how about tomorrow or next week—what would she be when the magic night was over?

"I—I caught him round the waist," returned Ernest. "He didn't get to use the gun. I leaped forward to bang him on that eye of his which was still kind of tender. My rush bowled him over. Then he got up and came for me low.... I didn't care. I had smelled blood, I guess. Anyway, it was soon running like water from both of us. We fought all over the place—" Ernest broke off.

Anne was silent. Ernest felt her quivering. He had a sudden realization at that moment that she would let him take her in his arms if he wished. He longed to crush her to him. But his courage had oozed away. And so that sweet moment passed!

"I suppose you think it is terrible in a girl like me that I don't think your fight with Hyslip disgusting," she said presently. "And I suppose I oughtn't gloat as I do. But Iowa, he—he—I must tell you and you must never tell anybody—not even Nebraskie— he insulted me—oh, in such a low-down way. He never even dreamed that his—his cheap advances were an outrage. He thinks he can maul a girl into submission. Since that night—it was right heah in this hammock—I've never been alone with him. I was scared to death of him. My high, wide and handsome talk was just a bluff."

"You should have told your father," returned Ernest, sternly.

"Not me. Dad dotes on Dude. But if I could have convinced him of the truth—he'd have shot Dude. So I kept my mouth shut. No one else but you knows. And, Iowa—"

"Please stop calling me that," interrupted Ernest, irritably. His nerves were on edge and he felt annoyed with himself for having let a glorious opportunity slip away—perhaps forever.

"Well, I can allow it," he said, in an effort to be facetious, "in your case, Anne, only when you say— *Iowa darling.*"

She gave a little start, as if she had suddenly found herself on a precipitous descent.

"Oh, indeed. In that case I'll have to call you Ernest," she returned, in a tone that made him regret he had given her a warning that she was on the verge of committing her genuine feelings. He swore he would not make another such blunder. And he concluded it would be wise, now that he had broken the spell, to make his departure.

"Anne, I'm fagged out. I think I'd better go now. You have your mail—there must be a dozen letters— and all your packages to open. I'll say good night."

She stirred and made a movement as if to rise, but suddenly pressed her arm close around his shoulder again. "Ernest, it's selfish of me to keep you even a moment longer. But I—I can't bear to have you leave me. I've never been so happy as I've been here tonight. Please believe me! So there! The murder is out.... But I'll let you go if you'll promise to take me up to Agua d'Oro Spring tomorrow."

"I—I'll have work to do," faltered Ernest weakly.

"You cain't work with those terrible bruised

hands," she protested. "I'll tell Siebert so. And I'll doctor them for you and bandage them. Will you come?"

"Of course I'll be overjoyed to go. But Anne, do you really think I should?"

"Why not? I often go riding with cowboys, though seldom with one alone, I'll admit. But Dad is away."

"What other cowboys have done or do is no concern of mine."

"You're thinking we might be seen and it would cause talk around heah?"

"Yes."

"Ernest, I thank you for thinking of it. No one else ever did. And just for that I shore won't care who sees us. And I'll tell Dad when he comes back. And if he fires you I'll meet you in the hills. So there, Ernest Howard!"

"Anne, you make me proud," he said huskily. "You scare me a little, too. But I'd feel a coward if I felt I couldn't go anywhere with you, or do anything for you—after what you said."

"I'm the coward," she murmured, and removing her arm she rose from the hammock.

Ernest got up then, knowing that the spell was broken. Together they walked around to the steps. He went down a step or two, then turned. She stood above him, her face pale in the starlight, her dark eyes unfathomable.

"I cain't help but l-like you," she said, and the grave way she spoke the words stirred him more deeply than anything in all his life.

"We're in the same boat," he said briskly, and left her standing there.

"Tomorrow mawnin', don't forget!" she called after him.

CHAPTER

13

*L*IKE a man pursued by the furies Ernest ran back through the pine woods to his bunkhouse. He was fated to find that its seclusion and the mantle of darkness were not protection against the conflicting tides of his feelings.

Only while removing his clothes was he suddenly conscious of the soreness of his body and of his many contusions and abrasions. Then he lay in the dark, trying to bring order out of chaos in his thoughts. But there was no order. There seemed to be nothing save love, to which he dared not and could not let himself succumb. So for hours he tossed in his bunk as in a nightmare. At last, exhausted mentally and physically he fell asleep.

He was awakened by Siebert's cheery call through the window: "Hey, son, air you daid? I been yellin' at you fer some time."

"That you, Hawk?" groaned Ernest.

"No one else. Will you get up an' have some breakfast? The outfit's gone."

"Course I'll get up.... that is, I guess I will.... Ouch!... Awww!... Stiffer than a board. Sore as a million boils."

"Haw! Haw! Don't look in the glass, Ioway. You've shore got the awfulest mug I ever seen."

Despite that admonition Ernest hobbled over to the mirror, from which he recoiled as though confronted by an apparition.

"O my Lord!" he wailed.

"Ioway, I'll let you off ridin' today," said the foreman consolingly.

"But I've got to ride," declared Ernest.

"I'm layin' you off, idiot. You got back from town two days early, so you've got some time coming."

"Hawk, I savvy. And much obliged. But I'm riding up to Agua d'Oro today."

"Oho! With our boss's daughter, I'll bet. You'd have a nerve, even if your face was fit to look at in broad daylight."

"Hawk, I've a notion Anne is sick of pretty men."

"Gawd, it's aboot time.... Ioway, I reckon you wouldn't listen to no advice."

"Not if it was against this ride."

"Wal, I wouldn't either if I was in your place. Only I hate to see you make a jackass of. Us western hombres can stand thet. But you're different, Ioway. It'll jest knock you plumb out when the time comes."

"What will?" queried Ernest, trying to get into a pair of new Levis.

"Aw, don't hand me thet kind of talk. You know what I mean. I'm tryin' to give you an honest hunch. Pretty soon you're gonna fall in love with Anne. An' then the trouble'll start."

"Gonna? ... Ha! Ha! Ha! Ha! ... No, I'm not, Hawk, old man. Nope, not, nix, never! Not *gonna*!"

"Wal, I'm darned glad to heah thet," said Siebert, perplexed, but not completely relieved.

"Not gonna. Not if I hung around Red Rock for years. I *have*!"

The anxious foreman threw up his hands. "I was afeared so. You've no more haid then any one else. ... Ioway, we're busted. Yesterday mawnin' I had an awful row with Hepford. Swore he'd fire me an' I said I hoped he would. He rode off to town mad as a Gila monster. Hyslip didn't come back. His hoss did. Nebraskie ain't come in neither. Bones Magill an' Lunky Pollard are fightin' sore over somethin'. Looks like my outfit's gone to hell."

"That'd be a blamed good thing," replied Ernest cheerily. "I'll tell you why someday."

"Wal, you beat me, Ioway," declared Siebert soberly, and left the bunkhouse, shaking his head.

Ernest got into his boots, a task that brought the cold sweat to his brow. He ventured another glance in the mirror. His eyes were wide open and uninflamed, and his nose, though scratched, did not look so very bad. Knots and bruises stood out everywhere else; his left ear was a swollen mass; one lip was puffed up and the other cut; his front teeth were sensitive.

"Well, all I can say is—if Anne Hepford can stand to look at that face in broad daylight— she loves me," he muttered. "That's all there is to it. . . . Damn the luck, I can't wash. I can't shave, I can't comb my hair. And I'll bet two bits I can't button my shirt."

His hands pained him most of all. His stiff fingers were like frozen members. He had been quite right about buttoning his shirt: he let it go open. But he managed to button the two lowest buttons of his vest. He labored over his necktie, and abandoned that for a new scarf. Then he went out to the cookshack for breakfast. Jeff was exceedingly nice to him this morning, very solicitous and very curious. He had as much trouble with eating as he had had with dressing, and finally he gave it up as a bad job. From there he went to the stables and got Pedro to saddle his horse. Leading the animal he walked up to the ranch house. He saw Anne waiting on the porch. Her pony stood, bridle down, by the fence.

"Ernest, I've been waiting an hour," she announced petulantly, as he reached the porch steps.

"Good morning, Anne. I'm sorry to be late. But I'm in pretty bad shape," replied Ernest, essaying a smile, which was a painful effort.

"Come up heah. Let me look at you," Anne demanded.

Ernest slowly mounted the steps. Anne looked like a slim rider in her blue overalls, boots and spurs. Her blouse was gray and she wore a red scarf. She somehow seemed vastly less dangerous in this garb.

"You look perfectly horrible," she cried.

"I feel worse than I look," he responded.

"Reckon I'll have to doctor you. I should have done it last night. Come in."

Ernest followed her into the dining room where she bade him sit by the table. She left the room to return presently, her hands full of bottles and tins and towels. A pleasant-faced Mexican woman brought in a pan of warm water. Anne threw aside her sombrero and, rolling her sleeves up to her shapely elbows, she managed to look very business-like.

"Tough luck some hombres have," she said dryly.

"Ahuh. But I wonder where Hyslip is," replied Ernest.

"I'd shore hate to say right out where I hope he is. . . . Let's see your hands first."

Ernest spread the ugly members out on the table. And without more ado Anne set to work. She washed the dirt and sand from the dried abrasions on his knuckles. They hurt about as fiercely as Ernest cared to be hurt. But when she felt him flinch she proceeded more tenderly. "I'll bet it hurts."

"Not so bad as some internal hurts I have," said he.

"Did Dude kick you in the ribs—or anything like?" she queried with sweet solicitude. But she had understood perfectly what Ernest meant.

"No. I was speaking of an emotional hurt. Something you wouldn't savvy, Anne Hepford."

"Maybe it's just as well for me that I'm a rowdy, a western hussy without any fine feelings, or the delicacy to diagnose emotional hurts," she replied with feigned sarcasm.

"Pardon me. I didn't mean anything of the kind," said Ernest stiffly.

"Then what did you mean?"

"You're a heartless, soulless girl."

She sighed. "That's all *you* know."

The soothing lotion she applied to Ernest's bruised right hand, and the soft bandages she carefully wound and tied expertly rendered this member once more human. Then she attended likewise to the other hand.

She proceeded to bathe his face and applied the aromatic salve to the sundry cuts and bruises.

"Doctor, have a look at that bump on my head," suggested Ernest.

"Gracious! It's as big as a goose egg. There's a cut, too, Ernest. The blood has matted your hair and dried.... This shore won't hurt at all."

The pain, as she said, was not unbearable, but it grew to be something of an ordeal to feel her hands on his head and brow.

"You've a well-*shaped* haid anyways, Iowa.... Excuse me, I forgot what I was supposed to remember. Yes, a good hand of nice wavy hair."

"Empty, though, you're thinking?"

"I haven't got you figured at all, Ernest," she said thoughtfully.

"Well, can I help you in your figuring?"

"No. It's rather pleasant to be kept guessing.... There. Thet's aboot all I can do in the way of easing your hurts, Ernest."

He placed a hand over his heart. "How about *this* hurt?" he asked.

She dropped her eyes. "I'm not a heart-doctor, Ernest."

"The cowboys call you a heartbreaker."

"How flattering! . . . I reckon you're in no danger with yours."

"Thanks for your kindness, Anne. I feel easier, especially my hands."

"Ernest, I reckon we'd better not ride today," she said. "Let's put it off until day after tomorrow."

"All right, just as you say," rejoined Ernest, somewhat puzzled. "It'd be better so far as I'm concerned. Are you sure it's not because you just couldn't bear looking at me?"

"What a kid you are!" she laughed, but there seemed to be a vague aloofness, an evasiveness about her.

"Will you ride out alone?" he asked.

"No. I won't be that mean, Io——. I keep forgetting not to call you Ioway. . . . Go rest up, Ernest. If Siebert wants you to work—and he shore is a driver—tell him you're laid off till Dad comes home. We'll have our ride Monday mawnin'. *Adios*."

She went with him into the hall, but no further. Ernest left, pondering what had suddenly come over her. It had surprised him to have her postpone the ride. He had thought that she really wanted to go. There was no understanding any woman, much less Anne Hepford.

When he got back to his room, and had removed boots and shirt, to lie back on his bunk, he discovered that he was extremely fatigued and a trifle feverish.

Perhaps Anne had observed his condition. He stretched out for a long rest and meditation, but he soon fell asleep.

Upon opening his eyes again he saw Nebraskie tiptoeing around the room, trying to be noiseless. The day was far spent, as Ernest could tell by the westering sun, shining through the window.

"Howdy, Nebraskie. Glad you're back."

"Aw, pard, I must hev waked you up," returned the cowboy, coming to the bunk and sitting down beside Ernest. "How air you?"

"Had a long sleep. I feel tiptop."

"Who tied your hands all up so nice an' neat?"

"Anne."

"Ahuh. How'd she take your looks?"

"She was so—so darned sweet that I'm completely off my nut again."

"Say, boy, you ain't never got back on it again. Wal, I'm darned glad. I always reckoned thet I savvied Anne better than these soft calves over in the other bunkhouse. They think she's—wal, you know. I'm tellin' you, Ernie, thet when it comes to the rub, Anne Hepford will surprise you. She'll turn out true western blue."

"Gosh, but you're a comforting fellow," returned Ernest fervently. "Almost you make me trust Anne."

"You'll be a damn fool if you don't, thet's all. No man gets nowhere with a gurl if he thinks she's only what the rest of them think."

"Nebraskie—did you find Daisy—all right?" asked Ernest, hesitantly.

"Yes, but shaky on her laigs. I wouldn't let her tell me nuthin'. I told her it didn't make a damn bit of difference to me what had happened."

"Nebraskie, you're one man in a thousand!" exclaimed Ernest admiringly. "And what did Dais say to that?"

"She's got spunk. She swore she'd tell me sometime. Then she flopped into my arms. An' cry—my, how thet kid did cry! Scared me, but I reckoned it was good fer her. So I jest held her, an' when she got over it I packed her into her room an' laid her on her bed. Then I went out an' tried to do somethin' with Brooks. But he was still daid to the world. I slept on his bed while he snored on the floor. He woke up sober, an' cross as a wet hen. I told him he'd better go out an' hunt up Hyslip. Wal, he went, an' I didn't see him fer a good while. In fact it was Dais who saw him fust. She'd got up an' was in the kitchen. I went in there when she called an' she pointed through the door. There was Brooks helpin' Hyslip on one of Brooks' hosses. It was pretty fur away, but Ernie, I shore saw what you done to thet hombre. I could hev yelled like an Injun. Dais jest shook at sight of him, I don't know what with. Thet worries me, pard. ...Wal, we watched Hyslip ride away, slumped in his saddle, an' he went toward town instead of Red Rock. Shore he's in no shape to ride to Holbrook. But mebbe he'd make Fisher's cabin. He'll hole up there. After thet Brooks sneaked away, red-faced an' ashamed, an' I stayed on with Dais....An' pard, considerin' everythin', I'm not so blue."

"Nebraskie, if I hadn't weakened for you long ago I would now, for your loyalty to that little girl," replied Ernest warmly.

"Wal, we're shore havin' hell with our gurls, ain't

we, but we'll stick....How aboot supper?"

"I'll go in. I didn't get up this morning, so missed seeing the outfit. Siebert told me he'd had a row with Hepford, who threatened to fire him when he got back from Holbrook. I'll tell you, Hawk was mighty upset. He said Magill and Pollard were sore, and in fact the whole outfit had gone to hell."

They went in to supper. Jeff, standing beyond the kitchen door, gave Ernest a knowing and warning wink. It failed to check the Iowan's desire to make a facetious remark, which was prompted, no doubt, by the ill-concealed resentment on the faces of the cowboys. All of them glared at him, except Bones Magill, who bent a surly visage over his plate. Before he had fairly seated himself across the table Magill leaped up.

"Fellers, I'll hev it out with him right heah," he declared sullenly.

"Wal, you damn rooster, if you want to get beat up same as Dude was, why we cain't stop you," replied Pollard in disgust.

"Say, you cowpokes, we wanta eat," said Nebraskie dryly, giving Ernest a nudge. "After thet we're willin' fer most anythin'."

Magill shook a fist across the table. "Howard, I'm gonna lick the daylights out of you."

"Indeed. News to me. May I ask what for?" replied Ernest, whose surprise was genuine.

" 'Cause you ketched my pard Hyslip drunk an' hammered him half to death," answered Bones belligerently.

"Who says I did?"

"It's all over, an' Jerry Blake rode in to tell us.

He seen Hyslip an' heerd how you did it."

"Bones, you're a liar. So's Jerry Blake. And Hyslip is a blankety-blank liar," retorted Ernest.

"All right. Come on outside."

"Delighted to oblige you, Bones. But you'll have to wait until after supper."

The cook came in carrying steaming victuals, the savory fragrance of which added considerably to Ernest's hunger.

"I ain't agonna eat or nuthin' till I lick you," shouted Magill, pushing back from the table.

Ernest, quick as a flash, reached and swung a long arm. His open hand smacked Bones such a forceful blow on the side of his head and cheek that the cowboy staggered back over the bench and fell to the floor. At this juncture Hawk Siebert came stalking in.

"Hey, what's up?"

"'Pears to me it's down," drawled Nebraskie, indicating the scrambling Magill. When he got to his feet to exhibit a flaming face, few questions were necessary.

"Who hit you, Bones?"

"It was thet d——loway tenderfoot," yelled Magill. "An' I'm gonna mop up this heah floor with him."

"Oh, you air. Wal, thet'll be interestin'," returned the foreman satirically. Then he looked at Ernest.

"Howard, did you hit him?"

"I slapped him, boss."

"What fer?"

"He accused me of beating Hyslip when he was drunk. And he got otherwise offensive. I politely said

I'd fight him after supper. Then he yowled across the table at me, so I slapped him one."

"Ahuh. . . . Wal, did you beat Hyslip when he was drunk?"

"No, I didn't," replied Ernest indignantly.

"Did you beat him at all?"

"That's different. Besides it's nobody's business."

Here Magill manifested most violently that he considered it his, and supplemented his assertion by some irritating profanity.

Ernest got up. "All right, if you feel that bad. Come on out."

Magill stamped at his heels, out of the door, and off the porch.

The outfit followed the two men out of the cookshack. But what ensued on the turf in front of the kitchen ended as quickly as it had begun. The Iowan strode back into the messroom, examining his bandaged hands, and straddled the seat.

"Now, fellows, let's eat in peace."

There came a muffled sound from the kitchen, very much like a suppressed laugh. Nebraskie bowed over his plate, his haste most obvious. The three other cowboys gazed blankly from Ernest to the door. Bones Magill did not appear. Siebert had been staring hard at Ernest, and his hawk eyes held a baffled expression. Once he glanced back to see if Magill was coming.

"Wal, I'll be doggoned. . . . Mebbe we *will* have peace. . . . Jeff, gimme some grub."

The meal progressed without further interruptions, and with few words. Ernest was busy with his apple pie when the three cronies of Magill ended their meal and got up.

"If you'll wait till I finish my pie, I'll be happy to accommodate any or all of you," said Ernest blandly. "Just in case you still think I took advantage of your pretty-faced pal Duke."

"Go to hell, Howard," replied Pollard.

Shep Davis gave Ernest a dangerous look. "Howard, I reckon you're a country-jake prize fighter, or suthin' like. But if you don't clear out of heah you'll be dodgin' bullets."

"Davis, you shut up," ordered Siebert loudly. "Don't let me heah any more talk like thet, or I'll fire you."

"Fire nuthin'," sneered Steve Monell. "You'll be gettin' the sack yourself before long."

"Is thet so?" snapped Siebert, leaping up. "Wal, I'm firin' *you* before I lose my authority. Right now! An' don't give me any more of your gab."

The three cowpokes stalked out. Pollard was heard to swear. "Blast you fellers anyhow. Givin' it away—"

When they had passed out of hearing, Siebert returned to his seat and finished his cup of coffee. Ernest consumed the last morsel of his pie. Then the three looked at each other.

"Hawk, there's shore a colored boy in the wood-pile," said Nebraskie.

"It do 'pear so," replied the foreman thoughtfully. "But I've heahed such talk before."

"Bones is only a blowhard. —Say, Ernie, what'd you do to him out there?"

"Nothing much. Just a punch or two. He's full of

wind, as you say," rejoined Ernest, with a laugh.

"Pollard is mean. But you needn't lose no sleep aboot him," went on Siebert. "Shep Davis, though, is a bad hombre. I didn't like his look."

"Neither did I," said Ernest shortly. "Well, I'm forewarned, and that's a lot."

"Boss, the Red Rock outfit is aboot to bust," declared Nebraskie, "an' fer my part I don't give a damn."

CHAPTER
14

*H*AWK Siebert lingered with Ernest and Nebraskie long after supper was over. Plainly he was discouraged and moody, though he showed but little of his feelings. Finally he got up to go and said: "Wal, there won't be much work till Hepford comes back. An' then, I reckon, none at all for some of us, leastways round heah."

After the foreman had left, Ernest asked Nebraskie what he made of the present situation. "Humph!" ejaculated that worthy. "Jest like the nose on your face, which in my case is shore plain. I've seen this sort of deal in many an outfit. Hyslip has undermined Siebert with the boss. Them cronies of Hyslip's hev heerd it an' couldn't keep from shootin' off their chins. Pretty soon you an' me an' Hawk will be lookin' fer new jobs. I'm sorry. Fer we was gettin' to be good friends."

"Yes, I'd hate to see us split up," returned Ernest. "But I don't think we will."

"What you mean, pard?"

"We'll get a job together."

"I'd like to know where. Shore I can go to Brooks. He needs me. But he cain't use you an' Hawk, too. An' fer thet matter things don't look rosy fer Brooks, either. He's worried. Hepford has long threatened to throw him off his ranch. An' I reckon now he's about ready fer any devilment."

"Nonsense. Hepford can't put Brooks off," declared Ernest in angry disgust.

"Why cain't he?" queried Nebraskie. "What you know aboot cattlemen an' ranges? If Brooks cain't be scared off he shore can be beat in court. Dais tells me he hasn't any papers fer thet hundred acres of land. He's got the water rights, though."

"Nebraskie, I don't know much about cattlemen or ranges," acknowledged Ernest ruefully. "But I—I just sort of feel that everything will work out fine."

"Ernie, you're a good-hearted boy," said Nebraskie soberly. "You make me feel more hopeful, somehow. Quittin' never helped nobody. An' mebbe it ain't as bad as Hawk an' me think. I shore hope not."

Ernest got the impression that Nebraskie was not confiding all of the facts of his chief source of trouble. He had a thoughtful brow and a sad eye. Ernest soon followed Nebraskie to bed, but it was to lie wakeful. Again the thought-provoking fact asserted itself—that he could at any hour precipitate a stunning denouement here at Red Rock, which would be fateful for his enemies and most welcome to his friends. But he was loth to do it. The situation was not yet ripe. He did not know enough about Hepford's operations. If he did not secure direct evidence of dishonest dealing he would surely lose considerable money. Ernest decided to go slower than ever and to leave no stone unturned in securing his proofs. Only one thing would rush him into claiming his property, and that was for Hepford to attempt to get rid of more cattle. He was sure he could prevent that, now.

Furthermore he did not want any change in the present situation between Anne Hepford and himself. He had believed in her despite many acts and words that might well have engendered distrust. He wanted that faith to persist and grow. Sooner or later it would be put to a test. He sensed that when the day came when he had to show his hand she might be as cold and mean as she once had been warm and sweet. Yet he wanted to postpone that fateful day. She did not know herself. She needed a terrific shock. Ernest wanted her to get it, but he was hesitant to bring that very contingency about. The situation itself would develop it, he felt. Love was blind, he knew, and he admitted that it must be particularly so in his case. Still his love thrived on the meager hopes that would not down that when the day came that her father's thievery was revealed, she would take it like the thoroughbred he felt in his heart she must be.

Next day inaugurated a waiting period at Red Rock. The cowboys did what they liked. Selby noted particularly that Steve Monell did not take himself off the ranch. He and his partners, however, avoided contact with Ernest and Hawk. Early in the day Nebraskie had ridden toward Brooks' place.

After cudgeling his brains Ernest evolved a perfectly valid excuse to go up to the ranch house. His ruse was so good that he chuckled. Wherefore he knocked at the wide-open front door and called: "Anybody home?"

"Who's anybody?" called Anne, from the little room on the right of the hall, which Hepford used as an office.

Ernest stalked in, bareheaded, and if his eyes had not shone before he espied Anne, he knew they did a moment after. She looked as fresh as a rose.

"Oh, it's you, handsome? I suspected as much," she said gaily. "What you want?"

The visitor stated the reason for his errand, which she saw through as if it had been transparent glass. She laughed but she certainly was not displeased.

"Lordy, you're a slick cowboy," she declared admiringly. "I'll bet you give me a jar someday."

"I hope I do," returned Ernest fervently, and laughed his relief. "What're you doing?"

"A lot of pesky letters and accounts for Dad. I'm a month behind."

"Then you won't go riding with me today?"

"No, I cain't. Dad may be home any day now. Perhaps tomorrow, Ernest."

"Really? But you'd like to go, wouldn't you, Anne?"

She smiled up at him. This was one of her unguarded moments, when she revealed more than she knew. Ernest gazed all around the little office, through the windows and door, then swiftly bent to kiss her.

"Ernest! You—you—" she expostulated, blushing scarlet, and pushing back her chair.

"I couldn't help it. You look so—so perfectly sweet."

She shook her red head dubiously. "It's never safe to give a cowboy an inch. He'll take a mile."

"Anne, if I'm not mistaken you've given me a little more than an inch," rejoined Ernest seriously.

"Perhaps I have," she said, dropping her eyes. "But I'm not sorry—if you're not."

"Me? I'm in the seventh heaven."

She checked a movement to stretch a hand toward him. The Iowan felt that his presence was not at all distasteful to her, even when she said, "Go away, Ernest. You're a most distracting boy. And I've a lot of work to do."

"Tell me you love me and I'll go."

"Well! The idea! You can't bribe me that way! I should say not!"

"Do you mean you'll not tell me or that you do not love me?"

"Both. Please go, Ernest. I'll get mad in a minute."

"That won't bother me. Let me help you at the work. I'm mighty handy with figures. Does your father trust you with his bookkeeping?"

"He does, with some of it," she answered. "But he's mighty finicky aboot some things. Look at that little blue book there. He forgot to lock it up before he left. I wouldn't dare look into it."

"Why not?"

"Because he forebade me—and he trusts me."

Ernest picked up the little blue book, which had rubber bands around it. His bandaged hands shook. This little book, he had a premonition, contained the information he needed to unmask Hepford's peculations. Anne snatched the book out of his hands.

"You're a nosey impertinent cowboy. Get out of heah," she burst, almost angrily.

"No offense, Anne. I'm just teasing. I should think though that you'd be keener to know *all* about your father's business."

"Why?" she queried sharply.

"Well, because he's so lax—so careless in his methods. So irresponsible, I might say. Any dumbhead of a cowboy can see that."

"You're no dumbhaid of a cowboy," she denied thoughtfully, her bright eyes studying him.

"Thanks. That's sure a compliment from you. I'll go now," he replied, and sauntered out.

"Ernest," she called.

He returned, but not saunteringly.

"I hope you've changed your mind about riding with me," he said.

"No. It was just—oh, well, never mind. I'll tell you tomorrow," she replied, and bent over the desk, with a tinge of color in her cheek.

"Fine. I won't have to think of an excuse to come tomorrow."

"You need never do that, Ernest. Only—I can't promise—anything more."

"Anne, that in itself is a promise. And it means a lot."

"You make too much of—of—little things," she protested.

"Is a kiss little?"

"But you stole that."

"Today, yes. But the other time?"

"I—I don't remember any other time.... Please go away."

Ernest left then, his blood racing, his head in a whirl. He strode off into the pine woods and sat under a great tree, trying to understand the green-eyed girl—and himself. If she did not care for him, if she was not affected somehow by his presence and talk, then he was either a conceited fool or she was the greatest dissembler in all the world—the unconscious, that betrayed Anne. It simply was not reasonable that she could be that way with all young men. Still, did he not have proof of the fact that she could? He suffered the sting of jealousy.

When that perturbing mood passed, however, he remembered the little blue book, which Anne had told him she had been forbidden to open. Of course it had never occurred to Hepford that his daughter would disclose its existence. The Iowan determined to see what was inside that little blue book, if he had to resort to most arbitrary means to get possession of it. After all, the book belonged to him, as well as the fixtures in the office, and the ranch house itself. He wished that Anne Hepford, too, belonged to him! Every turn of his mind led back to her.

All the next morning Ernest was on pins and needles, waiting for the afternoon, his hopes now soaring to the skies and then again cast down. Early in the afternoon he saw a stable boy leading Anne's pinto saddled and bridled, up to the ranch house.

Immediately Ernest rushed to saddle his own horse, which he had ready in a corral.

He could not avoid riding by the bunkhouse, where Monell and Davis were sitting on the porch, eagle-eyed and bitter.

"Ridin' fer a fall, tenderfoot!" called Monell.

"There's one born every minnit!" added Davis.

The Iowan gave them eye for eye, and halted his horse to call out:

"Say, you soreheads. Go take a look at Magill's mug. And then don't forget I'm always ready to accommodate if you want the same operation on yours."

They let the retort pass. But Ernest did not miss the gleam in Shep Davis' cold eye. He rode on, thoughtfully enough, and not until he espied Anne on the porch steps did he forget the disgruntled cowboys. He hurried to reach her side and dismounted.

"So heah you are. I thought you'd forgotten again," she said, in pretended pique.

"No chance of me ever forgetting anything that concerns you."

"Ernest! You're pale.... What has happened?" she asked, quickly, her green eyes widening.

"I just got sore at some of your cowboys, Monell and Davis."

"They're not *my* cowboys. I detest them both. What did they say?"

"Oh, never mind. It doesn't matter. I'm sorry my face gave me away. I'm not upset anymore, Anne."

"Ernest, please tell me," she cried imperiously.

At first he decided against telling her of his recent altercation, but he changed his mind, and related what had happened.

She flushed. "I don't blame you. What they think of me—" she stopped. Then she turned toward her horse.

"Let's forget it, Anne," he urged. "I want this to be a happy ride. I may never have another with you."

"Why not?"

"I'm to be discharged, so *they* say."

"Indeed. They know a lot. . . . Even so, Ernest, I'm worried. Things have changed heah. I don't understand Dad. He's changed, too. There's much kept from my ears. . . . But some things I don't understand get to my ears, too! Well, let's ride."

Ernest helped her to mount, despite her protest. "How many times have I told you I'm a western girl?" she asked with a pout.

"I know you are much better around horses than I'll ever be, but I can't help wanting to help you, no matter how awkward I am."

She gave him a long, quizzical look. "It isn't—I wonder if that isn't why I—I like you."

They rode off side by side, walking their horses through the pines. As they rode, Anne asked him many questions about himself, his family, and his life in Iowa. Ernest happily did not have to lie or evade queries, for fortunately she did not ask him anything embarrassing—why he had come to Arizona, for instance.

"Then your family and connections were not so poor as those of most boys who run away to make their fortunes?"

"No, not so very. . . . But I didn't run away."

"I'm sure you didn't, Ernest Howard. You must have a nice family."

"Yes. I think you'll love my mother and sister when you get to know them someday," he returned, looking at her out of the corner of his eye.

"How you talk!" she exclaimed. Then she spurred her horse and galloped on ahead of him. He did not catch up with her for a long while. Then he was to find that her mood had changed. Once more she had become strange and capricious. She would not ride up the mountain to the famous spring. She would not dismount to rest. She did not seem even to want to talk. But Ernest liked this mood. He had the feeling that something he had said must have touched her, and that she was ashamed of the wild, shallow, vain side of her nature.

On the return trip, which she started disappointingly soon, they rode through a dark pine grove when Ernest managed to reach her hand. She struggled to get free. But he held on. Suddenly she desisted and for a while they rode hand in hand, silent, she with pensive face, and he wondering if he were not wise and right to trust this gentle side of her. At any rate it emboldened him, and at the shadiest place in the grove he let go her hand and put his arm around her and drew her close. The horses halted stirrup to stirrup. Anne swayed so that her head rested on his shoulder, her face upturned, with eyes closed and lips parted. Ernest kissed her gently.

A long silent moment passed. Ernest knew that he ought not to disrupt it, but he had to speak. "Anne, I love you," he said, smiling down at her. "You must know it already. If not, you know it now!"

She gave a little start and then righted herself in the saddle.

"Oh, you've broken the spell!" she exclaimed, spurring her mount forward. This time the Iowan on his slower pony could not catch the fleet pinto. He was content to be beaten in that race, since he felt in his heart he had almost won in another.

But when he drew up at the porch he was amazed to see Anne confronting her father and Dude Hyslip. Hepford had a worn and harried look, which turned into a scowl at sight of Ernest. The dude cowboy preserved his reputation as to the neatness of his attire, but his visage was something else again. Selby was swift to grasp that it had excited Anne's pity. Anne's evident sympathy caused him to bow stiffly to Hepford.

"Howard, didn't I tell you not to go riding with Anne?" demanded the rancher.

"I don't remember it, sir."

"Dad, whether you did or not doesn't matter. I asked him to ride with me," spoke up Anne. "I'm old enough to choose my companions." Then she turned to Ernest. "Are you responsible for Hyslip's appearance?"

"Certainly not," retorted Ernest nettled. "If I were I'd be ashamed of myself."

"But he said you beat him!"

"We had a fight. He was responsible for that."

The Iowan was at a loss to understand Anne's obvious annoyance. Something had been said to her before his arrival. Then he observed Magill, Davis and Monell sitting in a row up on the porch. He had the feeling that one has when he has been caught in some act of guilt, and it made him coldly furious.

"Hyslip claims you found him asleep, after he had been drinking, and that you pounded him into senselessness," continued Anne in a coldly accusing voice.

"Mr. Hyslip always has been senseless. He was born that way," said Ernest tartly.

"You're dodging my question."

"Dodging nothing!...Anne Hepford, do you mean I'm to deny a baseless accusation like that? To *you*! I wouldn't stoop to it. Believe what you like about me," returned Ernest passionately, "even the foolishness this Texas ranger tells you!"

Hepford stepped down off the porch to confront Selby.

"Howard, you're takin' rather a high hand heah on my ranch. You may be a bully an' then again you may be only a wild tenderfoot. But if you want to clear yourself of somethin' pretty raw you'd better talk."

"Clear myself of what, sir?" demanded Ernest.

"Well, first off this charge Hyslip has brought against you."

"That's a dirty lie," flashed Selby, dismounting stiffly from his horse. "Let Hyslip come down here. He's not drunk or asleep now. I'd only be too glad to repeat the same treatment I handed out to him on two previous occasions."

Hyslip stirred uneasily, jingling his spurs. His eyes held a hateful light. "I'm no pugilist," he protested. "An' next time I fight you it'll be with a gun."

"Bah! You're only a bluff. You shot at me once when I didn't have a gun. You'd do it again. You're a coward, Hyslip. I think you're yellow clear through," rasped the Iowan.

At this juncture Hawk Siebert stepped out of the pines through which he had come unnoticed, and came forward. It was hardly possible that he had not heard Selby's accusation.

"What's comin' off heah?" he queried in a cool easy voice that steadied Ernest. He did not need to be told that Siebert was his friend.

"It seems I'm on trial," he replied, struggling to control his voice.

Hepford turned and repeated the charge Hyslip had made and intimated that he could handle the situation without any interference from his foreman.

"Wal, so long as I'm runnin' this outfit—" spoke up Siebert testily.

"You're not runnin' this outfit any more," interrupted Hepford. "Mebbe thet's news to you."

"Reckon it is."

"Hyslip is foreman now. I appointed him yesterday, in town."

"Without notice to me?" demanded Siebert, his dark face turning beet-red.

"You were not present when I made up my mind. Besides, thet didn't matter."

"Thanks, Hepford," drawled Siebert, stepping closer to fix his scornful eyes upon the rancher. "I'm glad to be free, even if my discharge ain't regular. As to thet, Hepford, there's a lot thet doesn't matter to you. An' I'm tellin' you straight to your face. You always was a queer sort of cattleman an' lately I've my own private idee aboot you and your shady deals with Anderson. An' I reckon I know why you want Hyslip in my place."

Hepford turned livid. It was Anne who broke the blank silence.

"Dad! Can you let him—or any man speak so to you?" she cried.

"Hepford," went on Siebert, "I cain't see if you've got a gun on you. But if you have don't try to throw it. I'd shoot your arm off. You'll hev to swaller what I said. An' some more. Your outfit is split. An' you owe thet to your dude cowboy foreman. He'd split any outfit. An' if you have an idee of hangin' on heah at Red Rock, with Hyslip handlin' cattle an' men— why you're crazy. But I'll gamble you've no such idee. Thet's aboot all I want to say. You're welcome to what little wages is comin' to me. I recommend you spend it fer a real ledger to keep cattle accounts in. Haw! Haw!"

Siebert ended with a snort of derision. Then he backed into the shrubbery, his hand still at his hip, and disappeared.

For a long moment there was deep silence. Then the issue seemed to shift to Anne and her father. It was evident that he was making a powerful and successful effort to overcome his angry shock. The natural color was returning to his livid face. When he faced his horrified daughter he was apparently master of the situation.

"There, you see," he said, with a deprecatory gesture. Ernest's keen eye saw his hand tremble. "My outfit is indeed split. But Siebert is to blame, not Hyslip. There's been friction for a long time. Siebert never liked my way of ranchin'. He wanted control.

An' now when I discharged him he showed his true color with those ugly hints aboot me."

"You should have shot him," declared Anne, her eyes flashing green fire.

Hepford laughed mirthlessly. "Siebert has had more to do with guns than I."

Suddenly Anne appeared to remember Ernest's presence. She turned and fastened cold, accusing eyes upon him.

"I am taking Hyslip's word," she said.

The Iowan bowed. "That's natural—for a girl like you."

"And what's that?"

"You're a vain, shallow girl, and the Dude is more likely your style. That was obvious to me from the beginning."

"Shore I was—in your case," she returned, her head lifting. Her eyes were proud, dark, fierce. "What did you expect?"

"I was a fool, of course. I believed you were honest, sincere, good, but against my better judgment. I should have believed the gossip of the range."

She shrank at that and could no longer meet his gaze.

Here Hyslip spoke up and Selby could see that he swaggered a little.

"Mr. Hepford, this fellow Howard is a slick talker. He's got around Anne, same as he did with Dais Brooks."

Ernest jumped forward as if he had been stung. But Hepford barred his way. He stood there, a prey to helpless rage and misery. What had happened seemed as unreal as it was unjust. After a moment, he was able to call upon some reservoir of strength and dignity. He regained control of his emotions enough, at least, for him to conceal his identity and not on the instant treat these people as they deserved. The greater his repression now, the greater his wrath when the time was ripe to strike!

"Mr. Hepford," he said quietly, "I accept my dismissal gladly, just as Siebert did his. I wish to say that under no circumstances would I work for a man like you."

His words, or perhaps the tone in which they were spoken, or the way he looked, had a striking effect upon both Hepford and his daughter. It was as if the young Iowan had suddenly become another person. He shot a pitying glance at Anne, then turned proudly away, leading his horse.

But once out of sight Ernest stumbled almost blindly along the path, his eyes unseeing, his hands clenched in the bridle, his throat dry. The reaction to the harrowing scene had left him numb and lower in spirit than any time in all his life.

Siebert was waiting for him at the bunkhouse, and as the Iowan slouched up he said: "Ahuh. I reckoned you'd get yours, too. An' thet shore means Nebraskie.... Say, boy, you're pale clean to your gills."

"I feel pale, Hawk. I'm licked. I'm sick. I'm so mad I could kill—"

"Don't holler. Somebody might heah you. Set down an' ease up. I'll look after your hoss."

Ernest flung himself down on the porch. It was indeed a sickening, hopeless moment. He felt that everything that mattered had gone from his life. All his recent hopes and plans had centered around Anne Hepford. In spite of all his former doubts of this girl, he had shut his eyes and opened his heart to her. Now when he had silenced all his doubts and lowered all his defenses, she had betrayed him. Only an hour ago she had yielded to him! Only an hour ago! Her rapt face, her closed eyelids, her upturned open red lips, sweet, alluring. And now—! What had possessed her, all in a moment, to change so completely, to champion that sneering, lying, cowardly Hyslip before her father and those hard-eyed cowboys? What had possessed her unless the sheer abandon of a vicious nature? How bitterly he reproached himself for ever having allowed himself to live even for a moment in his fool's paradise!

Siebert returned. "Say, Howard, it's more than losin' the job thet's diggin' you, ain't it?"

"Job! What do I care for that?"

"Ahuh. You're sweet on Hepford's girl—honest an' true, and she's played hell with you?"

"Yes. They were right—those damned, grinning cowpunchers," admitted Ernest. "They say I was riding to a fall—that a sucker was born every minute! They knew the girl they were talking about."

"Wal, I don't know. But they had your case figgered. Anne's bad medicine. Yet I'm shore she's not rotten clean through. You've got to shoulder a lot of blame yourself. Now you've jest got to stand it."

Ernest sat up. His battered spirits lifted a bit at the faint praise given Anne by his old Westerner. While he despised himself for still loving her so wildly that he could forgive her, he felt the shame that should have been hers for her betrayal.

"Ioway, we may as well pack an' borrow hosses, an' hit the trail," said Siebert. "We can stop at Brooks' tonight. I reckon Nebraskie is there right now. No use fer him to wait to be fired....An' then—wal, we can all talk it over with Sam, if he's sober. But good jobs air scarce on the range right now."

"Ha! Not for you and Nebraskie!" burst out Ernest. "And maybe even a tenderfoot like myself has a good job coming—soon as I want to grab it."

"Wal, boy, it's only natural you should talk kinda lighthaided," replied Siebert philosophically. He put a kind hand on the Iowan's shoulder. "I've sort of cottoned to you, Howard. An' I reckon I'd better look after you a spell. You might shoot Hyslip or do some other crazy thing. An' you know we three don't stand any too well with the Springertown sheriff."

"Hawk, you're my friend—honest, now?"

"Why shore I am. An' so is Nebraskie."

"I can trust you?"

"Me! Wal, thet's a fool question, son."

"If I confide in you, will you promise on your honor you won't tell Nebraskie?"

"Shore, Ernie, anythin' you like. But ain't you plumb excited an'—an'—"

"I'm out of my head all right. All the same I know what I'm saying."

"Shoot, then, cowboy," drawled the Westerner, with his warm smile.

"Hawk, I'm Ernest Howard Selby—the owner of Red Rock Ranch!"

15

*T*HE Iowan's revelation of his real identity had been spoken in a voice that was little more than a whisper. If he expected to bowl Siebert over in amazement he missed his guess, completely. The foreman started to laugh, but changed to sober gravity.

"Son, you're loco," he said kindly.

"Hell! You're as dumb as the rest of these Westerners," exclaimed Ernest, scrambling up. "Come inside."

Ernest closed the door behind Siebert and barred it; then he knelt to fish a bag out from under his bunk. This he unlocked. From the contents he selected a bunch of large imposing envelopes and stuffed them into Siebert's hands.

"There! Any one of those ought to convince you," he said.

Siebert opened one, glanced at it, back at Ernest, and then swiftly went back to perusing it.

"Wal, I'm a long-horned, three-legged son-of-a-gun! *I'm* the locoed one. You could knock me down with a tumbleweed.... Ernest Howard Selby!"

"Don't talk so loud. Yes, I'm Selby. And now you know why you and Nebraskie are not so unlucky after all."

"I reckon, if bein' friends to you means anything—either as tenderfoot Ernie Howard or as rancher Selby! Doggone! I'm flabbergasted, Ernest. What the hell do you mean, playin' this trick on Hepford?"

"Hawk, I was not so dead in earnest at first. But when I began to suspect him of crookedness then I set out to play my part in dead seriousness as a tenderfoot cowpuncher."

Siebert whistled long and low. The thing began to dawn clearly on him. He began to pace the floor. Now and then he would strike a fist in the palm of the other hand. Now and then he would break out in a chuckle. After a while he sat down again.

"You're a cute one! I always wondered aboot you. An' now I see everything plain as day. You wanted to get proof Hepford was stealin' your stock?"

"Yes. I have some, but not enough. We both *know* he's crooked, Hawk, but you can understand why I can't spring the trap until I have brass-bound, copper-lined, eighteen-carat proof that will stand up in a law court."

"Wal, it'll be hard to prove. He's covered his crooked tracks. I never worked fer a slicker cattleman than Hepford. I reckon I can tell how he works his deals. But, out here, in court words don't go far. His would be as strong as mine. Mebbe stronger. It's facts you want."

"He'll never get another dollar of mine, you can bet on that! Or another head of stock! And that reminds me, I want my wages."

"Shore. Go up to the house an' hit him for them. But don't lose your haid again, Ioway. This is a deep game now. Hepford would shoot you at the wink of an eye, 'specially if he knew who you are. An' Hyslip—look out fer him!"

"I will. I'll pack a gun, keep cool and watch them like a cat," returned Selby, buckling on his belt.

"My Gawd!" suddenly ejaculated Hawk.

"What's the matter now? I tell you I can take care of myself."

"It wasn't thet, son. I jest happened to think how you can get even with both Hepford an' Anne. They shore gave you a rotten deal. It'll be wuss fer Anne. She's good at heart, I'd swear. An' she always thought Red Rock was hers."

"Well, it isn't," rejoined Ernest grimly.

"Wal, wal! If she really has played fast an' loose with you, boy, she'll deserve to be ruined."

"If! My lord, Hawk, what do you want?" returned Ernest passionately. "Not a half hour—not a quarter before we rode in she—she let me kiss her. She wanted me to. And that's not the only time. . . . A minute later then—when she ran into her father and Hyslip—she changed. She was cold and hard. She took *his* lying word. She treated me as though I were a leper. She betrayed me before both him and her father."

"I was there, Ernest, hid in the pines. An' I seen an' heahed everythin'. Thet's why I stepped out. All the same, boy, I'd go slow. You own Red Rock—an' every hide an' hair on the ranch. You can turn them out any day. But before you ruin him an' disgrace her be shore she doesn't really care fer you."

"Hawk, you're a fine one to urge me to go slow!" cried Ernest.

"I'm fer givin' a woman the benefit of a doubt any time. Nobody knows why a woman does what she does. Anne might have betrayed you today *because* she loves you an' didn't want them to know."

"She *might* have, only she didn't," rejoined Ernest bitterly. "You wait here and think it over. I'll be back pronto."

"Remember my advice. An' while you're there ask if we can borrow a couple of hosses."

"Ha! Ha! Borrow my own horses. Sure, I'll do it, Hawk."

Ernest strode swiftly toward the ranch house, surer of himself and more self-possessed than he had been at any minute since he had come away from the scene in front of the porch. Still his bitterness remained. As he walked under the pines he felt a pang, like a blade in his heart. He would never be able to abide pine trees again.

The porch of the ranch house was vacant. He saw the office door open and at the same time heard voices. Boldly he mounted the steps and knocked.

"Who is it? Come in," called Hepford.

Ernest entered the doorway. The rancher sat at his desk and Hyslip stood beside him. Both men at sight of Ernest packing a gun gave an unmistakable start.

"I came for my wages," he announced quietly.

"Why, certainly, Howard," replied Hepford hurriedly. "What's comin' to you?"

The Iowan named the sum, smiling as he did so. Hepford counted out the money and handed it over.

"Much obliged. Siebert and I would like to borrow horses to ride out, as far as Brooks' ranch, anyway."

"You an' Siebert can walk," said Hyslip, with an ugly laugh. "I'm not lendin' any of my horses."

"Your horses!" Ernest quickly bit his tongue. "Hyslip, I'll bet ten thousand dollars that if you're not *carried* off this ranch inside a week you'll *walk* yourself."

Hepford laughed loudly, but he stared, too, as if this species of cowboy was something new to him.

"Ten thousand? Haw! Haw! When every dollar you got in the world is them twenty-six cartwheels we jest paid you!" sneered Hyslip, with a leer.

Selby felt the uselessness of speech with these men, at least until he could tell them what was boiling within him. But he gave Hepford a strange long look, and then a dark and meaningful one to Hyslip. His eyes dropped to the desk, upon which lay scattered papers and money. Ernest's pulse leaped as he caught sight of the little blue book. Then slowly he backed out of the office.

As he turned he gazed down the hall, arrested by the sound of a step. Anne stood there in the shadow. For an instant he was transfixed. Her face shone pale and out of it burned two great dark eyes which seemed to be filled with remorse. Wheeling, he rushed away, leaping clear down the steps, and he plunged through the shrubbery and into the grove.

Siebert sat on the bunk where he had left him in a brown study. "Lordy, you come ararin'."

Ernest exhibited his wages, which he still clutched in his hand.

"Hyslip said we could walk," he announced.

"Wal, I'm not surprised. What'd you say?"

"I offered to bet ten thousand dollars that inside of a week he'd either be carried off the ranch, or walk himself."

"Fine. I couldn't have done no better. Wal, I'll go fetch my bag."

"I've got two, Hawk, and you can help me carry the big one.... Wonder what Brooks will say. I'll bet Nebraskie will cuss."

Just before sunset the two dismissed employees of Red Rock toiled wearily up the lane that led to Brooks' homestead.

Daisy saw them first and she waved her sun bonnet. Next moment the burly form of Brooks appeared in the doorway. He ambled forward to meet them. Then Nebraskie showed up and he let out a howl.

"Sam, we want to work fer our board," said Siebert, as Brooks reached them. "Can you take us on?"

"Hell yes. But I'll do better than thet. What's up? Git fired or quit?"

"Which was it, Ernest?"

"I've a faint recollection that we were fired and that Hyslip, the new foreman, told us to walk. Glory, but these bags were heavy!"

They approached the house, to be met by Daisy, flushed and solicitous. She looked very pretty, Ernest noted. Nebraskie leaned against the door, a grin on his ruddy face.

"Laugh, you long, hungry-looking gazabo," declared Ernest. "You're out of a job, too."

So the fugitives were taken in and made much of, commiserated with and fed, and all the while avidly questioned. Ernest let Siebert do the talking, and at the news of Red Rock Brooks plainly was worried.

"It'd go hard with me to lose this home," he said, gloomily.

"Lose this home?" flashed Ernest with sudden passion. "Nobody at Red Rock can make you lose your place, Sam."

"Sam, you'll hev to make allowance fer the boy," drawled Siebert. "He's kind of loco, but his heart is all right."

They talked until long after dark. Daisy, who had been doing the supper dishes with Nebraskie, came in from the kitchen to announce it was bedtime.

"We got plenty of blankets," said Brooks. "You fellers can sleep out on the porch with Nebraskie."

After the lights were out, and all appeared settled for the night Nebraskie rolled over close to Ernest and whispered: "Pard, you shore must hev had a hell of a time with Anne."

"Heaven and hell, both, Nebraskie."

"I'm darned sorry. Reckon you mean she was sweet as sugar, then when you needed a friend she dished you cold fer Hyslip?"

"Nebraskie, old friend, you hit it square."

"Wal, damn her green eyes! I always had a sneakin' hope Anne was true blue, deep under."

"You're as bad as Hawk. She's got you fooled. Anne's just no good."

Nebraskie sighed. "Ernie, gurls hev a hard go of it, with fellers an'—an' all thet."

"Well, Nebraskie, I didn't mean to claim that *we* were angels."

"Air you bad hurt, pard?" went on Nebraskie in a low whisper.

"Pretty bad. Same as you with Dais."

"Wal, then, I'll be damned if I'd quit," replied Nebraskie, almost harshly, and rolling over, he went to sleep.

Ernest did not get to sleep for a long while. At first he thought of the kindness of these good friends and how he loved them and how he was going to reward them, when he took over the ranch. After that his thoughts reverted to the developments of the day, and over and over again he lived them, trying to see them clearly, to trace cause and effect. Vainly he sought for any hope where Anne was concerned. And every train of thought ended at the same dead end. He lay awake for hours, but at last sheer weariness brought on temporary oblivion.

In the morning, Nebraskie and Siebert went off with Brooks to do some ranch work, and Daisy was busy with her household duties. Ernest lounged around indoors and out, and finally he climbed high on a slope where he sat under a tree and gazed down the beautiful valley. The pasture land, the rolling fields, the green patches of alfalfa, the black slopes leading up to the red crags—these with all their beauty and peace, their loneliness and wildness brought little surcease to his soul.

The day ended without bringing him any nearer to a solution to his problem. At supper he had difficulty persuading Nebraskie not to ride down to Red Rock. He did not like the cowboy's cool tone, his gleaming eye. Nebraskie's complaint about wanting to collect his few possessions did not deceive Ernest. Siebert added his persuasions to Ernest's.

"All right. But folks, I gotta go someday. There's my wages, an' a saddle an' a bedroll. An' shore I want to pay my respects to the new foreman."

"Nebraskie Kemp!" cried Daisy, wild of eye. She had her fears and they were identical with Ernest's.

"Doggone it! You ain't my boss *yet*," complained Nebraskie.

"Well, it's aboot time I *was*—for your own sake," replied Daisy.

"Dais Brooks, I call your bluff!" burst out Nebraskie, as if suddenly inspired.

That was too much for Daisy, at least in the presence of the amused spectators, and, blushing, she ran out pursued by the grinning cowboy.

Up to midafternoon next day the situation was precisely the same as on the day before. Then Ernest, who had been sitting on the porch, espied two riders coming down the lane. A second glance identified them as Hyslip and Anne. For an instant Ernest was nonplussed. The next moment he was assailed by a feeling of unreasoning jealousy. He hurried into the house.

"Daisy, I see Hyslip riding in. Better let me meet him," he said.

The girl's face went white.

"Hyslip! Oh, I—I cain't see him," she faltered.

"You needn't," replied Ernest, shortly. "Shut the door after me."

He went out, greatly nettled that Daisy should show such agitation at the mere fact of Hyslip's approach. The little fool must still love him. Then Ernest forgot Daisy in the absorption of his own jealous curiosity and resentment. Hyslip, of course, had hatched up some excuse to call on Brooks. But why should Anne come with him? It was another of her mean tricks. It could not be just an accident. She halted at the gate while Hyslip rode on in. If she saw Ernest she gave no sign. It was impossible, however, for her not to see him. The distance was short and there were no trees intervening. Hyslip rode up and reined in before the door.

"I want to see Brooks," he announced.

"Nobody home. They're all out in the back field."

"Dais with them?"

"Yes. And so is Nebraskie. Take a tip from me. Don't ride out that way," replied Ernest. "Besides, to judge from your looks, this isn't such a healthy place for you to be."

"My business is not with any low-down cow-puncher," said Hyslip, flushing angrily. "You can tell Sam Brooks fer me thet he can get ready to move off the ranch."

"What ranch?" inquired Ernest instantly.

"Red Rock Ranch, thet's what."

"But this ranch isn't Red Rock. This is Brooks' ranch."

"He has no papers fer the land."

"So I've heard. But my—old Selby gave him the land. One hundred acres. And Brooks has papers for the water rights."

"You know a hell of a lot, Howard," sneered Hyslip. "Brooks cain't use the water if he doesn't own or lease the land. Hepford let him stay on heah. But I'm foreman of Red Rock now. An' off he goes!"

"Is that Hepford's order?" asked Ernest, stifling his fury.

"It's my order an' thet's enough," rejoined Hyslip, turning his horse.

Ernest took advantage of the occasion to walk beside him toward the gate. "I'll tell him, but I don't relish the job."

"You can save me the trouble of ridin' up heah again."

"Sure. I know I might be saving you more—"

"Howdy, Dais," interrupted Hyslip, waving his gauntleted hand at the front window, where Ernest's swift glance caught the girl's pale face and dark, strained eyes. Then she vanished.

"I reckon you savvy," continued Hyslip, and his look, as well as his tone of voice, conveyed more than enough to infuriate Ernest.

They reached the open gate. Hyslip rode through and Ernest put up the bars. Then he gazed over them at Hyslip and the girl beyond.

"I savvy a good deal, Hyslip," he asserted, his voice vibrating. "Brooks will never get off this land. And I advise you to stay off yourself—if you want to keep your yellow hide in one piece."

Anne wheeled her pinto in sudden haste. Ernest had caught only a fleeting glimpse of her face, but

enough to see that it wore a startled expression.
Hyslip swayed sidewise in his saddle, after the graceful fashion of riders and he sang mockingly:

> Son-of-a-gun from Ioway
> He stole my gurl aw-aay.

His mellow laugh rang out. Soon he caught up
with Anne, and riding beside her horse, he leaned to
catch her hand. She seemed to give hers willingly
enough. Then, hand in hand, they rode up the lane
together.

Ernest watched them in helpless rage. At last he
muttered: "Who could have—believed that—of her?
...She has settled it!"

Out of his agony of jealousy and betrayal had
come the decision to carry out relentlessly the purpose which he had so long hesitated to accomplish.

CHAPTER

16

NEBRASKIE rode in earlier than usual that evening. He brought the fragrance of the woods with him and there were pine needles conspicuously adhering to his rough garments.

"You don't look as if you'd been digging fence-post holes," observed Ernest.

"Sam an' Hawk hev been doin' thet," replied the rider.

"Where you been, Nebraskie?"

"Aw, jest ridin' around."

What would Nebraskie be doing that for, Ernest pondered? Then Nebraskie asked casually about the horsemen he had seen going down the road toward Red Rock.

"That was Hyslip and Anne," replied Selby, just as casually.

The cowboy swore fluently, then said, "Thet redhaided hussy! Is she playin' Hyslip's game?"

"I don't know, Nebraskie. I was sure surprised when I saw her riding off holding hands with Hyslip. She just must be plain rotten through and through."

"Naw, damn her. It ain't thet. She's jest bent on gallin' you an' she doesn't know how bad Hyslip really is. Somebody ought to tell her. Course Dais cain't. Fer thet matter Dais gits weak in the knees whenever Hyslip's name is spoke. It shore riles me. But Dais is honest. She *told* me. She said he charmed her like a snake charms a bird. If it wasn't fer thet, Ernie, old pard, I'd dish Dais tomorrow. But her heart is all right an' it's mine. I gotta stick to her. What worries me is thet Hyslip might ride in heah someday an' ketch Dais alone. I reckon he was just lookin' the place over today an' fetched Anne along."

"That may be. But he said he came over to put Brooks off the ranch."

"The hell you say! He'll do it, too, Ernie, if we leave him alone. The law is on Hepford's side. Brooks has no deed or patent for this ground. He never even homesteaded it."

"Well, Nebraskie, you'll be pleased to know that we won't leave Mr. Hyslip alone," replied Ernest cheerfully.

"Now you're talkin'. Gosh, but you're a comfortin' pard to have around, Ernie. I jest don't know what I done afore you came!"

"Thanks. I'm happy to return the compliment. ...Now let's do a little figuring. For the present Brooks and Siebert can keep busy building that much-needed fence. You and I will take turns watching this house. From up in the woods there, where we can see the road each way."

"Ahuh. It's a smart idee. Let him ride up an' find Dais alone, huh? ... Ernie, I feel it in my bones thet he'll come, too."

"Sure he'll come. Today when they got here Anne stayed out there by the gate. I had seen them coming and told Daisy to shut the door. Well, when Hyslip rode in I lied—said everybody was away. Told him Daisy was out with you and that he'd better not show himself. But, Daisy, the darn little fool, showed *herself* at the window. Hyslip saw her. And say, but was he cocky! Told me I savvied the case all right. And he rode away singing that Iowa song."

"Ahuh. I'm glad you told me, Ernest," replied Nebraskie. "Reckon it's wuss than I feared."

He clanked into the house, leaving Selby sitting there. A moment later, Ernest heard Nebraskie's stern voice and then the sound of Daisy's weeping. Not wishing to overhear what was being said in the house, he got up from his seat on the porch, and moved to a bench under a pine. Presently Nebraskie came out again, white to the lips.

"Whar air you, Ernest? ..." he called. Then he espied Ernest and stalked over to where he sat in the shade of the big pine. Squatting down beside his friend he wiped his perspiring face with a grimy scarf. But he seemed otherwise composed.

"It is wuss, Ernie," he began steadily. "I jumped Dais good an' hard. She swore she didn't remember peepin' out at Hyslip an' couldn't tell why she did it. But she confessed thet she was turrible afeared he

had got her into trouble. She *had* to confess it an'
was glad when it was out. But she cried somethin'
pitiful. I was sort of floored. Then I asked her if she
loved Hyslip. She said she hated him, an' she shore
looked it. Then I asked her if she loved me. An' she
swore she did.... So I told her thet was enough. We'd
ride to town soon an' git married. Then Hyslip would
leave her alone."

The Iowan cursed under his breath. After a moment he replied: "That's exactly what I'd do, Nebraskie."

"Shore, I knowed you would.... Wal, it's a hell
of a note. But now my hash is settled, I'm worryin'
aboot you."

"Never mind me, Nebraskie. My hash is settled,
too."

On the second afternoon after the day of that
conversation, Ernest was sitting on the hillside
watching the road when he espied Hepford's buckboard rattling along in a cloud of dust behind the
spirited blacks. Soon he recognized the occupants.
Hepford was one, and the other Hyslip, who held the
reins. At first Ernest thought they were coming to
Brooks' ranch, but they passed by the lane, and went
on swiftly and soon were out of sight.

"Going to town," soliloquized Ernest. And he became very thoughtful. Suddenly he jumped up, ex-
claiming, "It's my chance!"

He would go down to Red Rock Ranch and under
cover of darkness, in the absence of Hepford and his
new henchman, secure that little blue book which

he believed he required to substantiate his demands on the rancher.

Ernest did not return to the house. Keeping under cover of the woods he made a wide detour, circling above the end of the Brooks farm, and came back into the trail that led down on the west side of the valley. He made his way slowly, cautiously and watchfully. Some of Hyslip's riders might be encountered along the trail, and Ernest did not intend to be seen. The sun had long set when he reached a point opposite and above the ranch house. Here he waited. His gaze wandered with pride over the broad acres, where the long purple shadows were creeping. The wide green pastures were dotted with a hundred head of horses; far beyond, in the larger pasture, cattle grazed. Somewhere cows were lowing and calves bawling; a burro brayed his raucous call to his mate; the baaing of lambs came from the lowlands beyond the house. It was a very beautiful ranch scene, and the sights and sounds of it swelled Ernest's heart. It was his, and he would soon come into his own. At that moment his heart held no pity. He had been cheated by the father and flouted by the daughter. The time had passed to allow a crown of red hair and a pair of green eyes to stand between him and his own.

Far above the opposite slope the last gold-red rays of the sun shone on the mountain peaks. This touch of wild grandeur was all that Red Rock needed. The peaceful valley was insulated by rugged timbered heights. Ernest watched the purple shadow lengthen, the twilight deepen to dusk, the dusk to night. Then he moved down from his covert, to enter the pine grove which surrounded the house. Here he proceeded cautiously. The barking of a dog halted him; again a man stalking down the road made him freeze behind the trunk of a pine.

At length he reached the shrubbery that grew thickly on the north and east side of the house. Once in this dense shelter he felt safe. From its shadows he peered out to discover that there was a light in the little office. His keen ear caught light footsteps. No doubt Anne was in the office. It surely could not be either Hepford or Hyslip. Ernest did not care about any one else, but he dreaded the thought of meeting Anne. If he happened to encounter either Hyslip or Hepford it would mean gunplay. He had prepared himself, and when his hand touched the cold butt of his six-shooter he felt reassured. This was no child's play. Squatting down noiselessly, he composed himself to wait for the light to go out in that office window.

He sat there until his limbs were cramped. Time was no object; he had no sense of hurry. Still the moments began to drag. Presently he got up and moved out across the open yard in front of the house, careful not to cross the beam of the one lighted window. The shadow was impenetrable. He had to feel his way, consequently had little fear of being seen. At length coming to the high porch steps he drew himself up until he could see into the window. The first thing he caught sight of was Anne's red hair shining in the lamplight. He suffered a sharp pang. Farther up he drew himself. Now he could see Anne sitting at the desk, with her head resting on her folded arms. It was a posture of complete despair. The most

callous heart would have been moved by that brief
glimpse of dejection and sorrow. What could have
happened, he wondered. She was not working nor
writing. Again Ernest raised himself to take a keener
and longer look. Presently the bowed shoulders of
the girl began to shake as though she were sobbing.
Her actions were those of a person who had given
herself up to grief and hopelessness. Ernest abandoned his position, and gliding back to his covert he
settled himself once more to watch and wait and to
think.

Something had occurred that had brought sorrow to this proud and strong-willed girl. Was it something that had to do with her father? With him? With
Hyslip? Not that it could change his resolve one whit,
he determined. Still he felt his cold savage mood
disrupted. Could Anne by any chance actually be
feeling remorse? Once he would have known it to be
quite possible. A girl of her nature had the moods of
April. He even found himself hoping that she was
suffering. This thought was followed by the realization that if she were not the fact was certain that
very shortly she would be.

He grew restless, nervous and then uncertain.
He could not recapture his cool, determined strength
of mind. Sight of Anne's unhappiness had upset him.
Bitterly he accused himself of being a softhearted
weakling. But it was no go. Now almost he wanted
to abandon his quest. Almost he wanted to go away
and leave Red Rock to her. But enough of his purpose
remained to tell him that this was sentimental nonsense.

He was still struggling with himself when all at

once the light went out. Ernest caught his breath. At last! He heard a door close and steps retreating into the interior of the house. He waited what seemed a long time. Perhaps it was not so very long as time goes, but it seemed like hours. At any rate he could not wait longer. He drew off his boots.

Soundlessly he slipped out of the bushes, peering all around him, listening like a hunted deer. Then he mounted the porch steps. The office door was locked. Evidently it had been locked while Anne was in there. Then he tried the window. It held fast. This was bad, but he was prepared for that eventuality. His hunting knife, which he wore at his belt, possessed a heavy, stout blade. He inserted this between the frame and sill, and pried. A crack followed, so loud that it startled him. Again he froze to a listening, watching posture. Nothing happened.

Again he bent to the window. It opened easily, but he had trouble in holding it up while he slipped inside. Then he lowered it. His next move was to feel at the door, to find the lock and unbolt it. Slowly and carefully he opened the door. He tiptoed to the desk and bent over it, feeling with careful, swift hands.

Suddenly they came in contact with a soft, damp object. A handkerchief! Anne had left it there. Ernest caught a faint well-remembered perfume. It shook his nerve, even more than had sight of her. The handkerchief was wet with her tears. On an impulse he stuffed the bit of linen inside his shirt.

Then to his task he bent swiftly. The desk was bare. He felt in the little open compartments. One article after another he touched, handled, discarded.

At last his eager hand came in contact with a small ledger held shut by rubber bands. He put the book in his pocket. Yet to make doubly sure he went all over the desk again, outside and inside. He had what he wanted.

His exultation died a sudden violent death. Rapid hoofbeats transfixed him. Horses were approaching at a swift gait. Then he heard a halloa, so close at hand that his blood turned to ice in his veins.

He stepped to the door. In the gloom he saw the black team and buckboard come to a halt, right at the foot of the porch steps. A man leaped out.

"Tell the boys, pronto," called Hepford harshly. "Send Pedro for the team. But tell him not to unhitch. Hurry now."

The man ran off. Hepford moved to get out of the buckboard. Ernest's mind worked with the swiftness of lightning. His first thought was to walk boldly down the steps to confront Hepford. But the rancher was excited. Something had happened. Ernest would have to kill him. Next he decided to cross the porch and leap off in the shadow. But this would not do. He took the only retreat left open.

Gliding out he slipped down the dark hallway. His intent was to go through the house and out at the back. But he bumped into a door that would not open. He felt like a trapped wolf.

Hepford's quick footsteps sounded on the porch. Ernest advanced along the wall, feeling at the left side for a door. At the same moment he heard distant shouts. Suddenly his shaking hand came to an offset in the wall. A door! He found the door knob. Softly he turned it while peering down the hallway toward the porch. The door opened into a lighted room. Like a flash Ernest slipped in, and closing the door locked it behind him. Only then did he look up—in time to see Anne Hepford sit bolt upright in bed.

CHAPTER

17

E*RNEST* made a sharp gesture, which ended with his fingers to his lips. But that did not prevent Anne from crying out: "Ernest!" He made a hissing sound as he whispered to her to keep still.

"What does this mean!" she exclaimed, her look of surprise turning into anger and indignation.

He advanced with long strides, to halt at the foot of her bed. Here the lamplight shone full on him. Anne's big eyes widened as they swept from his bare head to his stocking feet, his menacing posture, his gun. She sank back with a gasp.

"In God's name!...What're you doing in my room? What are you going to do to me?"

Her fright gave Ernest a cue. He had nothing in mind on the instant but to keep her quiet.

"That depends," he replied, very low and fiercely.

She sat up again, her red hair tumbling around her white face and bare shoulders. Her terror, her agitation, tended to make her appear more beautiful than Ernest had ever seen her. It occurred to him that his sudden entrance and his attitude might well have made her think he had broken into her room to revenge himself upon her for her cruelty to him.

"Ernest—you—you wouldn't—" she began, and lifted a shaking hand.

"I'd do anything, Anne Hepford," he whispered threateningly, bending over the bed, fixing her with his eyes. He meant to frighten her until she helped him out of this dilemma. "You made me love you to distraction. Then you betrayed me—scorned me before your father—and that damned blackguard!" he whispered hoarsely.

"Oh—but wait—listen! Ernest," she begged wildly. "I'm not so vile as you think. When we got back—from that ride we took everybody ridiculed me. I was furious anyhow—because I—I began to see I really cared. I wouldn't give in to it. I encouraged Hyslip again....And when I saw you at Brooks' I wanted to make you feel as miserable as I was.... But I was sorry. That settled me. Tonight I wrote you—telling you how wrong I was to hurt you—how sorry I was that I had done all this to you. You must believe me, Ernest."

"Anne Hepford, you're lying," he retorted, not needing now to feign anger.

"No, Ernest. I've got the letter under my pillow."

She turned and tumbling the pillows extracted a letter, which she held out.

The intruder eagerly leaned over the bed to snatch the letter from her fingers. A glance showed that it was addressed to him. The envelope was thick, and undoubtedly its contents occupied many pages. Slowly he dropped the missive into his pocket. His doubt of her remained as great as all the pain she had caused him. He willed himself not to yield to her charm, to her lies, only to be humiliated all over again. Yet the sweet loveliness of her, as she lay helpless there in bed, made him catch his breath.

"So you've taken to writing letters now? Why don't you get the Dude to deliver them for you?" he asked harshly.

"Oh, please, Ernest," she pleaded. "I know I deserve—oh, Ernest, I've been heartless. But I know how wrong I was. I don't ask you to forgive me—just to believe me. It's all in that letter. I confessed. I told the truth at last—how I found out that I really cared for you—hated myself for my blindness, my stubbornness—begged you to understand—asked you to come back to Red Rock and I'd make everything all right."

"Anne, what you say is impossible."

"Indeed it's not. It's all in that letter—and if you just cain't believe me, read it heah and now. I don't blame you. I—I've been a liar—a flirt—a cat—a coward. But, Ernest, I didn't know myself—I didn't."

"If it's true—it's too late!" he said, turning away in order that she might not see his face.

She sat up, and reaching for her dressing gown, she slipped the coverlet back and moved to the foot of the bed. Her glance fell to the floor. She was flushing scarlet now.

"Not too late, Ernest. Oh, don't say that—not if you still—"

Heavy footsteps and a knocking on the door silenced her. Ernest drew back. He suddenly realized what an awkward position he was in, and what a compromising situation it must be for the girl.

"Anne, are you awake?" called her father's voice.

"Oh! That you, Dad? Yes, I'm awake, but I'm in bed," she replied in tones that sounded unnatural to Ernest.

"Let me in."

It was then a subtle change passed over her. The startled look left her eyes.

"But, Dad, I told you. I'm in bed. I don't want to get up."

"Reckon you needn't. You have that money safe?"

"Yes. I hid it away."

"All right. Never mind now. I'll probably be out all night. . . . Anne, somethin' terrible's happened."

"What?"

"Young Howard killed Hyslip. . . . The cowboys think it was murder."

Anne's horrified gaze transfixed him. "Oh Dad— how awful!" she cried huskily.

"Wal, it was awful fer Hyslip an' it'll be awful fer Howard if we catch him," responded Hepford grimly. "It'll mean a lynchin'. I'm sorry to have to tell you, Anne. But you had somethin' to do with it. I told you to let that tenderfoot alone. I sensed that he was different from the start. Not a cowboy at all, not even a Westerner. He was out of his haid over you.... But no use to rail. It's too late now. Let this be a lesson to you. Go to sleep, if you can. I'll tell you everythin' tomorrow."

He ceased and his heavy footsteps sounded down the hall. Voices came from the porch. There were others outside.

Ernest's heart, which had been in his throat, resumed its natural position. His consternation and then terror had all been for Nebraskie. In a flash he realized what had happened. Hepford and Hyslip had not gone to town. No doubt Hyslip had returned instead to Brooks' ranch, there to run into Nebraskie. Then in some way Hepford, and perhaps others deliberately had mixed up Ernest's name in the case.

All of a sudden Ernest became aware of Anne. While those thoughts had flashed through his mind he had forgotten her and where he was. She came sliding unsteadily along the bed, and reaching the footboard she raised herself to her knees and clasped Ernest with nerveless hands. Her face was ghastly white, her eyes were strained and full of dark terror.

"Oh, my God, I know now—why you said it's too late," she moaned. "I drove you to do it. I don't blame you. *I'm* to blame. Oh, Ernest why, *why* didn't you wait? Why didn't you come to me sooner? I can see it all now. Hyslip crowed over you. Aboot me! The damned conceited fool! And you killed him! Oh, may God forgive me!"

Ernest put his arms around her and held her close, doubting his own senses. But he could feel her throbbing heart; he could see the tragic despair in her great eyes.

"Anne, hush. Your father—or someone else may hear you. My life is in danger," he whispered. "You heard what he said about a lynching."

"Yes—yes." She clung to him then straining and trembling and shivering as with a chill. It was on Ernest's lips to tell her that he had not killed Hyslip, to assure her of his innocence, but he was powerless to resist the moment. What more would she say? What would she do? Again he was finding himself convinced that in spite of all that had happened, this beautiful girl truly loved him. It seemed preposterous, incomprehensible, yet she might. She might prove it in some glorious way.

She drew back from him a little, and he could see her gathering her courage.

"We must leave Red Rock at once," she whispered.

"You would go with me?"

"Heaven help us! Yes, I'll go. Once across the territory line you'll be safe. But if you're caught now—Dad and his outfit will hang you. Oh, they hate you, Ernest, for some reason I can't figure out.... We must go at once."

"Anne, you'd really—run off with me?" he asked wonderingly.

"I told you. Yes, yes. I will. I must. I'd never let you go alone."

"But why?"

"Because I've ruined you.... And because I—I love you, Ernest." She put her arms around his neck and kissed him.

"But Anne. Think. Don't take a step like this—

just out of remorse or sense of pity. You'd have to marry me."

"I'd want you to, of course, Ernest. But I'll go whether you marry me or not. I'll give my life. I'll pay. I'm a new Anne Hepford. And I know what I'm doing. You killed a man because of me. But he deserved to die. I want you to live—for me."

"We'd be very poor, Anne. You've been used to everything you wanted. If you do this rash thing and afterward regret it—"

"I ask only to get away from them.... Ernest, you do love me still? I didn't make you despise me?"

No dream of love he had ever had could equal the sweetness and passion of her voice, the entreaty in her face.

"Anne, I love you more madly than ever. Still, I beg you once again. Think of what you're doing."

"Kiss me," she whispered, holding up her mouth. Her lips clung to his. Then with a quick movement she broke from him.

"I'll let you out this window," she said swiftly. "Keep in the dark. Find your shoes. I'll dress, pack a few things and meet you in fifteen minutes. Let's see. I'll go through the grove, down by the road. Wait for me near the big pine. I must try to get horses, if I can."

She turned down the lamp till the room was almost dark. Then she slid up the blind. The window was open. All appeared dark and quiet outside. "Now," she whispered, "and for my sake don't let anyone see you."

Without a word more Ernest slipped out, while she knelt to help him, clasp him, and kiss him once more. As her lips left his cheek they formed the word: "Darling." Then her hold loosened. Ernest dropped to the soft turf. The dim light from the window vanished.

He stood there for an instant like a man in a trance. How dark the night! How still! He was trembling all over. He listened. The sound of faint hoof beats came to his listening ears. Stealthily he moved, making no sound. He parted the leaves of the shrubbery and moved noiselessly through them, away from the house, into the grove. He found his shoes and put them on. He had to feel for the trunks of the pines. One by one he passed through them, gradually gaining control over his faculties, as he crept toward the road. At the edge of the grove he stopped to make sure of his further course. He knew the way as well as if it had been daylight. Across the open to the left several of the bunkhouses showed lights from their windows. He crossed the wide dark space to the right of the grove, and gained the high vine-covered fence. He slipped along this to the end, where it turned at right angles, forming one side of the barnyard. He had only to go round the barn to the lane. Then as he listened the sound of hoofs came again, louder now, followed by the crunch of wheels on gravel. Someone was bringing the buckboard from the house. It was coming too slowly to be driven. Suddenly the sounds were drowned by the rush of horses from the other direction. Several riders galloped by, toward the ranch house. Ernest saw the dark forms.

He did not have a great while to think and plan. Absolutely, beyond any equivocation he would take

Anne at her word, elope with her, marry her, and let the rest take care of itself. Exultation swelled his heart. But they could not walk. He must procure horses. Perhaps it would not be the best course to wait until Anne joined him. Nevertheless he waited. Soon in the gloom dim forms appeared—Pedro leading the team, still hitched to the buckboard. The Mexican lad was humming a tune. He went by, continuing on into the barnyard.

Ernest took advantage of his opportunity, and passing the barn, hurried down the lane. The customary quiet of the ranch at this hour appeared to have been disrupted. The sound of distant voices came to his ear and the pounding of boots on wooden floors. The cowboys were moving to and fro. Ernest worried about the three horsemen who had passed. He wished they would return. However, he reflected, they could have gone on toward Springertown.

He did not proceed more than halfway to the big pine that stood close to the road, but waited just out of sight of the barn, and listened with all his might, peering impatiently into the gloom. He was sure Anne would come. He had dispelled his last doubt of her. And he thanked God that his faith had persisted, despite all appearances, despite his own weak pretenses up to the very end. Yet how wrong he had been that day at Brooks' farm. She had only been distraught. Her vanity and her pride had succumbed to her love for a tenderfoot masquerading as a penniless cowboy. Ernest blessed the deception he had practiced. Otherwise he might never have won her. It had taken the tragedy of Hyslip's killing to make a woman of her.

Suddenly his keen ear caught the sound of light swift steps. His blood raced. She was coming. Sure as the stars shone she was coming to meet him, to go away with him, to share what she deemed would be his vicissitudes. Then a dark flitting shadow emerged from the gloom. He waited until he recognized it. She wore a black coat and carried a small bag. Ernest stepped out from his hiding place. She shied like a frightened colt. Then he spoke her name softly, reassuring her. Joining her, he took her bag.

"I'm late. But I had—some narrow—escapes," she whispered, her breath coming in little gasps. "I got out easy enough. Dad has men there. I—I listened a moment—at my door....Now, we must have horses."

"Pedro just led the buckboard into the barnyard," said Ernest.

"Good. I'll get it. Wait at the gate for me. Have it open." She was gone before Ernest had a reply ready. He obeyed her, hurrying down the lane. She could do anything with Pedro, or any of the other hired hands for that matter. Before he reached the gate he heard the buckboard coming, the horses at a brisk trot. Ernest ran to open the gate.

The black team approached almost to where he stood. Anne slowed up, but did not stop. "Jump in!" she called, with an excited little laugh. Ernest leaped aboard. Then with Anne grasping the reins they went at a rapid clip down the road. "I told Pedro not to tell until the team was missed. And then that I was going to Springertown. That'll put Dad off the track. He'll be wild—but not half as wild as he'll be when he discovers the loss of something else."

Ernest put his arm around her slender waist. "We're off. I don't care where. Oh, Anne, it's too wonderful to be true."

"Well, it's true enough," she replied grimly. "You talk sort of funny for a man who's been hunted for a murder."

"What could you expect? It's turned out you don't hate me—but love me."

"Ernest, you've got to use your haid now, love or no love," she replied seriously. "I'm hoping in the excitement that the cowboys won't think of tracking the buckboard but haid straight for Springertown. But even if they do they cain't catch us. We'll have an all night start."

"Where are we going, Anne?" he asked.

"We turn off aboot ten miles beyond Brooks' ranch. It's a fairly good road, but not much used. Short cut to Snowflake. Showdown, Pine Hill and the New Mexico line. I reckon it'll be pretty safe. No word can reach those towns of your—your fight with Hyslip, before we get there. And once across the line we'll be safe from Dad's outfit."

"Your father has it in for me. I never knew exactly why."

"He never liked you. He was suspicious of you at first. Swore you were no cowboy. Though you might be snooping. Hyslip he always doted on. Wanted me to marry him! Fancy that—the skylarking dude! And of course Hyslip's cronies will be daid set to catch you. They'd not wait for a sheriff, but lynch you, Ernest. Dad would stand by to see them do it, too."

"Without proof that I—I killed Hyslip?" queried Ernest.

"Proof? They must have that.... When are you going to tell me what—how it happened?"

"Not until we are married and safe."

"Maybe you'd better never tell me.... Say, we'll soon be to Brooks' lane. We want to watch careful heah." She urged the team to a swifter gait, until Ernest saw that they were fairly flying along the road. The night was clear and cold; the stars shone white; the cool wind swept his heated face.

"I'll bet it will be cold later," he said.

"Shore will. There's a heavy robe under the seat. Get it out. You don't have a coat. It'll be mighty cold before morning, I reckon."

Ernest drew it forth and spread it over their laps. "There's a sack of grain under the seat."

"Good. Do you know, it's strange about this. Dad set off for Holbrook, intending to be gone several days and—" Anne broke off, and though Ernest did not know just what she was about to divulge he refrained from questioning her.

They were silent for a while. Ernest kept a sharp watch.

"We passed the lane then. Bars down. Somebody forgot. Brooks never leaves the bars down," he remarked presently.

She slackened the rapid pace of the blacks and kept them to a trot. Ernest felt the need of gloves and coat, for the motion of the buckboard caused the robe to slide down continually. He found his thoughts recurring to the reported killing of Hyslip, growing far more concerned about Nebraskie's welfare than his own. But he was satisfied that Nebraskie surely must have had justification for his act. When the truth was known Hyslip would not be mourned or even defended. Hepford must have some private reason for his championship of the dude cowboy and for implicating Ernest in his killing. Siebert had hinted of that very thing, openly in his retort to the rancher. Ernest put that out of his mind for the present. He had all he could do to play his part. He wanted to carry his deception up to the time of his actual marriage with Anne, and if possible, beyond that, clear to the hour when he would be able to confront Hepford and claim ownership of Red Rock Ranch.

That was going to be a thrilling moment when he revealed his true identity to Anne. He tried to picture her surprise when she learned that she had married a wealthy rancher instead of a poor fence-post hole digger. And perhaps after she recovered from the shock she would not regret too deeply that she was the wife of Ernest Howard Selby. How to avoid discovery when they were being married caused Ernest some concern. It would be difficult, unless he could hurry the ceremony and trust to his bride's excitement to conceal the fact that her husband's name was Selby instead of Howard.

From time to time Anne would turn to peer into his face. He could see her dark eyes and the shadowy smile on her pale face. "Don't worry, Ernest. I got you into this and I'll get you out."

"I'm not worrying. I'm too happy to fret—and don't care a darn what happens after."

"After what?"

"After we're married. Which will be tomorrow."

She laughed. "So you're more concerned aboot making me your wife than getting away from my dad's outfit or the sheriff?"

"Reckon I am. If I can have you for my wife one single day I'll cheerfully stand to be hanged."

"Well, I won't. I want you forever....Lordy, Ernest, isn't it wonderful that we love each other! If we only had known sooner!"

"I did. I told you. I begged you. Couldn't you guess I was not the kind of man to trifle with?"

"I figured you absolutely wrong. So did everybody else, especially Hyslip."

"You sure did. I'm a bad hombre," replied Ernest coolly. "I'll surprise you yet, too."

"Don't, please. This once is enough for me. I'm punished for all time."

So they talked on, with frequent intervals of silence, and the miles slid past under the buckboard wheels. Presently they turned off the main road, and after that Anne showed great relief. She conserved the strength of the horses, and did not halt them for a rest until long after midnight. It was at the edge of a pine forest, where the road passed under great spreading branches. A brook babbled from somewhere in the darkness and the wind sighed in the tree tops.

"We'd better rest the team and build a fire to warm ourselves," suggested Anne practically.

"Have you any matches?" asked Ernest.

"No. But shore you must have?"

"Nary a match."

"Cain't you build a fire without matches?"

"Anne, I'm no wizard."

"Reckon I'll even have to keep you warm, Mr. Tenderfoot."

She drove off the road, into the black shadow of a great pine. Anne insisted that they put the two horse blankets over the horses, and use the rug themselves. So presently Ernest found himself, as one in a dream, under the robe with Anne, his head resting on the sack of grain, and his shoulder serving as a pillow for Anne. In fact she was in his arms, almost, and her hair brushed his face.

"This isn't so bad—for runaways," she said softly.

"I think you'd better pinch me to see if I'm awake."

"You'd better sleep some."

"Sleep!"

"Shore. I intend to. It's no time to be sentimental and romantic, Ernest darling. We'll have plenty of time for that after we get you out of the clutches of the lynching party."

Ernest said no more, and lay there marveling, all too conscious of Anne's warm presence. She made only one movement, and that was to take off her gloves. Her left hand nestled at Ernest's neck and her fingers were like ice. A short time afterward, Selby knew from her deep breathing she had fallen asleep. He saw the stars shining through the dark lacy foliage and he listened to the keening of the wind in the big pines overhead. He wondered what the next day would bring forth, though for his part he never wanted it to dawn. Then hours later it seemed to him that the dark star-studded canopy faded, and even the sweet proximity of Anne passed into oblivion.

WHEN Ernest awoke the sky was gray and cold. His movement disturbed Anne, who sat up looking wildly about her. But it took her, at most, only an instant to connect the present with the past. She threw back the rug, laughing gaily. "I was shore snug and warm. Roll out, cowboy. You don't seem to be a very ambitious bridegroom."

Ernest rolled out with all the alacrity that his cramped limbs would allow.

"Where're my gloves? ... Oh, dear, I lay on my hat. ... Ernest, we must feed the horses and be on our way even though we'll have to go breakfastless ourselves. There's water heah, but I doubt if the horses will drink."

Ernest set the bag of grain upright. "That was a darn sight harder pillow than you had," he observed.

"Oh, my pillow was fine—that is, after its internal machinery calmed down. Ernest, at first your heart was beating like a trip hammer."

"Humph! Why shouldn't it? Never before did it serve as a pillow for such a beautiful and bewitching head."

"Honest?"

"Yes, honest," he added, shortly.

"Well, I've plenty reason to love you, and that's one more. I knew it, though, without your telling me."

"Who's the sentimental one now? What'll we feed the horses with?"

"Nose bags. They must be under the back seat."

It was just daylight when they were finally ready to start. As Anne turned the buckboard back into the road she appeared to discover something on the ground.

"Ernest, we didn't make those tracks," she observed.

Whereupon he discovered both wheel and hoof tracks in the sandy soil.

"Look pretty fresh to me," he said.

"They shore were made yesterday. Now who the deuce could be ahaid of us? . . . Ernest, I don't like that for a cent."

"What do we care so long as they're ahead."

"It might be somebody who'll spread the news."

"That's so. What'll we do?"

"Risk it and go on."

So they did, and the sky reddened in the east, the sun rose to make the frosty grass sparkle, and the beautiful woodland awoke with life of bird and squirrel. Ernest saw deer, and horses that he was sure must be wild. His enthusiasm did not communicate itself to Anne, who looked serious, and seemed to be shy now that it was broad daylight. She drove for a while, after which Ernest asked to take the reins. And as he was by no means a good driver he had his hands full with the spirited team. On good stretches of road, however, he did well enough. Once Anne remarked that she might make a Westerner out of him, after all. At length they came to a brook, where the horses drank. Ernest tumbled out and did likewise. But Anne averred she would prefer to remain famished until she could have a cup of coffee and some toast.

They climbed a long gradual slope over a wooded hill, and went on down into more open range country. Selby looked in vain for fences and ranches, but espied neither, and did not see even any signs of cattle until nearly noon. Then they began to descend into lower country, where the rocks and pines vanished, and the cedars of the desert began to manifest themselves. Here cattle dotted the open patches, and at length they came to the first ranch.

"I don't know how far it is yet, but we ought to be coming to Snowflake soon," said Anne anxiously. "I was over this road once years ago."

Her anxiety communicated itself to Ernest, who showed his concern by urging the team forward. The blacks, however, still did not appear to tire.

"How many miles have we come?" he asked once.

"I reckon sixty miles, if not more. This time tomorrow we'll be over the line."

"Anne, we'll be over the matrimonial line today, if I can find a preacher."

She blushed scarlet. "You're shore in a hurry to make me Mrs. Ernest Howard."

"Hurry's no name for it."

"Are you afraid I'll change my mind?"

"You're a bewildering girl you'll have to admit. I'll take no more chances."

"Ernest, have no fear. You'll never lose me now," she replied wistfully.

From the top of a hill they espied a pretty village down in a valley. Anne said that it was Snowflake. Its green confines covered considerable space, out of which white and gray houses showed, and a church spire, and a large brick edifice.

"Good! I see a church," crowed Ernest, urging the team faster.

"But, darling, there—there is a jail heah, too," faltered Anne.

"Who cares? We can have the preacher come in and marry us there, as well as anywhere."

"You beat me all hollow," she returned, puzzled by his careless gaiety, yet at the same time gratified.

So they drove on down into Snowflake, which to Ernest appeared to be a very pretty town, and by no means the little hamlet he had expected it to be.

They entered the town by a long main street, far down which straggled two rows of buildings. The outskirts, however, consisted of small cottages, set well back among trees and gardens. A boy, astride an old gray black-spotted horse, came by.

"Hey, sonny, is there a preacher in this town?" asked Ernest.

"Yes, sir, a new one, just come. Parson Peabody. He lives in thet there house there—where you see the buggy hitched—next the church."

"Thanks, sonny. Here's a dollar," replied Ernest, gratefully, and he flipped the silver coin to the boy, who dexterously caught it.

"Gee! Much obliged, mister. I bet you're gonna git married."

Ernest was trying to prepare himself for the ordeal ahead. He occupied himself with driving the blacks, and did not look at Anne until they drew up before the house which the boy had pointed out to them. He reined in the team behind the buggy, and was about to step out when Anne clutched his arm.

"Look!" she whispered, in sudden agitation. Ernest looked down the street, naturally expecting to see a posse riding toward them. But the street was vacant and sleepy in the late afternoon sun. Indeed the whole town appeared to be taking a siesta.

"It's Nebraskie and my cousin Dais Brooks," cried Anne.

"Whatever does this mean?"

Ernest wheeled swiftly. Coming down the path from the house were three figures, two of whom were those of his friend and Daisy. Nebraskie was dressed in his best, and it took only another glance to tell that Daisy was also. Ernest sagged on the buckboard seat and stared, utterly thunderstruck.

Then Nebraskie showed sudden excitement. He had discovered the presence of the buckboard and its occupants, and came running up to the gate. He looked paler than Ernest had ever seen him.

"Fer Gawd's sake, Ernie, is it you?" he demanded.

"I think—it is, Nebraskie—but I'm not sure—of anything anymore," replied Selby haltingly.

"An' is thet Anne with you?"

"Yes, I guess so. It *was*," replied the Iowan, turning to see that Anne was hiding behind him.

"Did you heah what happened—aboot me?"

"No. I've not heard anything," replied Ernest, studying the cowboy's stern visage.

"What'd you foller us fer, then?"

"Nebraskie, we didn't follow you. We had not the remotest notion you were here," rejoined Selby, in a voice that permitted no doubt.

"Pard, if I'm loco I seen thet buckboard an' team yestiddy as late as four o'clock. An' heah they air in Snowflake."

"That may be, Nebraskie. But it doesn't prove you're not loco."

"Whatinhell—excuse me, Parson," burst out Nebraskie, as Daisy and the third member of the trio joined him. "Ernie, what on earth are *you* heah fer?"

"For one thing—Anne and I want to get married," replied Ernest loftily.

"*Whoopee!*" yelled the cowboy. "Thet's what Dais an' I come fer and we done it! We're married!"

Ernest leaped out of the buckboard and strode to the gate. Daisy's strained, pale face, telltale as always, grew rosy. "Congratulations, pard. I'm sure glad. . . . Daisy, I'm going to kiss you. I always wanted to, you know." And Ernest did so quite heartily. "You've got the best fellow in the world. . . . Anne, come out of it. Here's your own cousin, with my best friend—and they're married."

"I—I'm not blind," faltered Anne, and she clambered unsteadily out of the buckboard. Her face was pearly white, and her big green eyes were wide with mingled astonishment and pleasure. "Dais, I'm happy for you. I wish you joy," she said, and took the girl in her arms.

"Oh, Anne!" cried Daisy, in a strangled voice, and she clung to her cousin. Ernest's keen senses gathered that there was more agitation here, on the part of both girls, than a mere marriage could account for.

"Hey, come heah, Anne," broke in Nebraskie. "Ernie kissed Dais, an' I'm shore gonna kiss you. Same as he, I always wanted to." And he certainly made good use of his opportunity.

Still the tension did not relax. Ernest felt it, and guessed the reason, though he was sorely perplexed at Nebraskie's advent here in Snowflake. But that could be cleared up in due time. The exigency of the moment called for quick wit and action.

"Parson, will you marry us?" asked Ernest, turning to the mild-eyed, pleasant-faced clergyman, who stood by, taking in the scene with amused interest.

"Surely, if the young lady is over eighteen," was the reply. "This is my second day here in Snowflake. And this will be the second wedding ceremony. I consider it propitious."

"You have a marriage certificate?" inquired Ernest hurriedly.

"Assuredly. Come right in," replied the minister. "Your friends can be witnesses."

"Anne, I'll go in and—and fix it with the minister," said Selby, and he did not try to conceal his excitement. His voice actually thickened and broke.

"You come in when I call....Nebraskie, pard, hang on to her. Don't let her run."

"Shore, I'll hang on to her, Ioway," replied the cowboy, and he put a long arm around Anne.

Ernest turned to look at the three smiling people at the gate. Sight of them there was too good to be true. Then he hurried the preacher into the house.

"You are a very impetuous young man," observed the minister smilingly.

"Parson, if you knew the trouble and heartbreak it's taken to win that girl!" burst out Ernest. "But hurry, give me a certificate to fill out....Here's twenty dollars. All I've got with me....Ah! Thank you."

Ernest grasped the paper held out to him, and seating himself at the desk began to fill it out. The minister bent over him. "It's customary for me to do that, young man. But it's all right....Miss Anne Hepford, aged twenty....And Ernest Howard Selby—aged twenty-four. Very well. Call the others in."

Ernest went to the door. "Come on, Nebraskie. You and Dais fetch her in."

Nebraskie and the two girls hurried into the front parlor of the parsonage. Ernest, despite his agitation, managed to meet them composedly. Anne was far from pale now. As her eyes met Ernest's he felt a sweet warm rush of emotion.

"Have you a ring ready?" asked the parson, as he took up a Bible, which lay open on the table.

"No," replied Ernest blankly. The blood fled back to his heart. Delay here would be fatal, not only to the marriage, but to the identity he wished to conceal.

Daisy came to the rescue. "Take mine, Ernest.

...Nebraskie forgot to get one so we used this."

"By gosh, pard, we've gotta buy us some rings when we get to Flaggerstown."

The parson took the ring, and straightway began to read the service. Ernest was keyed up tightly as he waited, his mouth dry, his veins bursting for the minister to begin. Presently came the query: "Do you, Ernest, take this woman—"

"Yes!" he burst out loudly, and to his joy the minister passed over the interruption, and went on. The end came swiftly. Anne held out a trembling hand to receive the ring on her finger, and her "Yes" came sweetly and demurely from her heart. It was over. She was his wife. The room seemed to whirl about him. He embraced Anne in a rush of love and gratitude, careless of the onlookers.

"Oh, it's too good to be true!" he exclaimed softly. "Here, Anne, sit down and sign your name.... Hurry, dearest.... There! Sign there!" He hung over her, and she wrote her name without a glance at the contents of the document. Then Ernest lifted her up and took the paper from her hands, and as one beside himself, while the others smiled, he dashed his own name down and handed the certificate to the minister. In another moment the ceremony was ended without a hitch. Selby folded the precious paper and waved it at Anne.

"You're my wife. Here's my proof. And I'm the happiest man in the world."

"Yes. I—I'm happy, too, but Ernest, we must go—you know. We must hurry."

"Surely," replied Ernest, as he buttoned his vest over the marriage certificate that now reposed safely in his pocket. "But we must have something to eat first. I'm starved. I didn't feel it before, but I do now."

"Same heah," corroborated Nebraskie. "What's the hurry? We're all married now an' nothin' cain happen. There's a hotel heah. Let's eat."

Anne still seemed to be a bit dazed. Between them they led her outdoors. The preacher followed as far as the gate, pleased with the happiness he had bestowed, and there he bade them good-by. Once seated again in the buckboard Anne begged: "Ernest, let's not stop heah. We must hurry."

"But child, there's no risk. No one save Nebraskie and Daisy know we're here."

"Any minute some one might come."

"Sure. Only the chance is slim. We can't go without eating forever."

So he prevailed upon her, and they drove to the hotel. While the girls went upstairs Ernest and Nebraskie took the horses round to the barn.

"Might as wal unhitch, pard," said Nebraskie. "We'll spend the night heah."

"Suits me," replied Ernest shortly.

"Say, you're shore loco," went on Nebraskie, his keen gray eyes on his friend. "What's eatin' you?"

"A lot," replied Ernest.

"You heahed aboot me?"

"Not a damn word. I told you," flashed Ernest.

"Wal, you needn't jump down my throat. Doggone it, I reckon I done you a good turn."

They saw to the needs of the horses; and then Nebraskie dragged Ernest into a stall, and after peering around to make sure they were alone, he whispered: "Now spill it, you blank-faced idjit!"

Ernest drew a long breath. "Yesterday afternoon—or when was it?—I saw Hepford and Hyslip drive by Brooks' place. And I jumped at my chance to—to go down to Red Rock. I went. Waited till dark. Then I slipped down to the house. I—I busted into Anne's room—"

"Whatinhell fer? My Gawd, Ernie, I'm worried aboot you," interrupted Nebraskie, red in the face.

"Shut up. This is my turn to talk," went on Ernest. "I busted into Anne's room. She was in bed. She'd been reading. She was scared stiff. . . . Well, that was what I wanted. I was aiming to scare her—among other things. We were having it hot and heavy—she sure I had come to kill her—or worse—because she had treated me so rotten—when Hepford knocked on the door. It was good I'd locked it. He wanted to come in, but she wouldn't let him. Then he said there had been hell to pay—in substance that *I* had killed Hyslip—that they were going to lynch me. He went away—and then—well, Nebraskie, I just can't tell you what did happen. But it turned out that Anne really loved me and swore she would run off with me—get me across the state border. I never told her that *I* didn't kill Hyslip. I knew you did and I was sure sick about it. But I let her believe I had because I wanted to see how she'd take it. . . . She was great, Nebraskie. She helped me outside, met me down in the lane, she stole the buckboard, she drove all night—and here we are!"

Nebraskie gripped Ernest with stiff fingers. His eyes shone like fire.

"Didn't I tell you she was game? Thet she'd come out true? But, Gawd Almighty man! You cain't let her think thet you're a murderer any longer. Fer I killed Hyslip an' it was a job I'm shore proud of."

"For Lord's sake, tell me!" cried Ernest passionately.

"I came back to the ranch aboot four o'clock," began Nebraskie, cool and easy. "Sam an' Hawk was with me, but they put the hosses away while I went to the house. I heahed Dais cry out. An' I heahed a tusslin'. The door was shet. I peeped in the winder, an' there was Dude Hyslip with Dais in his arms. I looked long enough to make shore Dais was fightin' him. An' pard, thank Gawd she was—like a little wild-cat! Hyslip always had Dais locoed, but when it come to the pinch she was game.... Wal, I was lookin' around fer somethin' to bust in the door when Sam an' Hawk arrived. 'What's up,' they says. An' I said, 'Bust open thet door damn quick!' When the two of them flopped agin it—smash! It gave in. Sam lodged agin the doorpost, but Hawk fell in. An' thet crazy fool shot him. I had just enough sense left not to face the open door. So I ran to the winder. I shot Hyslip through the glass, but hit him low down. He came out a yellin'. An' he shot at Sam jest as I bored him agin. Funny how nervous I was, pard. It turned out afterward thet either of them shots would hev done fer him, in time. But Hyslip was shore waivin' his gun on me when I killed him."

"Good Lord!" ejaculated Ernest, in mingled relief and horror. "But don't say he killed Hawk?"

"Nope, Hawk got it through the shoulder an' a madder man I never seen. Dais was in a faint. Wal, we fixed Hawk up temperary. Meanwhile Dais come round of her own accord. Brooks hitched up the wagon an' packed Hawk off to Holbrook, tellin' us to foller. After Dais an' I'd thought it over we decided to come over heah an' git married, so's to have thet done when we got to town....We left Hyslip lyin' where he fell....I reckon now thet heah's whut happened. Hyslip an' Hepford split up fer some reason. Hyslip went back to Brooks' house, an' findin' Dais alone he lost his haid agin. Then Hepford must hev come back later, an' he jest put the blame on you. Or mebbe Magill an' Davis or Pollard did the little job. An' I reckon thet's aboot all."

"It's bad enough, but thank Heaven you can't be held!...Nebraskie, you're going on to Holbrook, then?"

"Shore. It'll save some investigatin'."

"Hepford put a posse after me, sure as you're born. Suppose they happen along here?"

"Wal, I'd stop them darn pronto. Reckon, though, thet ain't likely. Let's go in an' tell Anne the truth."

"Perhaps Daisy has already."

"No siree. I told Dais to keep mum."

Upon returning to the hotel Ernest and his friend found their wives in their separate rooms. Anne had her hat and coat on and seemed nervously anxious to leave Snowflake without delay.

"Well, let's see Nebraskie and Daisy first. Then if you still want to hurry away, we'll start pronto," replied her husband.

"Ernest—how you talk! I'm shore Daisy knows. She acted so strange. She couldn't keep the tears out of her eyes."

Ernest crossed the hall with Anne and led her into the presence of Daisy and Nebraskie. It was a large light room. Nebraskie looked cool and relaxed, Daisy nervously solicitous.

Anne opened the conversation. "Daisy, you and your husband are on a honeymoon. . . . But Ernest and I—are fleeing for his life. As he won't tell you I must. He—"

"Now, Anne, jest wait a little," interposed Nebraskie, in his drawling voice. "Shore there's a mistake around heah somewheres. There cain't be any need of you two fleein'. Cause—"

"But Nebraskie, my dad has set his men on Ernest's trail," cried Anne, her eyes desperate and dark with anxiety. "They hate Ernest. They'll hang him!"

"Aw, thet's a bit exaggerated, Anne. What on earth fer?"

"Ernest killed Hyslip. It—was my fault. Oh, I was rotten to Ernest. I know he's innocent of murder. He shot Hyslip in self-defense. But *they* won't believe that. They won't give my—my husband a chance. We won't be safe until we're across the line."

"Anne, darling, wait. Let us say a word. You haven't considered that maybe—perhaps your father—made a mistake," interrupted Ernest.

"Mistake! What aboot?" returned Anne, nonplussed. She gazed from one to the other. And when Daisy began to cry she turned to comfort her.

"Why shore—aboot this heah killin' of Hyslip," said Nebraskie, feeling his way. "My pard Ernie, now, he couldn't hev done it, Anne. He jest couldn't."

"Why—why not?" she implored weakly, a terrible hope in her eyes.

"Wal, in the first place Ernie wasn't around when it happened. . . . I was the one who killed Hyslip."

Anne gave a gasp, and reeling, would have fallen if Nebraskie had not caught her in his arms.

CHAPTER
19

STRICKEN with remorse Ernest took his wife's unconscious form out of Kemp's arms and laid her on the bed. Daisy removed her hat, and the two of them managed to get her coat off, after which they bathed her white face with cold water. At length her eyelids flickered, then opened, to reveal two tragic green wells of consciousness.

"There! She's come to," whispered Daisy.

"Aw, I'm shore glad. She looked daid. Think of Anne Hepford keelin' over like thet."

"Anne, darling—you fainted," said Ernest, greatly relieved, as he held her hands.

Nebraskie drew Daisy away. "Say, folks, we'll go have a special dinner fixed up." And he left with Daisy in a haste that gave evidence of his great concern.

"All right, but not too soon," called the Iowan after them, and then closed the door. When he returned to the bed it was to discover a new Anne Hepford.

"Ernest, is—it—true?" she faltered.

"Is what true, honey?"

"That you didn't—kill Hyslip?"

"Certainly it's true, I'm happy to confess. But, darling, I never *said* I did."

"You didn't deny it."

"No. I let you think so."

"Oh, why did you deceive me?" she asked, reproachfully.

Ernest leaned over, holding her hands, and gazing deep into the eyes that at last expressed her true soul.

"Well, you took it for granted. You were so shocked, you blamed yourself so passionately that I just couldn't bear to tell you," explained Ernest.

"Ernest, you are pretty wonderful, too. I don't know just how—but you are," she replied dreamily, and she slipped a hand free to touch his cheek tenderly. "You were cruel. You've no idea of the torture I endured."

"I endured some myself, little wife," he said, significantly.

"I'd forgotten. I *am* your wife....Oh, thank God you didn't kill that cowboy. Ernest, I'm no chicken-hearted girl. I'm western. I'm not afraid of death—or of a man who takes a life in a just cause. But the fact that I thought I was to blame is what crucified me."

"I might have done it. I packed a gun for that very reason."

"But you didn't.... Let me up, dear.... I feel giddy."

Ernest led her to a big chair, and sitting down he drew Anne into his lap. It was not many moments before the natural ruddy color had been restored to her cheeks.

"They might come back," she whispered, protesting.

"Who cares? Anne, I can't get used to the idea you love me and that I've the right to embrace you and kiss you whenever I like," he rejoined.

"If I remember correctly you did something of— of that sort before you had any right at all.... Oh, I tried to fight against you. To my shame I confess it— after that first time I—I was crazy for your kisses."

"Glory be! And you never let me guess it!" cried Ernest ruefully.

"You acted as if you did.... Ernest, please tell me where, why and how Nebraskie killed Hyslip?"

Ernest took rather a long time for his recital of Nebraskie's story.

"Served him right!" she flashed, with green fire in her eyes. "Ernest, I was always afraid of him. When I rode with him I was careful never to get off my horse. I rode, and that's all, believe me.... I'm sorry for Daisy. Poor kid! She shore was hypnotized by that cowboy.... It might have been worse. I think Nebraskie is a noble fellow. He must love her dearly. It will come out all right in the end."

"I hope so.... And that *our* love and marriage does the same."

"We shore have a lot to think of," she said, with an arm around his neck. "Reckon I ought to be scared stiff of what's ahaid of us. But I'm not. I can work. You'd never believe it, Ernest, but I can cook, bake, wash, sew. Honest, I can. Reckon I was born to be a cowboy's wife. We'll pioneer it somewhere. I can chop wood, too, and I believe I could handle a plow."

"I hope you don't have to be a drudge for me. Maybe we'll find a way. Don't you think you could make a rancher out of me?"

"I shore could. Only," she sighed, "it can't be Red Rock now! When I think of how I love Red Rock— that always it seemed mine—I feel sort of sick. Imagine, Ernest. When the news first came that the new owner of Red Rock was coming out to take charge— I—made up my mind to marry him! Young or old, I meant to. That shows you how I love that ranch. And now—"

"My, what a calculating creature you were! And I'll bet you'd have done it, too. No man could resist you, Anne. But you married me, a poor cowboy instead," he ended exultantly.

"So it appears. I'm not sorry, Ernest. I'll never have any regrets. It'll be the making of me."

"It'll have to be the making of us both. But Anne, let's postpone talking about all them serious things for the present. At least until—"

"How can we, you goose? Our problems begin now. I feel so free—so happy at the release from that terror for you—why, I can face anything."

"Even life with a poverty-stricken, would-be cowboy?" he asked smilingly.

"Yes, as long as that poverty-stricken, would-be cowboy is you," she nodded gravely, smoothing his hair.

"You make me feel very humble—and very proud, my dear," said her husband in a voice that was little above a whisper.

"Ah—I—I—reckon it doesn't make—any difference now," whispered Anne, surrendering to his embrace.

The simplicity of Anne's statement brought Ernest sharply to his senses.

"Anne, I—I must tell you something—we can't be really husband and wife truly—until—"

"What do you mean?" she queried, aghast, while the red mantled from neck to temples.

"Simply this. I won't—I can't take advantage of your love and your becoming my wife—in all that implies—until I can do so honestly. It's a horrible temptation to continue as we are. But—"

"*Ernest!*" she cried, clasping him wildly.

"Anne, I've deceived you—basely."

"Aboot Hyslip? But I know now."

"Not that. Something very much worse. I hope you'll still love me—but you might not."

"Oh, what is it?"

"I can't tell you yet."

"Ernest, it's not—you love some one else?"

"No, not that."

"You never loved any other girl?"

"Honestly, I never did."

"There's no reason why I cain't be your wife?"

"No, indeed."

"Then what in the world have you done?"

"I won't tell you now."

"When?"

"Well, in a few days. After we go to Holbrook

and disprove the charge your father laid upon me. And have it out with him."

"Pooh! You're afraid of Dad?" she exclaimed, in sudden relief.

"Yes, I am, a little. He'll be a bad customer. He never liked me. And Hyslip and his cronies hated me. Naturally that set Hepford even more against me. Then the day we came back from our ride—I was mighty upset. I was determined to find out something to his discredit. Siebert's talk told me a lot."

"Shore it told me a lot, too," rejoined Anne bitterly. "It justified my fears. If I'd had any sense I'd have realized Dad was being dishonest. I knew in my heart, when he drew all that cash out of the bank, and told me we'd leave Red Rock presently—I knew he was dishonest. Siebert knew it, too."

"Well, dear, *I* know it, also," returned Ernest. "He had discharged me. *You* had flouted me. I determined to get proof of my suspicions. It was partly for that reason that I broke into your house....Anne, I stole the little blue book you wouldn't let me look into. I stole it that night. Here it is in my pocket now."

"So that was it!" she murmured.

"Yes. Hepford drove up to the porch. Almost surprised me in his office. I couldn't get by, so I ran down the hall. That was how I happened to come into your bedroom. Oh, what a lucky thing for me! But if you'd only known it—my heart was in my throat."

"Then it was not to—to revenge yourself on me that you came?"

"Indeed it was not."

"How things come aboot! But I'm glad—Ernest—*glad*.... When you burst in there—white as a sheet—with eyes like black blades—I just wilted. I thought you'd come to—well—to do something after Hyslip's style. And now that I'm your wife I can confess.... No! I won't confess that. Someday, maybe."

"Anne, I think I can guess. And talk about your savages! But I loved you too deeply for revenge—or anything like that. No, I went to the ranch house to steal this little book."

As he took it out of his pocket a thick envelope came with it. "What's this? Oh, your letter. I must read it. But I no longer need it to prove to me that you are true blue. I'll never need any proof of that any more, darling."

"Read it, Ernest, but not now. First let's see what's in Dad's book."

"No. It might make you unhappy," returned Ernest, replacing both letter and book in his pocket. "That can wait."

"Ernest, I'm a thief, too," confessed Anne boldly.

"How so?"

"Dad entrusted me that wallet of money he drew from the bank last time he was in town. When he leaves the house he always does that—well, *we* had to have money. So I fetched it with me."

"Anne, you stole for me!"

"I shore did. It hurts now that you're not a fugitive from the law. I reckon I'll have to return it to Dad—even though I feel I ought to keep it for the new owner of Red Rock, when he comes. He'd probably reward me, Ernest. And you and I must have enough money to get away with. We cain't stay heah."

"I'm not sure what we can do. Where's that wallet, Anne?"

"In my bag."

"I'll get it," decided Ernest with alacrity, and disengaging himself from Anne he left the room to cross the hall into their room. His fingers were not steady as he opened Anne's bag. What a complication of events! He found a large leather wallet, so full that it appeared about to burst. Ernest could not resist opening it far enough to see if the contents really were money. His eyes popped. Closing the wallet he raced with it back to Anne, scarcely thinking to conceal his exultancy.

"I declare, Anne, this is great," he said, waving the wallet.

"Ernest, are *you* going to give in to temptation?" she queried, with grave concern. "Even if Dad has been dishonest that's no reason for *us* to be. Because I stole the money. And if *you* make me keep it you'll be dishonest too."

"What'll we do, darling?" he asked, boldly, realizing that here was the supreme test of Anne Hepford. "I gave my last dollar to marry you. We'll have a long hard fight before we can have a home—and all the things you're accustomed to."

"Ernest! You frighten me.... I'd have been glad to spend it—every dollar—to save your life—or a long term in jail. But you're free. We're both young, strong, and we've got brains. We won't steal, Ernest. But we might fairly put that money away—in the bank—for its rightful owner."

Ernest shouted out loud in his gladness, and his

antics opened Anne's eyes wide. "Are you plain loco, boy?"

"I'm just so glad I'll—I'll burst. You can't understand how I feel. But that you'd steal to save me and won't steal to make us rich—what can I say! You're wonderful."

"Am I? Love is blind, Ernest....Put that wallet away before Nebraskie and Daisy come back."

Ernest had difficulty in stuffing it into his inside coat pocket, and then it bulged noticeably. "Lordy, I can't wait to count it."

"I did," laughed Anne.

"How much is here?"

"Guess."

"Several thousand, I'm sure."

"Do you think a big rancher makes so much over a little money as that? Ernest, there's over forty thousand dollars in that wallet!"

Selby sat down suddenly, his eyes popping.

"No!"

"Shore is. We'll count it again when we're alone. I don't know if it's a good idea, though. You might—"

A knock on the door interrupted them.

"That you, Nebraskie? Come in," shouted Ernest gaily.

The door opened, to admit the lanky cowboy and Daisy. They were all eyes.

"Wal, Anne, you come to fine, I'm glad to see. An' say, pard, what's eatin' you?"

"Starvation. Is the dinner near ready?"

"You bet. An' it's gonna be a humdinger. Come on. Let's forget our troubles."

Notwithstanding Nebraskie's enthusiasm, and a bountiful spread by the landlady, the dinner was not a marked success. Ernest, despite his assertion that he was starved, had to force himself to eat. And the girls were evidently too excited to be hungry. Conversation lagged.

"Wal," drawled Nebraskie, "you gurls shore hev long faces an' dewy eyes. What's the matter? There ain't nuthin' wrong. If what people say is true—thet the consummashun of women's happiness is gettin' married—you both ought to be turrible full of joy."

"I am, Nebraskie," declared Anne, smiling through her tears. "But it's a little too soon—right now."

"Don't be a fool," retorted Daisy, giving her husband a disapproving look. "How can we be gay?"

"Ioway, let's you an' me celebrate," said the cowboy, turning to Ernest. "Mebbe if we got ourselves good an' drunk our wives would lose their glum faces, anyhow."

"It's no laughing matter, Nebraskie," declared Ernest. "You're only bluffing. Deep down in your gizzard you've got bridegroom jitters yourself."

At the conclusion of the dinner, Ernest suggested that they go on toward Holbrook. There were still several hours of daylight. They could drive until late and stop at some ranch house; then get into town by noon next day.

"What-at?" demanded Nebraskie. "Sleep in some stall or haymow—on the first night of our honeymoon—when we could stay at this heah nice quiet hotel?"

"Be reasonable, pard. To be sure it's our honeymoon, but you'll allow, no ordinary one," protested Ernest.

"Ioway, I been dreamin' an' prayin' fer this ever since I laid eyes on Dais," protested the cowboy, in his turn.

"Nebraskie, I've entertained something of the same hope ever since I saw Anne," went on Ernest, with a laugh at the evident embarrassment of the two brides. "Listen now, you Romeo. There are some things to settle up before we start on this honeymoon."

"What, fer instance?"

"Well, this late escapade of yours—ridding Red Rock of a very undesirable individual. And looking out for new jobs to come back to—*after* our honeymoon. Let's go on to Holbrook, then back to Red Rock, and then, after everything is fixed up fine, have our honeymoon."

"The four of us?" asked Daisy eagerly, her dark eyes shining. "Oh, I'd love that."

"It does sound nice. I—I believe I approve," added Anne, who evidently wanted to help Ernest, but was not completely sure he was not out of his mind.

Nebraskie stared hard at his friend.

"We might even raise money enough to go to California," went on Ernest, trying to be casual.

"Wal, pard, *now* I savvy what turned Anne's haid. It's your silver tongue," burst out Nebraskie, in admiration mixed with wistfulness. "My Gawd, I wisht we could. But I'm near broke. An' you *air* broke. Dais hasn't any money. Have you, Anne?"

"I reckon Ernest can raise some. But wouldn't

we be crazy to spend it on honeymooning, when there's no more in sight?"

"Shore we'd be crazy," admitted the cowboy. "But I'd like to go thet crazy once....As fer a job, Ioway, I'm goin' to work with Dais's father. It'll be slow buildin' up a payin' ranch, but I see somethin' shore ahead, anyway."

"Cowboy, the way to make money out of Brooks' place is to irrigate, put most of the land in alfalfa, and run your cattle out on the range," said Ernest, most businesslike.

"I'm a son-of-a-gun," ejaculated Nebraskie. "Never thought of thet. Neither did Sam. Ioway, you're not such a dunce at thet. It's a darn good idee."

Anne was so pleased with Ernest's sound ideas that her face grew tender.

"It is indeed," she said. "That is precisely what Dad meant to do with the farm, when he'd driven Brooks off."

"Oh, I'll be a rancher someday," said Ernest, laconically. "How could I help it, with such a wife? ... Well, Nebraskie, shall we forego our honeymoon, and get to moving toward town?"

"Shore. I reckon I'm gonna stick to you like a plaster, from now on," rejoined Nebraskie.

While the two were hitching up Nebraskie observed thoughtfully: "Ioway, you're the damnedest, originalest, mysteriest, best pard I ever had."

Soon they were driving north on another road. They passed several ranches before dark, but after night fell they did not come to another until it was so late that Nebraskie advised not awakening the owner. They drove on to a cedar woods, where they built a fire, unhitched the horses, and made camp under a clump of cedars. They managed to keep warm, at least. Dawn came presently, and soon afterward they were traveling swiftly on the last lap of their journey. Before noon they were in Holbrook.

CHAPTER
20

*W*HEN Ernest thought what he was going to do, now that he had arrived at Holbrook, he found himself at a loss. As he drove the buckboard up the main street he espied Nebraskie's rig halting in front of the hotel, where several other vehicles stood. Two or three men strode across the pavement to meet Nebraskie. One of them he recognized to be Brooks.

When Ernest hauled up beside them the rancher's broad face was wreathed in smiles. A quick glance at Nebraskie and Daisy satisfied Ernest that all was well.

"Wal, an' what air you doin' heah?" queried Brooks in surprise.

"I've been getting married, Sam," replied Ernest happily. "Nebraskie hasn't got a corner on all the girls."

"Fer the land's sake!" exploded the rancher, throwing up his hands. "You ain't gone an' married Anne Hepford?"

"I should think one look at her would be suffi-cient to convince you," replied the Iowan blandly.

It would have been, but Brooks took more than one. "Wal, I'll be doggoned! . . . Howard, you're a lucky cuss. As for you Anne, wal, I reckon, if looks count much you're as happy as you air lucky. Bless you both."

"Tell me pronto. How's Hawk?" interrupted Er-nest.

"He's all right. Little lame in his shoulder, but nothin' serious for a tough customer like him. I'm pickin' him up at Babbitt's. We're drivin' off right away. Jest almost missed you."

"Then—there's no—no trouble ahead for Ne-braskie?"

"Nope. None in the least. Siebert an' me fixed thet. The sheriff drove out this mawnin' fer Red Rock. We're to meet him there."

"Well!" ejaculated Ernest with a deep sigh of relief.

Brooks turned to Nebraskie: "I reckon, son, you'd better go along with us."

"Shore, Sam. We'll hev somethin' to eat, an' ketch up with you."

"I'll stop at Miller's."

Ernest leaped at a solution to his problem. "Anne, you go along with Daisy and Nebraskie. I'll follow as quickly as—"

"See heah," exploded Nebraskie. "Ain't we gonna ever hev any honeymoon at all?"

"Leave that to me," retorted the Iowan, laughing.

"Wal, all right, if you'll promise thet after the fuss an' funeral are over we'll go off somewhere an' be happy fer a coupla days anyhow."

"I promise, Nebraskie."

"Darling, for a brand new married man, you seem rather anxious to get rid of your wife," interposed Anne, her large eyes studying him quizzically.

"It does look a little that way," rejoined Ernest, laughing. "But, dearest, I imagine your father will not take our marriage as calmly as Daisy's father did hers. Wouldn't it be better for you to see him first?"

"Yes, it shore would," replied Anne, a little grimly. "But you forget. What'll I say aboot the money?"

"Oh!" Ernest certainly had to think hard. "Anne, you must pretend surprise at its absence. Then— when I come down I'll explain."

Anne gazed at him dubiously, but his frankness disarmed her for the moment.

"Very well. I—I reckon you're right," she conceded thoughtfully. "I don't want to stay heah an hour longer than necessary, with that storm hanging over my haid."

Ernest leaped out to help her down. She whispered, her hand on his: "If you didn't come—back it'd—kill me."

"Anne!"

She said no more but when she got up between Daisy and Nebraskie she gave him a long look that he would remember as long as he lived.

"Ioway, when'll you come?" queried Nebraskie. "We ain't gonna start our honeymoon till you do.

Shore if we did it'd plumb kill Anne. I heahed her say so."

"Well, let's go if we're going," cried Anne sharply, and Daisy pummeled Nebraskie with a vigorous little fist. Reluctantly, the cowboy took up the reins and clucked to the horses.

"Wal, I'm so glad over thet I could bust," declared Brooks, fervently, as he watched them drive down the street. Anne looked back once more before the buggy disappeared down the road.

"So long, Sam. I've got some things to do," said the Iowan quietly. "I'll see you at home, maybe to-morrow, or next day surely."

Ernest first called upon his lawyer, Jefford Smith, who was greatly pleased to see him.

"I was trying to make up my mind to go down to Red Rock," said Smith, after greeting him. "You are delaying too long. Hepford is planning on shipping cattle to New Mexico. He has acquired a ranch there."

"Well, a lot has happened to prevent me. One thing of which was—I fell in love with Hepford's daughter."

"No?"

"And I married her, too," declared Ernest.

The lawyer was thunderstruck. "Good heavens, young man! Unless you mean to let Hepford get away with wholesale robbery, you've surely complicated the case."

"Mr. Smith, I won't let him get away with any more property. But of course I won't put him in jail or even disgrace him. That, of course, is for his daughter's sake."

"You're very magnanimous. Excuse me, but is she deserving of such a sacrifice?" returned the lawyer bluntly.

"She's worth more."

"Hepford has robbed you of approximately two hundred thousand dollars."

"Sure that hurts. But I've got nearly forty thousand of it back. At least I have the money. The disposition of it depends on your judgment."

"How on earth did you get such a sum from him?" demanded the astonished attorney.

"Well, he entrusted it to Anne, his daughter, and I took it."

"Good. Put it in the bank at once."

"I will, sir. . . . And I have something else. I stole a little blue book, a private ledger in which Hepford kept his personal accounts. Can you recall the statements in my uncle's papers, which I showed you?"

"Yes, enough to make comparisons. Let me see this ledger."

It did not take the keen lawyer long to digest the contents of the little book. Closing it, he said, "You have him pat. Now what are your instructions?"

"How soon can you leave for Red Rock?"

"Right away."

"I must rest the horses. Say tomorrow morning early."

"The earlier the better."

"Daylight then, at the hotel. . . . Oh, yes, there's one more thing. I need some money."

"I can lend you any reasonable sum. But why not draw on that you have? It's yours. There will never be any court proceedings."

"Gosh!" ejaculated Ernest, and rushed away.

On his way to the bank he happened to think that to deposit such a sum of money as he had in his possession might very well rouse suspicion on the part of the bank officials. There was only one bank in town. Hepford had drawn the identical sum there not very long before. Ernest decided he would risk less by carrying it on his person.

His first errand was to the jeweler's. And this was an occasion. Not for nothing had he looked so long at Anne's fingers, nor studied the ring Daisy had loaned her to be married with. He purchased a gold wedding ring, and then a solitaire ring, the stone in which was a very beautiful blue-white diamond, the finest the jeweler had in stock. Then, such was Ernest's exultation, he bought another solitaire that he would tender to Nebraskie to give Daisy. He felt hugely delighted with himself.

From the jeweler's he repaired to the emporium where he had once obtained chaps, gloves, spurs and sombrero. He was remembered.

"Want something rich in cowboy togs," he said. "No flash or phony stuff."

There appeared to be a vast assortment of things for riders of the range. What an extravagant class cowboys were! Ernest bought boots with high tops of decorated kangaroo leather, as soft as kid; silver-mounted Mexican spurs, fringed buckskin gloves; a sombrero that felt like an umbrella; corduroys, blouse and scarf; and lastly a black leather gun belt and holster containing a white bone-handled gun.

"Some Texas Jack died heah sudden with his boots on, an' I got these," explained the merchant.

"Second hand, yes, but all the better for a little wear."

Ernest carried his purchases to his hotel room, thinking the while how his new regalia would make Anne gasp and those Red Rock cowboys stare and gape. His mental state was such that he could scarcely eat and he almost forgot to order the buckboard fetched round at dawn. It seemed no time at all when he was awakened by a thumping on his door. Through the window he could see that another day was dawning—a day that perhaps was to be a very important one in his life.

Hepford's black team was noted for its swift trips to town and back. By three o'clock in the afternoon Ernest halted where Brooks' lane branched off the Red Rock road.

"Now, Mr. Smith," said Ernest, "you drive on to the ranch. Leave the horses at the barn and go hunt up Hepford. Tell him simply this—that the new owner of Red Rock will be there pronto, you are his lawyer, and you want to know what he's going to do about an accounting. I'll get my papers and follow you immediately."

"I like the job.... But, does your wife know *you* are young Selby?"

"She does not. Don't you tell her or anybody."

"Very good. I'll expect you shortly after I arrive," returned the lawyer, and then he drove on.

Ernest strode rapidly down the lane, absorbed in thought. He had planned exactly what to do and say, how he was going to act, up to a certain point. That point was when he finally found himself alone with Anne. As he thought of that moment his heart came up in his throat. When he stooped to slide between the bars of Brooks' gate his ear was assailed by a stentorian: "Whoopee!"

Nebraskie was standing in the open door. "Folks, come heah," he called to those within. "It's Ioaway. Look at him!"

They flocked outside—Nebraskie, Daisy, Siebert and Brooks, to gather around the newcomer.

"Howdy, boy," drawled Siebert, with his hawk eyes twinkling.

"How're you, boss?" flashed Ernest, his quick eyes noting no change in the foreman, except a slight pallor.

"Me? Aw, I'm plumb fine."

"Brooks, how'd it all come out? About the sheriff?"

"They was heah yestiddy," replied the rancher cheerily. "Looked around some, at these bullet holes in the doorpost. Then they packed Hyslip off to Springer. I made shore they'd stop at Hepford's to tell him the news."

"Will you hitch up your two-seater and take us all down to Red Rock?" asked Ernest eagerly.

"Shore I'll hitch up. But what fer do you want us to go—me in particular?"

"Sam, the boy figgers he may need his friends," put in Siebert persuasively.

"Wal, then, shore I'll go," replied the rancher, and he moved away toward the barn.

Nebraskie walked round and round Ernest, gazing with experienced eyes, as he inspected the Iowan's new outfit.

"You locoed son-of-a-gun from Ioway!...Silver

spurs an' Mex at thet! Kangaroo tops! An' them velvet pants!...Peep at thet gun, Hawk! Look at it!...Ernie, I'm shore knocked flat to think you'd go in debt like this."

"Come here, you long lean cowpuncher," retorted Ernest, dragging him aside. "Look! Is this what you wanted?" And Ernest produced the diamond solitaire. The cowboy's eyes popped, his jaw dropped, for only a moment, when his back was toward the others.

"Dais, come heah," he drawled, his old cool easy self again. "Looka heah....Gimme your hand. I ast loway to fetch this to you....Doggone! It fits perfect."

After one little joyous scream Daisy became petrified. Ernest left them to their amazed rapture. He did not want to betray then the emotion that gripped him. But Nebraskie soon caught him, swung a long arm round his shoulders.

"Pard, did ya rob the bank?"

"No," laughed Ernest.

"Hold up anybody?"

"Well, not quite."

"Went in debt fer us! My Gawd, pard! I reckon ya got the same fer Anne."

"Sure did. Look again, pard."

Nebraskie gazed mutely. At last he burst out: "Jumpin' bronchos! We're ruined. It'll take all our lives to pay them debts. But I'm game. I'd 'a' done it myself."

Not until the two-seated wagon had reached the Red Rock corrals and barns did Selby again acquire the cool self-control that he had determined to show now that the big moment had come. The time had arrived for the big showdown, when Red Rock was to become his own.

They reached the long bunkhouse, upon the porch of which lounged the cowboys Lunky Pollard, Steve Monell, Bones Magill and Shep Davis. They were staring at the arrival of Brooks' two-seater with wide-open eyes.

"Sam, I'll get off heah an' pack my duds, roll my bed an' get my saddle," said Nebraskie.

"Hadn't Hawk better get down too?" queried Brooks in a low tone.

"Reckon I had, Nebraskie," replied the foreman.

"What fer?" asked the cowboy mildly.

"Wal, Shep, anyhow, is a bad hombre. He looks ugly."

"You go with my husband," said Daisy peremptorily to Siebert.

"Wal, reckon all the rest of my life now I gotta be chapparooned," complained Nebraskie. "But if you want to know it, those boys won't kick up nothin'. They'd been all right but fer Hyslip."

"You're talkin' sense there, Nebraskie."

They got out and slowly walked toward the bunkhouse. Ernest watched them long enough to assure himself there was no need for concern, then he braced himself for the ordeal at hand. Brooks reined in his team before the big ranch house, that had never before seemed so impressive to its new owner.

"You follow me," said Ernest, to father and daughter, and leaped out of the wagon to go quickly up the steps.

The office door was open. Ernest looked in to

see the room was vacant. He heard voices in the living room. Entering he espied Anne standing beside the open fireplace. She looked grave. Mr. Smith sat opposite, and Hepford, white and shaken, halted in his pacing the floor before the porch windows.

"Get out of heah!" he almost shouted. "You cain't pull the wool over my eyes as you did over Anne's. She's confessed she's your wife. It wasn't necessary for you to come. Get out of heah, an' take her with you. I've business with this lawyer. We're expectin' the new owner of Red Rock."

"Mr. Hepford, he has come," interposed Smith, rising.

"What?" snapped Hepford.

"Young Selby has arrived," returned the lawyer, indicating Ernest. "This young man you once employed as a cowboy is Ernest Howard Selby."

"WHA-AAT!" shouted Hepford, with a roar that was like a thunderclap, and indeed his face resembled a thundercloud.

"Yes, Mr. Hepford I am Ernest Selby," spoke up Ernest composedly, and he stepped forward to hand the small valise that contained his papers to the lawyer.

Hepford suddenly turned white and flopped into a chair, a beaten man. Ernest took a fleeting glance at Anne. That one glance was enough. Another would have unnerved him completely. As he turned again to face the two men he saw her, out of the corner of his eye, walk with bowed head out of the room. How he had to fight to keep from rushing after her.

"Mr. Hepford," said Smith, in a professional tone, "you will go over these papers with me."

"To hell—with papers!" muttered the rancher thickly. "If this Iowa tenderfoot is Selby's nephew— why thet's enough for me. I quit. I'll get out at once, this very night."

"Very good, but there are some other matters we have to wind up first. I was just suggesting before Selby's arrival—" went on Smith.

"Let's make it short and sweet," interrupted Selby, and at that moment he was glad to see Hawk Siebert come in quietly. "Mr. Hepford, I've had the great good fortune to win the hand of your daughter. Naturally I have no intention of ruining you or of making her unhappy. We need not even go over your irregularities, such as I have proof of in a little blue ledger I appropriated from your desk. . . . I have, also, the forty thousand dollars you entrusted to Anne. She believed I had killed Hyslip and took the money so that we could get out of the country. If you withdraw claim to that, and this ranch, and all your other Arizona interests in the bank and otherwise, I will exact no more. There will be no publicity whatever."

"Howard, I—I'll do thet," responded Hepford thickly, staring with astonishment at Ernest.

"That's all then," returned Ernest shortly. "Mr. Smith, you settle with him—to insure what I ask."

Whereupon Ernest stalked past Siebert out into the hall. "Wait outside for me, Hawk."

As once before Ernest found the door of Anne's room unlocked. He went in and shut it behind him, and proceeded to the bed where she lay, face down, her red hair tumbling about her like fire, her graceful body relaxed.

"Anne," he called, trying to control his voice a moment longer.

She stirred, she turned. Great tragic eyes transfixed him.

"So—this is your revenge?" she whispered hoarsely.

"Yes."

"You fooled me?"

"I did indeed."

She rose to a half-sitting posture, so that the afternoon sunlight, filtering through foliage and window shone on her pale agonized face.

"You—you took your opportunity—you let me believe—you made me love you—you *married* me—you even—even took me as your wife—all for revenge?"

Ernest parried that question by asking one himself. He dared no longer risk this delicious proof of her love, her abasement.

"Anne, did I make you love me?"

"Yes, heaven help me, you did. But don't be mean enough to gloat over me heah. I—I've deserved this."

He walked round the bed and sat down beside her. Taking her hand, he swiftly slipped two rings on her third finger.

"There! There's some more of my revenge!"

She stared uncomprehendingly. But the pallor of her face receded in a wave of color.

"Anne, darling," he whispered, stealing an arm around her. "I've settled with your dad. No fuss, no trouble! He took me up pronto. There'll be no disgrace, no publicity. He is welcome to his ranch in New Mexico."

"Iowa! What—what—" she faltered.

"Say, you're a 'turrible dumbhaid,' to use Nebraskie's words," chided Ernest, as she broke off. "For a girl who has made as many conquests as you have—you're being pretty dense right now."

"But—your re—venge?"

"Revenge. What for?"

"For my hateful low-down treatment of you—that killed your love."

"But it didn't, Anne."

"You still—love me?" she whispered. "You are really Ernest Selby—no poor grub-line tenderfoot cowboy after all?"

"Love you. Ha! Ha! That's an understatement. I worship you. Why, all this has turned out wonderfully. You are a true-blue western girl. You proved you loved me, just for myself. Besides that, you're the loveliest girl in all the world. And I'm the luckiest, happiest man in that same world."

"I'm your wife," she breathed.

"Yes, and just as you said, you've become mistress of Red Rock—even if you had to marry the owner."

"Oh! . . . Oh! . . ." she cried, shutting her eyes. Her face began to change convulsively.

"Kiss me," said Ernest passionately. She kissed him, but it was he who found her lips, and they were quivering.

"Ernest—I—I don't deserve it—I—I don't," she went on brokenly, and then bursting into tears she fell back upon the bed, her face hidden in the pillow.

"Darling, there's nothing to cry over," began Ernest, and then left off, realizing that perhaps there was a good deal. He stroked her shining mass of red hair.

"Well, honey, you have a good cry, if you want," he said, rising. "I'll go out and fire that bunch of cowboys."

As he went out he found the living room empty, but he heard Smith and Hepford in the office, the door of which was shut. Hawk waited for him outside, and Daisy, with her father nervously paced the porch.

"Come on, all of you. See the fun," called Ernest, gaily. And he led them at no slight pace around the house and through the pine woods.

"What you up to, boy?" drawled Hawk, half anxiously.

"You mustn't miss this," replied Ernest.

"Wal, Dais an' me air tryin' darn hard to miss nothin', but if you ask me we're shore plumb mysticated," added Brooks.

Soon they reached the bunkhouse where the cowboys stood and sat around. Their former lethargy had vanished. Ernest, leading his little band, halted before them.

"Say, you punchers, do you recollect that when Hawk and I got fired your pard Hyslip made us walk off this ranch?" demanded Ernest.

Shep Davis was cool and civil enough to reply: "Shore, we recollect thet."

"Well, was it regular or a low-down trick?"

"Reckon it was low-down all right."

"Listen then," went on Ernest, after an impressive pause, during which four pairs of eyes stared intently at him. "For my part I think you're pretty much of a no-good quartet. But Hawk swears it was Hyslip that spoiled you. So does Nebraskie. I'm willing to give you the benefit of the doubt.... Would you rather pack up and walk off this ranch, as Hawk and I did, or apologize to me and swear you'll be better fellows, and stay on here at higher wages?"

Nothing could have been clearer than the fact that those four astounded cowboys thought Ernest was crazy.

"Boys, wake up," added Hawk. "This is the new owner of Red Rock Ranch—Ernest Howard Selby."

Davis was the first to recover. He leaped up, his dark face brightening, and he made a move as if to offer his hand, but on second thought withdrew it.

"Hawk, I might hev knowed.... Mr. Selby, I ain't so low-down but what I appreciate a man. I'll accept your offer an' shore reckon I can answer fer my pards."

Just then Nebraskie came stamping out on the porch, his cherubic face expressive of his wonderment.

"Whatinhell's goin' on out heah?" he demanded. "Somebody's loco shore."

Ernest actually leaped to confront him.

"Shut up. You're fired!"

"Huh?" ejaculated Nebraskie.

"You're fired."

"Who's firin' me?"

"I am."

"*You*!...My Gawd! Dais—Hawk, the pore boy has gone dotty."

"You're fired, you long lean wild-eyed bridegroom," shouted Ernest, warming to the enjoyment of this moment. "Pack up and rustle. You're fired.... But you're hired again. You're a partner with Sam Brooks and me in the new development of Red Rock Ranch."

Nebraskie was past speech. He gazed stupidly from Ernest to Hawk. That worthy laughed.

"Nebraskie, let me introduce you to the new owner of Red Rock—Ernest Howard Selby."

A full moment passed in silence while Nebraskie looked from one friend to another.

"It's true, Nebraskie, pard," added Ernest. "Now, you and Dais go home pronto. Pack up for that honeymoon. We leave tomorrow for California."

Ernest turned away from that radiantly happy visage, and as he leaped off the porch he bumped into Daisy. Her face was so rapt that he stopped to plant a kiss full on her smiling lips. Then he rushed toward his ranch house, and as he hurried back to his wife his ears were assailed by Nebraskie's high tenor voice, that never before had rung with such a glad, rich note:

> Son-of-a-gun from Ioway
> He stoled my h-heart awa-ay!

Zane Grey, author of over 80 books, was born in Ohio in 1872. His writing career spanned over 35 years until his death in 1939 in Altadena, CA. A prolific writer, Zane Grey left behind enough unpublished manuscripts to last another fourteen years. Hailed as the true spirit of the American West, Zane Grey's work has entertained four generations of readers.